MW00882393

Praise

"I couldn't hug this story tight enough! 5 stars!"

T.L. MANNING, AUTHOR OF THE SIX FEET HIGH SERIES,
AND CURSED SERIES. ASD MOM OF 15 YEARS.

"...one of the best portrayals of high functioning
autism I've read in a long while if not ever."

SHANNON, TRIPLE A BOOK BLOG, ASD MOM

"What would you do if you found out you may die soon?
Well, if you're Prudence Penderhaus, you get brave."

TONYA ALLEN, ABIBLIOPHOBIA ANONYMOUS

"...sarcasm, sass and a whole lot of heart wrapped in
a big red headed burrito. Pru is a true hero.
I can't wait for the next one."

RAVIN TIJA MAURICE, AUTHOR OF THE PROPHECY GIRL
AND THE AFFLICTED SERIES

17 marigold LANE

the odd boy

a prudence penderhaus novel by

r.m. gilmore

mac
gille
mhur
publishing

17 Marigold Lane by *R.M. Gilmore*
© 2019 R.M. Gilmore *All rights reserved.*
2019 Revised Edition

Editor: Becky Johnson
Design: RMGraphX

MacGilleMhur Publishing

Paperback ISBN-13: 978-0-9989908-9-7

Publisher's Cataloging-in-Publication Data

Names: Gilmore, R.M., author.
Title: 17 Marigold Lane / R. M. Gilmore.
Series: Prudence Penderhaus.
Description: Dallas, OR: MacGilleMhur Publishing, 2019.
Summary: Prudence Penderhaus, a high school senior diagnosed with cancer, uncovers an odd boy and small-town corruption under dreary Pacific Northwest skies.
Identifiers: LCCN 2019908222 | ISBN 978-0-9989908-9-7
Subjects: LCSH Cancer--Fiction. | Terminally ill--Fiction. | Child abuse--Fiction. | Friendship--Fiction. | Love stories. | Bildungsroman. | Mystery fiction. | BISAC YOUNG ADULT FICTION / Mysteries & Detective Stories | YOUNG ADULT FICTION / Loners & Outcasts | YOUNG ADULT FICTION / Coming of Age
Classification: LCC PZ7.1.G573 Se 2019 | DDC 813.6--dc23

And still, after all these years…
For Nicky, Jack, and Skyler.

acknowledgements

Thanks to the help of Shannon Pell, attorney, Jennifer Pell, RN, and Casey Oliver, wrongful conviction advocate and law student, for making this book *mostly* accurate.

Sincere thanks to Stacey Ekparian for sharing her child's journey to defeating cancer and giving Prudence's story life.

Continued love and gratitude to my students who gave me the chance to know and love them. They allowed me to create a complex character like Cassius Shooster.

To Becky, Peggy, Tara, and Ravin for making sure this book wasn't a mess of nonsense. Thanks for having my back.

To my readers, weirdos who have loved me through it all. Don't stop being weird.

Thank you to my daughter, who allows me to be her mom even though I'm *so lame*.

My husband Kyle... you know.

17 marigold LANE

1

I'D CRIED FOR THE BETTER PART OF THE NIGHT. SLEEP hadn't even been a thought. How could I possibly? How could anyone?

I blinked against a beam of escaped light blaring through my window as thick autumn clouds passed over the sun. The ragged corners of my eyes burned. I glanced at the clock; six twenty-one. I shouldn't have cared about school, but habit and a desperate need for normalcy called me out from under Nan Lil's quilt.

Stumbling to my dresser, I caught sight of myself in the mirror and cringed at my own horrendous reflection. Puffy lids covered bloodshot eyes. My nose was raw from clearing away snot with my sleeve. I stared into my own murky eyes, lost in time. For the last twenty-four hours, time had been a fleeting idea.

I examined my lightly freckled face and wondered how

I'd look in a month. Six. A year? The word "malignant" played over and over in my head, and suddenly my post-bawl face didn't seem so bad.

Whether it was a conscious effort or some primal instinct to refute mortality, my brain couldn't comprehend the words Dr. Harris had said. Part of me held out hope that he was wrong. The other half of me wanted to scream, curse God, rip my red hair from its roots, and leap from my second-story window. Unfortunately, that fall wouldn't kill me. Knowing my luck, I'd break my back and live the rest of my short life in a wheelchair. Suicide attempts aside, there was nothing I could do but wait. Wait for treatment, wait for news, wait to die.

In the bathroom, I splashed cold water on my face. The rims of my eyes stung from salty tears running over them for hours on end. My freckles, which usually stood out against my ivory skin, were hidden behind a mask of splotchy red. I considered putting on makeup, but nixed the idea at the thought of black streaks on my face when the crying started again. It would, of course. There'd be a lot more crying to come.

I should get dressed. It was getting later every second I stood there feeling sorry for myself. School sucked but it was better than sitting at home thinking all day.

Back at the dresser and none the prettier, I pulled my snot-stained sweater over my head, catching a glimpse of the culprit—the murderer—in my reflection. The assailant. The bastard that would likely kill me before I even had a chance to really live. Eighty percent survival rate for those in the low-risk zone. Unfortunately, that wasn't me. I was too old, it was too large, it was encroaching on the bone and lymph and showed no signs of slowing down.

I lifted my arm above my head and exposed the golf-ball-sized tumor that had made itself at home on my bicep near my armpit. What had begun as nothing more than a knot, a pimple on the underside of my scrawny wing, had become a killer seemingly overnight. Taking over the muscle in a matter of a few months, the nearby lymph soon after, it was quickly making its way to the bone where it would take up shop, seeping its toxins into my body. Spreading until I was one walking cancer giant.

The scissors that sat in a jar of pencils on my dresser silently called my name. My fingers trembled with the need to take those scissors and cut that ruthless thing from my body. It was an invader, an intruder, a burglar intent on stealing from me the one thing that couldn't be bought, sold, or bartered. I wanted it gone. Out of my body. "Eradicated" seemed the most fitting word.

My Fiskars would've been no match for the tenacity of the thing, the big C, the naughty word no one wanted to mention but everyone knew. He who shall remain unnamed. The doctor, a young, handsome oncologist, was my only hope, my Obi-Wan.

"You're up." My mom's husky voice whispered from my half-open door. Why she whispered, I didn't know, but she hadn't spoken at full volume since we'd stepped foot in Marysville General yesterday morning.

"Yeah, it's six thirty." My alarm had gone off long ago, and any other day I'd have been in the bathroom trying to do something with my thick head of red hair.

"I just didn't think you'd be going to school today."

I shrugged my bare shoulders. "What else am I supposed to do?"

"Take some time to rest. Get your thoughts together maybe. You've got to be exhausted. Why don't you stay home and sleep today?"

"Mom." I sighed. "If I stay home today, all I'll do is sit and think about it. I don't want to think about it." She opened her mouth to say more, but I knew what she was going to say and added my two cents before she had a chance to jump my case. "Right now. I don't want to think about it right now." I looked away from her sullen face and back at my own. "I just need time."

I felt her move closer before her squishy arms wrapped around my middle. She buried her face against my back. Tears slowly dripped down my skin, just above my bra hooks, but she never made a sound. Getting my height from my dad, my petite, round mom hadn't stood past my chest in years, so I was grateful for the hug from behind. Having my sobbing mother bury her face between my boobs would have only made the tragically awkward moment so much worse.

"Mom, I'll be fine. If I need to, I'll just come home," I reassured her.

Mom sniffed back tears and left my back cold and wet. "I'll drive you."

I shook my head. "I want to walk."

"Pru, it looks like it might rain." She pushed, but I wasn't budging.

I pulled a clean hoodie over my head. "I don't care."

Rain was a constant during autumn in Flintlock. It was nearly unavoidable. Which worked in my favor because walking in the rain was a welcome alternative to riding in the car with my sobbing mother for all of the two minutes it took to get to Flintlock High School from my house. I needed time to think about anything other than what I should have been thinking about, and the fifteen-minute—if I stopped to smell every flower—meandering walk would work.

"Fine," she said under her breath and waved her hand in my direction. She didn't look at me again as she walked out my door and down the hall.

If I were any sort of daughter, I'd have followed her to her room where she was likely crying into her dated rose-patterned pillow. But I didn't. She needed time too. Even though she didn't think so. Her bawling had gone on all night as well and hadn't done me any good in the end. She had every right to behave exactly like she was. Her only baby girl had just been diagnosed with cancer; what parent wouldn't be a blubbering mess? Or worse. I had a feeling it would get worse, for both of us.

I said bye through Mom's closed door, and she

mumbled something back to me. My long legs allowed me to take the stairs two at a time, but it didn't bring an arrogant grin to my face as it had just yesterday. The old door closed loudly behind me. I didn't bother to lock it. In a town like Flintlock, there was really no need to lock anything up.

The October wind sent a chill through my jeans and down my legs. Fall was usually my favorite time of year, and blustery weather tended to bring out my inner weirdo, but the paper skeletons and cotton-fiber webs flittering in the wind from house eaves just didn't hold the same wonder as they had only the day before. Dreary gray clouds loomed overhead, and I slumped in my hooded sweater, fully expecting a single cloud to open up and dump rain on my funeral parade.

My street, Marigold Lane, was one of the oldest in Flintlock. Houses on Marigold, mine included, were nearing their hundred-something birthday—give or take a decade. There were other parts of town that were newer, but very few places were more recent than thirty years. My faded canary-yellow two-story Victorian sat four from the corner. Next door, Mrs. Callaway, a widow and perpetual cat lady, waved at me from her pristine white porch while three cats rubbed their fat bodies over her spindly ankles. The gingerbread house two doors from mine sat vacant since Mr. Horowitz died this summer. Weeds jutted up between the cracks in the aging front walk, around masses of decaying leaves and storm debris, making the vacancy obvious. On the corner, where Marigold Lane meets Thyme Drive, the Shoosters' matte-brown Victorian-Tudor mash-up finally had its moment to fit in with the cheery, "hi, neighbor" street.

Historically haunted and feared by all kids under twelve in Flintlock, the old dark house was like Herman Munster at a Halloween party. Jack-o'-lanterns smiled from the front porch surrounded by rubber spiders, making pretty for the holiday, but unaware of its year-around creepiness. I'd never been inside, but I'd heard there was an honest-to-goodness coffin in the living room. I always wanted to know for sure, but like every kid in Flintlock, I was too chicken to go see for myself. In fact, no one I knew of had actually ever been inside the old place to verify the rumors. A town like Flintlock was good for two things: community and bullshit. Honestly, the two went hand in hand.

Most days I eyed the house cautiously as I passed, curious, but still well aware of the stigma that surrounded it. Anxiously anticipating rain, huddled in my favorite sweater, I stood on the corner of Marigold and Thyme and stared at that place full-on.

The windows were dark. By all outward appearances, no one was home. I'd never seen Mrs. Shooster in all my seventeen years, but always figured Mr. Shooster was some kind of salesman or something because he was often away for long periods. I assumed his absence was the reason behind the regular tall grass and chipping paint, but told myself there was no reason outside medical disability that his wife couldn't at least work around the yard.

As I stood there, blatantly watching the house, feeling a little like Ray Peterson spying on his new creepy neighbors, I began to realize how rude it was when kids would point and stare and dare each other to go up to the door. Unlike the murderous family in *The 'Burbs*, these neighbors weren't new, and regardless of the local lore, I doubted they had bones in their backyard. In fact, as far as I knew, they'd lived in that house longer than I'd been alive.

The distant first-period bell of Flintlock High clanged up the street. I glanced down Thyme toward the school. First period wasn't required, but I wanted the college credit, so I sucked it up and decided to spend my senior year going to school an hour early. That was before… this. Why did I even care to go? It wasn't exactly like anyone missed me. It wasn't like I didn't have a damn good excuse.

From the corner of my eye, I caught movement in an upstairs window of the Shoosters' house. My eyes shot toward the window, searching for any sign of life. A dark curtain slammed shut and piqued my interest even further. Was that the elusive Mrs. Shooster watching from on high? Would she open the door if I knocked? The muscles in my skinny legs twitched, trying to unwittingly force me through the old metal gate and to the door.

"What are you thinking?" I muttered under my breath and groaned at my own stupidity. I'd walked past that house more times than I could count, and not once had I seen someone—or something—inside. I had seen Mr. Shooster twice, hurrying out to his tan Volvo early in the morning. He was taller than me, maybe thinner too, with a mop of jet-black hair on top of his head. "You're not thinking, that's the problem." I shook my head and looked down at my oversized feet. Same old me, perpetually alone and consistently boring.

Screeching tires drew my attention back to the street. A red sixties' muscle car, spotted with gray primer, fishtailed down Thyme toward Marigold. I held my breath and waited for the inevitable.

Brady Miles, captain of everything sports related and complete a-hole, gripped the steering wheel. I saw Morgan Pennington's big round head hanging out the passenger window a second before his thick arm jutted out and threw something in my direction.

"Lurrrrrrch!" Morgan bellowed their favorite nickname for me as his Big Gulp cup collided with my shoulder. Syrupy dark liquid that I could only guess was Coke splattered across my side and soaked my hair. "Go on in, loser, they've been looking for a new butler," he yelled as they drove right past, leaving me humiliated and sticky.

Any other day I'd have let it go, turned the other

cheek, and let them get away with treating me like I was their personal insult receptacle. Today was not that day. I pulled in a gulp of air and sucked back tears.

I'd been called Lurch since the fifth grade when Morgan decided it was unacceptable that a girl be inches taller than his stocky frame. Seven years later, the name had just become a part of who I was. There was no reason to start crying over it now—none other than the huge, monolithic, disastrous impending death I had weighing over my head.

I kicked the empty plastic cup at my feet. "What a waste of a dollar thirty-nine."

I looked back to the house. At least Morgan had been clever in his insult. Me being Lurch and the house looking as though Morticia and Gomez should be standing on the porch, it made a lot of sense. Maybe it was where I belonged all along. A freak should stay with the freaks. Right?

My heart fluttered, and something in me flipped like a switch. "Prudence Penderhaus, you get your chickenshit butt up that walk and knock on that door," I told myself out loud.

I took a deep breath and swung open the gate. Without thinking it through, I stomped up the walk and to the door. I lifted my fist to knock but hesitated. What I was going to say when someone answered hadn't even crossed my mind. I was more concerned with finally proving those jerks wrong and doing something spectacular before the bastard in my arm finally overtook me. "You're dying anyway, dummy. What's the worst that could happen?" I knocked, too fast and too hard to be pleasant and neighborly.

I'd been standing on the porch for a full minute when thunder bellowed overhead. The soda on my skin was drying into a sticky mess that my hair seemed to be having an intimate relationship with. Another minute passed, and a faint voice came through the other side of the door.

Deep and mumbling, I couldn't make out the words. Or even if they were speaking to me. I pushed my clean ear to the wood and strained to hear. The sounds of movement from inside were all that came through.

"Hello?" I said right against the door.

"Why are you here?" a voice said back.

I didn't know how to answer. I couldn't just say, "Because I heard you have a coffin in your living room."

"Um, I, uh…" I cleared my throat. "My name is Pru, uh, Prudence Penderhaus. I live a few houses down." Silence. "Can I use your bathroom quickly?" No reply. "You see I've got a mess of sticky soda in my hair, and I'd just like to use your sink to rinse it out before I head to school." Still quiet from inside. "I'm already late, and I need to hurry so I won't take up much of your time. I'd really appreciate it if I—"

The door opened, and I was suddenly standing in front of a Mr. Shooster replica. Only he wasn't the forty-some-odd-year-old man I'd seen before. The tall, lanky thing should have been in my graduating class from the looks of it, but in my life, I'd never seen him.

"Could use your loo?" I finished softly.

"You're wet."

If he were a blond, I'd have called him Riff Raff. Instead I said, "Yeah, it's soda."

"What flavor?" he asked with a straight face.

The importance of flavor didn't seem to take precedence, but I didn't want to upset the controller of my entry. "Coke, I think."

He nodded, and his floppy black hair bounced at the crown. "Coke has twenty-six tablespoons of sugar."

"Yeah, it's getting pretty sticky. Can I come in and use your sink before my hair is permanently glued to my neck?" His black eyes watched my mouth move but refused to meet mine.

"Soda isn't glue. It's a beverage."

"Right." I stared at him, examining his face, wondering why I'd never seen him before, and he stared at his feet.

His chest rose and fell with panting breaths while he mumbled something inaudible. An awkward span of time past before he finally pulled in a deep breath and moved from the doorway. Without looking at me, he pointed toward a darkened room behind the staircase.

His oddly literal interpretations and monotone speech made me wonder if he'd just done a bunch of drugs or something. Perhaps 17 Marigold Lane was a drug den and that's why no one ever left. A quick glance around the front room proved that hypothesis was unlikely. I'd never heard of a drug lord collecting rose-covered things.

I hovered in the doorway, processing too many thoughts at once. All I'd wanted was to do something no one in Flintlock had ever done, to my knowledge, and I was doing it. I was going to find out once and for all if the rumors were true about that old house. But in doing so, I unlocked a sea of new questions. The most prominent of course was, who was this odd boy?

The boy's shoulders stiffened. The longer I stood there the more uncomfortable he appeared. "Are you going?" he asked, his rumbling voice low and hurried.

I nodded and moved past him, clearing the door. "Thank you." I smiled and tried to meet his eyes. He shut the door softly and scurried around to watch me from the other side of the stairs. He'd clearly been trying to stay quiet so of course my sneakers squeaked on the hardwood floor on my way to the bathroom.

I moved slowly, trying to take in everything I could see. The bathroom door was open just a few feet ahead, behind the staircase and to the right of a small sitting room filled with old, pretty things. The inside didn't match the outside like I'd assumed it would. Cluttered with rose-covered knickknacks but nicely decorated and well-kept, the room had little space for a sofa let alone a coffin. *Perhaps*, I thought, *it's in another room deeper in the house.* As much as I wanted to find that coffin, a new curiosity was building about the strange boy who'd invited me in.

The bathroom was plain, no soaps shaped like shells or monogrammed towels. Just a sink and a toilet surrounded by dark brown, striped wallpaper and one mirror above the sink. I caught my reflection in the mirror and grimaced. It was a wonder the boy hadn't turned me away thinking I was some sort of bum trying to use his facilities to clean up. My face hadn't changed much since I'd walked out of the house, but added now was the drowned-rat look my fiery hair had taken on, thanks to the twenty-six tablespoons of sugar and caramel coloring.

I cleaned up the best I could. My sweater would need a run through the old Maytag, but my hair and skin came clean just fine. I looked at myself one last time. I'd had the same face for going on ten years, only growing in height and wisdom. I'd never gone anywhere or done anything spectacular. I played no instrument or sport. I didn't act, and I couldn't sing. My only vice consisted of racks upon racks of movies and books, most left to me by my dad. While other kids snuck out to meet up at the well just off Beaker Street to drink beer and smoke cigarettes, I sat at home alone with my movies. Every third Saturday, Angus Libbit, ten years old and already as handsome as his father and just as willful, came to watch movies with me until the wee hours when his parents finished their town meeting and mixer. I was always just Prudence Penderhaus. Odd and painfully average all rolled up into one six-foot-tall redheaded burrito. Adding "dead girl walking" to the list of things that set me apart from my peers, I decided then and there that was the last time I'd be *just* Prudence Penderhaus.

"If I'm going out, I'm going out with a bang." I nodded once at myself in the mirror and set out to do just that.

I cracked the door open and peered out into the cluttered sitting room. Quietly, I slid through the door and closed it softly behind me. I peeked around the staircase, near the front door, looking for the boy. Mr. Shooster's look-alike had left me to my own devices at some point during my bathroom epiphany. The coast was clear, or clear enough for me, anyhow.

I hugged the other side of the staircase and made my way through the narrow hallway and toward what I thought was the entrance to the family room. I pushed the swinging door enough to see what was on the other side but not enough to be obvious. A stark white kitchen, practically immaculate, sat seemingly unused beyond the swinging door. Through the kitchen was another door, the type with a knob. It was the only option other than up the stairs.

I crossed the kitchen stealthily, making every attempt to not squeak my sneakers, let out a long breath, and turned the creaky brass knob. The sounds of a television roared to life as if the knob itself controlled the volume. I pushed the door further and poked my head into the room. A solid brown couch sat in the center, facing the television. A matching recliner was angled with its back toward the door and aimed directly at *The Maury Show*.

A stark contrast to the rose-cluttered sitting room, this room was free of clutter. No knickknacks or family photos on any wall or surface. Not a print or pattern to be seen. Even the walls were painted a boring white like the kitchen. And no coffin. No further doors or entryways led to other rooms where one could be hidden. A tiny smile twitched at the corners of my mouth at the thought that I, Prudence *freaking* Penderhaus, had debunked the decades-long rumor all by my lonesome.

A loud and abrupt snort came from the recliner, and I yipped, slamming a hand over my offending mouth. The snort was followed by even, rumbling snores. Someone was sleeping in the chair. My age-old curiosity mingled with my newly found courage and, heart thudding in my chest, I left the security of the doorway to investigate Sleeping Beauty.

I pressed each toe of my sneaker to the ground, soft and deliberate like a black-and-white slapstick Laurel and Hardy mystery. I cleared the space in a handful of steps, even with my silly walk. Height occasionally had its perks. Looking down my nose, literally, over the top of the chair, I could see only a mass of auburn hair riddled with straggly grey strands jutting out at random. A hefty chest and rotund belly rose and fell with each breath. An empty bottle of wine lay across her lap.

"Hello, Mrs. Shooster," I whispered, hardly audible over the shocked *Maury* audience.

The digital clock on the cable box glowed 7:21 a.m.

First period was well underway, and there I was standing unlawfully in the living room of the scariest house in Flintlock. My stomach fluttered with excitement. I was scared to die, terrified in fact, but ironically, it seemed the prospect of dying had unleashed an inner badass I didn't even know existed.

I tiptoed back out the way I'd come in and left the door the way I'd found it.

Just beyond the swinging kitchen door, cut into the wall, looked to be a door with no knob, which for some strange reason brought Kathy Bates to mind. I tapped my fingers against my thigh, debating on testing the door, which I made a bet with myself was a basement. Rationale got the better of me, and I made my way to the front door.

I reached for the knob. Fully ready to leave, satisfied with my discovery, or lack thereof, and head on to school. I stopped. What was keeping me from checking out more rooms? If I were to run back and spread the word that the Shooster place did not in fact house a coffin, only to make myself a fool in the end when someone bigger and badder than me came through and found a shiny, dark wood casket up in some room on the second floor.

My wet hair flopped over my shoulder as I slowly turned to look up the stairs. What was up there? A coffin? Something else? The odd boy had disappeared somewhere in the house, finding him to say thank you would be the neighborly thing to do. Wouldn't it?

I took each carpeted step covertly and with ease, or

at least that was what I had drummed up in my head. I felt like Nancy Drew, but it was more likely I looked like Mr. Bean. At the landing, I had four choices. Two to the left, one to the right, and another directly in front of me. I caught a tiger by its toe and chose left. The short hall matched the living room. No knickknacks or pictures on the walls, not even a lowly cobweb in a distant corner. Choosing left again, I pressed my ear to the door. Hearing nothing, I turned the knob over and pushed it open. A clichéd creak squeaked from the hinges, and my breath caught in my throat. I stopped, frozen, and waited to get busted. Silence filled the house; the only noise was the thrumming of my own heartbeat in my ears. When no paratroopers descended from the ceiling, I pushed the door open all the way. In the dim light coming from behind dark curtains, I made out a large desk and bookcase in the far corner, a side table next to the door, and a shelf with more books and awards on the wall to my left. An office filled with office stuff. No coffin.

Moving on to door number two and confident I was alone on the second floor, I opened the door with less caution. The room, painted a dark blue, obviously belonged to a boy. A bed in one corner, simple desk in the other, and an entire wall taken up by racks and racks of movies. My jaw dropped to my shoes, instantly covetous of the collection. Ignoring the rest of the room, my vast feet shuffled me toward the racks. I eyed each case, touching every title I'd seen, and coveting those I hadn't.

Hundreds of cases, DVD and VHS alike, each categorized first by genre, then alphabetically by title. My skin turned a Hulk shade of green with envy. It took everything I had not to pull cases from the rack, shove them into my backpack, and run like hell home for a movie marathon of epic proportions.

"Hands down," a rumbling voice demanded from the door.

Both of my hands slammed to my sides so fast they slapped against my jeans. I spun toward the door. "Oh, I'm sorry. I just... I was... I wanted to thank you for letting me use your restroom." I let out a heavy breath.

Shooster junior stood in the doorway. Loomed might be a better term. "Are you spying on me?"

"What?" *Not you, exactly.* "No. No. I just needed your bathroom." I changed the subject. "You have a really awesome collection." I pointed to the racks without touching anything. "I love movies too. I don't have this many, but someday I'll have a collection like this." I admired the cases one more time.

We were both quiet for at least a minute, maybe two. He watched me cautiously as I eyed his collection.

"Kids with backpacks like yours stand on the sidewalk and look at my house." I looked at my feet, sorry I'd been one of those kids today. "I can see them from my window. They laugh and push each other to the gate. They always run away." His dark, intense eyes stared at the side of my face. "You didn't run away."

I closed my eyes and took a deep breath. "Kids can be really cruel. Trust me." I'd seen it firsthand and could probably pick out the exact kids he was referring to if given a lineup.

"Do they laugh at you too?"

I nodded and chuckled. "I wish all they did was laugh."

The boy snapped his fingers near his ear a few times and looked at my feet. "You have big feet."

I swallowed hard and looked at my feet too. I did have big feet. They needed to support a big body; it was only natural. But most people didn't see it that way. Just another Penderhaus oddity. "Yeah." He was the strangest boy I'd met in my life, and even he had something to say about me. Maybe I was better off stuck in a cancer ward for the next year until I died.

The boy loped across the room, stood next to me—close enough to smell his soap—and set his clodhopper next to mine. "I have big feet too."

Chortling around a sorrow that had begun to set in, I agreed without luster. "Yeah, you do."

We stood next to each other, him standing a surprising few inches taller than me, until the awkwardness was on the verge of unbearable. "Why are you here?"

"I heard you had a coffin in your living room." I slapped my hand over my mouth. There was no reason to tell him the truth. It slipped out before I could get a handle on it.

"I don't." His matter-of-fact tone was strange in the

context of the conversation.

"I know that now," I said and shrugged sheepishly. I looked up at him from the corner of my eye. "Why don't I know you?" His own peculiarity aside, it was the mystery surrounding his existence that kept me standing there like a big gangly drowned rat.

"Because we've only just met," he said. His supercilious tone left me waiting for him to add the word duh at the end.

"No, I mean, why have I never seen you before? Like, ever." I turned my head to look at him, to study his face. He refused to look at me.

"Would you like to watch a movie with me?" he asked after a long, awkward silence.

His socially weird offer caught me off guard. "Really?" I asked. Aside from Bonnie Templeton and maybe Marlin Sheave, most people my age didn't willingly hang out with me. Not to mention the fact that I'd entered his house with the intent to uncover a fictitious coffin, propagating further ridicule of his home. I don't think I would have been so willing to hang out with the person who'd done that to me.

"I'm going to watch a movie. You can watch it with me." He still stood shoulder to shoulder with me, talking at the doorway. "No person is ever here to watch with me." His awkward cadence and stance brought a smile to my face. He acted how I felt. Gawky and kooky. Standing in his creepy old house, we could've easily added mysterious and altogether ooky to the list of our shared idiosyncrasies.

"I'm supposed to be at school...." I let my thought hang in the air, unwilling to outright declare I would certainly skip school for reasons far less intriguing. Inside, I was giddy as a schoolgirl—*whatever that means*—to choose one of his many videos. Slyly, I eyed each one and pushed aside the eerie feeling I'd been harboring over standing in the spook house. "Won't your mom be mad?"

He shrugged off my comment and left me to stand in front of the A-G rack. "My mom will sleep in her recliner until my dad comes home from his job at MileStone GenTech Incorporated at 5:00 p.m.," he said, revealing Mr. Shooster was likely not a salesman, but rather a fancy-pants scientist of some sort. Or maybe a janitor, but I doubted it.

The boy's peculiar speech tempo and tone intrigued me more than it might've our peers. Should the boy have attended Flintlock High, he would've likely been a *just* kid like me.

Letting out a long breath, I eyed the movies one last time. *Screw school. This is better.* "Can I pick the movie?" I asked with a smile that was so wide it hurt my cheeks.

"Yes, but I want to watch something without color today. It's a colorless sort of day." His deep voice rumbled in his chest and matched the size of his body. It wouldn't have taken long for him to become Lurch too. Mr. and Mrs. Lurch. That would've been a joy to grow up with.

With the choices I had at my disposal, the minor black-and-white request would be easily met. I nodded to his wish and stuck out my hand to shake his. "My name is Prudence Penderhaus." I figured we might as well know what to call each other if we were to spend the morning together. "I'm glad I decided to weasel my way into your home."

The boy looked at my hand like it was a foreign object. "My name is Cassius Shooster. Why is your hand pointed at me?"

I pulled my barely there ginger brows in toward the center. "To shake hands." I heard my tone come out patronizing, but it was too late to turn back.

"I know what shaking hands is. Why are you doing it?" He shot back in the same tone I'd given him.

"Because we're coming together as friends for the first time. It's what people do...." I let the last few words mumble out as I looked away from his intense stare and let out a long breath.

I took his long hand and put it in mine. His hand was warm, almost hot. My slender fingers wrapped around his hand; he didn't match my grip.

"Have you never shaken hands before?" It seemed an odd question, but it was exactly how he came across.

"No."

"Not even your dad?"

He shook his head.

Our hands stayed locked together longer than one

would consider a casual handshake. I couldn't believe he'd never, not once. As the seconds ticked on, and the moment grew awkward, he pulled his hand from mine and turned away. He snapped his fingers near his ear again. His solemn expression worried me more than the snapping, as though perhaps his invitation was out of pity more than friendship.

He stammered, "You can sit on my bed. The television is right there." He pointed at the wall at the foot of his bed.

I smiled, nodded. "Okay."

Fighting the overwhelming urge to know everything there was to know about him, I put all my focus into finding the perfect movie. His organization was impeccable and made for an easy search. I finally selected a Lugosi classic in honor of the coming holiday, though I had three others in mind before coming to a decision.

Cassius didn't say a word while he put the disc in the player and sat beside me on his bed. Tucking his long legs over and under, avoiding touching my legs with his, the entire show of sitting became a minute-long period of awkward limbs and personal space. The credits rolled, and Cassius snapped his fingers again. As the first lines began, he quoted each of them without fault, impressively matching the accent and rhythm. In all honesty, I was annoyed at first, as I hate Chatty Cathies during movies. After twenty minutes or so of watching the story play out through him, I decided to join in. I'd seen it plenty of times and knew it well enough to keep up. He didn't seem to like having a partner at first, but that didn't stop me. I smiled at him and recited a set of lines, waiting for his response. Before long, he and I were spouting off verbatim as though we'd been reading the script on stage. At my urging, we added dramatic movements and facial expressions to sell the scene.

In those moments, I felt, for once in my life, I had found someone who really understood what it was like to be the odd duck. There was a part of me that hoped Cassius had finally found that someone too. Bonnie had always been a good friend, and I'd known Marlin since kindergarten, but neither of them really got me. When it came down to the nitty-gritty weirdo, they'd never get it. Not in the same way someone like Cassius Shooster could. *Freaks should stick with freaks.*

Considering a budding friendship with another soul seemingly so similar to mine made my heart flutter and ache in the same breath. I'd possibly lived houses away from Cassius Shooster for seventeen years, and the day I met him for the first time just so happened to be the day after I was diagnosed with stage three cancer. I believe they call that irony. The universal kick in the crotch.

2

THUNDER RUMBLED OVER THE HOUSE. FROM THE SOUND OF it, lightning was inevitable and hard rain was only moments away. Though Flintlock was perpetually wet, it was rare a bolt of lightning scratched across the sky.

I fought against my excited urge to get up and look out the window to take in the specter. Just my luck, someone of authority would spot my truant face in the window and my life as I knew it would be over. Well, okay, maybe that was an overstatement, the situation being what it was.

Cassius scooted off the edge of the bed to exchange one Lugosi film for another. The clock on the desk showed quarter to eleven. I'd officially ditched school for the first time. I was spending my day in the spook house of Flintlock with a boy no one knew existed. In a matter of hours, I'd gone from cancer-riddled loser to kind of a badass. As I sat there listening to the impending storm, I felt cool for the first time in my short life.

I wished Morgan and Brady and the lot of them could've seen me doing something no one in the history of Flintlock had ever done. At the same time, I wanted Cassius and 17 Marigold Lane to be my secret—a sanctuary to hide away from the world that I never really understood. And never really understood me.

"It's raining." It was the first thing Cassius had said that wasn't part of the movie in over an hour. I'd been lost in a vision of badassery when he'd moved from the foot of his bed to the window. I hadn't even seen him do it.

"Oh, yeah? Is there lightning?" I heard myself and cringed at how eager I was over the stupid lightning.

"Yes… and thunder too." He fidgeted with the hem of his sweater sleeves. "Want to come stand here and watch it with me?" He spoke quickly and didn't look in my direction, which was fine with me. If he wasn't looking at me, he couldn't see the stupid grin on my face.

Hell yes I wanted to stand with him at the window. But I didn't. I was doing well enough to stifle my weird, surrounded by a room of movies and movie memorabilia, a mecca for pop culture buffs like me.

I'd spent the morning playing a game with myself, finding hidden gems all over the room that I'd missed initially. I knew if I wasn't sitting on my hands, I'd be up trying to play with everything, and I got the distinct impression Cassius wasn't okay with people touching his things.

"Do you like storms?" I asked instead of joining him at the window. I was still dying with curiosity to know everything about the secret boy, while equally trying desperately not to geek out and freak him out. "Flintlock gets its fair share. When I was a kid, I was terribly afraid of thunder, like hide-under-the-covers scared, but my dad told me how it worked, and it made the whole thing interesting instead of scary." Now I was just the weirdo who watched the skies hoping for rain. "Science does that sort of thing."

He tucked his head, raising his broad shoulders. "I don't like thunder. It's loud."

I shrugged. "I don't like balloons popping," I admitted nonchalantly, not understanding the weight of his words at first. Thunder rolled through the atmosphere again and Cassius flinched. "How about we watch the movie? We'll turn it up really loud so we can't hear the thunder as much." I nodded at *White Zombie* playing on the television. "We can pretend it's just part of the movie. I think Lugosi would love it." I felt suddenly like a cheerleader, which was so far from my parameter of abilities it was actually somewhat comical. To be honest, he seemed a bit too old to be afraid of lightning and thunder.

"Bella Lugosi died in 1956, Prudence," Cassius grumbled and flopped on the bed, repeating his gawky limb and space dance before settling in. As the movie played on, the storm grew. He and I laughed and joked as much as the situation would allow—I forced a lot of it, honestly, he wasn't one for idle conversation—for an hour before the storm finally cut the power. In a snap, darkness took over his room. Lightning crackled across the sky, lighting his room for a blink before it collapsed back into darkness.

Cassius stiffened, tucked his head, and clapped his hands over his ears. From deep within his chest, a whining hum.

I laid my hand on his shoulder and he immediately jerked away like my ice-cold hand was a hot poker. "Cassius, are you okay?" I asked idiotically, knowing full well he was not anything of the sort.

"There's no light," he grumbled between his whining, his face practically buried in his lap.

Even ten-year-old Angus Libbit wasn't that afraid of the dark. The whining noise was constant and aggravating my sense; I had no idea how he was making it.

"It happens all the time in these old houses." Fear rolled over his body, thick enough to touch. Desperate to stop the whining, I thought quickly of something comforting to say. "When our lights go out, my mom lights the candles in the living room and brings a lantern to the bathroom. We read books or tell stories to pass the time until the power comes back on." That was a bunch of bullshit. In reality, Mom would stick our only candle in the bathroom so we didn't fall in, and I spent my time struggling to read a book on the toilet with the one candle. All the while she'd be reminding herself to pick up batteries for the flashlights and another box of emergency candles, which she never actually did. All of that had been my dad's job. "What do you guys do when the lights go out?"

His hunched back rose and fell a few times before he finally answered me. "I wait alone until it stops or my dad comes in to get me. He comes home at 5:00 p.m. It's not 5:00 p.m."

"Not for a couple of hours still, but that's okay. What about your mom? Do you want me to get her?" I was beginning to feel more like a babysitter than a peer.

His whining had transformed into a grumbling hum, hauntingly deep. "Mom drinks all the wine and sleeps until Dad comes home at 5:00 p.m.," he mumbled into his folded arms pressed against his legs. "It's not 5:00 p.m."

"So you said," I said under my breath. It seemed Ma and Pa Shooster weren't exactly your typical uppity homeschool parents. "Well, what do you need me to do?" I put my hand on his shoulder, and he shoved it away again. A ping of rejection hit my gut. He flipped the hood of his sweater over his head, shutting me out. After a moment of staring at the back of his hooded head, I murmured, "I'll just go," and lifted myself from the bed.

He didn't even look up, hands over his head, completely ignoring my exit. I moved slowly, hoping he'd come out of whatever he was going through and we could continue our day. If he didn't, if he just let me walk out the door, would he answer it again tomorrow? Would this be my one and only visit with Cassius Shooster?

I slung my backpack over my good shoulder—
backpack application had become one of my most
difficult tasks. I struggled with the strap, eyeing Cassius
who didn't budge. I turned to walk out the door. Cyan
lightning scratched across the sky, and thunder clapped
only a second later. The strange boy who had, only a
moment before, refused to acknowledge my existence
leapt from the bed, closing his impressive wingspan
around my middle as he fell to his knees.

"It's too loud," he pleaded, his face buried against my
back.

I swallowed and considered what to say. I'd never
seen a teenage boy behave that way and wondered if
his obvious—there was no other reason I could see—
sheltered existence played a major role in his strange
behavior. Did Flintlock's constant rain keep the poor kid
huddled under his covers until Papa Shooster came home
at 5:00 p.m.? What did Daddy do that was so spectacular
to save the situation?

I grabbed for anything, anxious to get Cassius off
the floor and not buried into my back. "Do you have a
flashlight?"

He pulled in a shuddered breath and said quickly, "I
have a flashlight in the second drawer of the blue dresser
on the left side of the room."

I started to move toward the dresser, but he refused to
release his grip. I thought initially about just dragging him
with me like a football player refusing the tackle at the

goal line. But he wasn't exactly light, and I wasn't exactly fit. "Cassius, I need you to let me go so I can go get it."

I patted his arm and reluctantly he let go. His precise instructions allowed quick retrieval of said flashlight. Cassius, sitting back on his heels, still kneeling on the floor where I'd left him, paid me zero attention as I took my spot back on the bed.

"Hey, Cassius, why don't you come here and sit with me?" I smiled, but it clearly didn't reach my voice. I wanted nothing more than to rewind and go back to before whatever it was he was doing. "Come on," I urged.

He shimmied on his knees to the bed, unfolding his long legs at the last second to slink onto the bed. Hood still slid over his head, face nearly buried in his own lap.

"What do you need?" I wanted to ask, but ultimately it sounded pushy and overbearing and all too mothering for a peer-to-peer encounter, so I didn't.

Pulling a card from years of babysitting, I slipped the blankets over our heads while we sat facing each other crisscross on his bed. His eyes were closed when I flipped the flashlight on, pointing it upward so to not inadvertently blind either of us.

Heart doing some odd semblance of summersaults in my chest, I fought a festering urge to rip the hood from his head and force him to look at me. Instead, I said the dumbest thing I could have possibly said. "Cassius, look, we're in a fort." I smiled and giggled embarrassingly, but he opened his terrified eyes.

Dark pools of oil stared at me for a moment that seemed to never end. "This is my bed, not a fort," he said. I laughed at his literal understanding and felt a hot blush hit my cheeks. "Hey, it's really bright in here." He looked around the small space we'd created with our tall bodies under the covers.

"Yup. Now you can see everything you need to see, and you're guarded from the dreaded thunder outside." I tapped the fabric over my head as evidence of our fortress of solitude.

"You are a nice girl, Prudence, but this is a sheet." His tone didn't give away the intention behind the comment.

"Thanks, I think." I was fairly certain he'd just called me an idiot.

I watched glittering dust float through the beam of light. To call the silence spread between us awkward would have been a hyperbole. In fact, it was the most comfortable silence I'd ever been party to.

Cassius was the first to break. "Why did you think I have a coffin in my house?" It was a valid question he seemed to have taken his time processing first.

I laughed, discomfort bubbling back up to the surface, and looked away from his piercing dark-chocolate eyes. "That's just the word on the street."

"Which street?"

I shrugged and searched for a sensible answer to his question. "All of them."

"There's no coffin here."

I ran my hand over the glittering beam of light. "I know, Cass."

"It's Cassius." He angrily cut me off short.

"Sorry," I mumbled, not knowing what I'd done to tick him off. "I just thought… since you're my friend, I could call you Cass. You can call me Pru."

He seemed confused. "Your name is Prudence."

"Yes, but my friends, the few I have, call me Pru. It's a nickname. Don't your friends call you something other than Cassius?"

"What friends?"

The question hurt more than it might've someone not in the same sinking lifeboat. "Not even your mom?" I found it hard to believe his own mother had always called him Cassius and nothing else.

"My mom's name is Beatrice." I stared at him, mouth agape, utterly unsure why he'd said that. "She doesn't call me anything," he blurted and looked away.

I blinked, stomach sinking to my butt cheeks. "What's that mean?"

"Nothing." He huffed. "My mother doesn't talk to me." *Snap, snap* went his fingers.

I didn't bother to hide the shocked disbelief in my voice. "*Ever?*" He shook his head, sending his black mop of hair flopping around his face. How could a mother not speak to her son? Like, ever? "What do you do up here all day?" I flashed on his racks of movies and things started to make sense. What had I inadvertently barged in on?

Cassius shoulders raised at least six inches. "I watch movies. I listen to music. I read books. I look out the window at the kids in backpacks that laugh at my house." His impressive Adam's apple bobbed over a voice too deep for a boy. He swallowed and grumbled, "I look out the window... at you." His list of daily activities left me feeling worse for him than I'd ever felt for myself, but it was his mention of watching me that clanged noisily through my soul.

My stomach fluttered, a million monarchs let loose in my gut. I brought a trembling, boney finger to my chest. "You watched *me*?" The idea that someone had been watching me without my knowledge tugged at the primitive instinctual part of my human. I shoved it aside, wholeheartedly assuming Cassius Shooster was anything but predatory.

"You know something, Cassius..." I sighed, almost unwilling to defend those snot-faced hooligans I knew would soon be tromping down my street. "Those kids don't even know you're up here." He huffed, puffing gold dust out of the beam of light. "*I* didn't know you lived here. And I've lived three houses away for almost eighteen years." The idea was practically improbable in real life, a made-for-TV movie at best, and yet, there I sat. "How long have you lived here? I knew your dad had a wife, but I'd never seen her. Your house is...." I stopped when my brain caught up to my mouth. All of the things I'd been holding back had rushed out. Well, almost all of them. I chose my next words carefully as it was becoming more obvious he had a hard time understanding nuances for whatever reason. "Scary." I left it at that. He surely could understand scary just from the movies he liked to watch.

"My mom tells my dad I'm scary." He looked away from me and shrugged his wide shoulders, completely ignoring the question I'd snuck in. "*Too* scary, she says. Too scary for school, I heard her say once." He breathed, shallow but enough to disturb the dust beam. "Dangerous." Those monarchs in my gut all died and crashed down at once. "I don't think I'm dangerous."

We sat in silence for a while. "Me either."

The thunder had died down and the pitter-patter of rain against the window filled the quiet. I could have sat in that void for hours, in the quiet. He was so still. When he wasn't talking or snapping, his stillness could have been misconstrued as unsettling. I found it soothing—away from the busybodies of school.

Cassius sat in that numbing quiet alone every day before that day. For hours. Days. Years?

"Do you want to go outside?" I asked.

His black eyes grabbed the light, gleaming back at me like a wild animal caught in the darkness. "In the *front*?" I nodded and smiled, thinking I was a genius, but his face twisted into a mask of fear. "Mom says to stay inside." His breath came in heaving puffs. "Don't open the door. Don't go into the rose room. Never, ever in the front."

It couldn't have been possible. How could parents

keep a child indoors for *years*? Not even a trip to the dentist? It seemed my assumption of a sheltered life had been an understatement. Cassius had been, from what I put together, trapped inside that house for his entire life with a woman who refused to acknowledge his existence, and his only companion his dad. Until the day I knocked on his door drenched in cola.

That, I do believe, is what they call kismet.

I bit my cheek and set myself up for a poor decision. "That changes today." I flung the covers off our heads and leapt from the bed. "Cassius Shooster, you are far too excellent a human being to be trapped inside this dank old house." I reached out and took his large hand in mine, yanking him from the bed. He helped of course by actually getting up; there would have been no way I could have moved that boy on my own.

Flashlight in hand, I trotted along the hallway with my odd boy in tow. The tension in his body ran right down to his fingertips. My guess was it was the first time he'd held hands with a girl, probably with anyone. First trip outside, first girly hand.

Life was full of firsts. First bike ride. First dance. First kiss. I'd never met another soul in my life who hadn't left their house. Ever. I couldn't sit back and allow that to continue. His day—the rest of his life, or mine—would be filled with firsts if I had anything to do with it. His first visitor. His first friend. His first trip outside to play in the rain.

We reached the front door, the infamous rose room to our right, and his heels set. I pulled, but he didn't move an inch. "There are rules," he said, his head shaking. "Cassius follows the rules." He was talking only to himself—repeating something ingrained in him for too many years to undo in just one afternoon.

I met his eyes, holding his face with my hands on either side. I'd never felt as powerful in my life as I did in that moment. "Prudence Penderhaus followed the rules every day for seventeen years, and it got her nowhere." *But dead.* "I changed that today, and it brought me right here to you. If that's not fate, I don't know what is. There's a whole world out there waiting for you, Cassius. Come see it... with me." The smile on my face spread so wide, my eyes crinkled at the edges.

Cassius didn't smile back. He really hadn't genuinely smiled since the moment I'd met him. He looked over his shoulder like someone would be coming for him any minute. "It's raining. I'll be wet."

"That's the point," I urged, and pulled him hard once more as I opened the front door.

Cassius and I tumbled out onto the porch. His expression played out an internal war of fear and wonder. The rain fell softly, and the wind blew under the eave, sprinkling our cheeks. The front door slammed shut behind us, and in that moment, Cassius Shooster broke his first rule. Ever.

He didn't catch fire or sparkle or anything of the sort

when we stepped outside so I could probably also rule out that vampire rumor—the lesser of the rumors, but valid in its own right.

Tugging on his hand, I pulled him off the porch and into the gentle, cool drops of rain. They fell perfectly against my skin, as if something above had sent them down to earth just for us. Cassius's deep eyes sparkled while he took in the world. His expression, a confused muddle of worry and joy, turned the corners of my smile down. After being overloaded by thunder, I worried he wouldn't be able to handle being outside. That the idea of rule breaking would send him scurrying back inside, never to emerge again. Never to see me again.

Using the moment to prove the world was nothing to fear, I let go of his hand and spread my arms wide. Turning my face to the sky, I closed my eyes and opened my mouth to catch the drops. I spun as though I were ten again. Laughter tickled the back of my throat, and I nearly lost myself in the moment of silence and rain.

A laugh that didn't belong to me brought me back to earth. I opened my eyes to find Cassius, arms wide, mouth open to the sky, and spinning like—I assumed—he'd never spun in his life. His smile brought dimples I hadn't known existed to his cheeks. Happiness filled my heart at seeing him enjoy something so mundane. Most everyone had played in the rain at some point in their life. Not Cassius Shooster. I'd rectified that, and it made me feel good to be a human being. Good to be alive.

My hair, wet and stuck to my head, surely looked like a drenched cat, but Cassius didn't seem to care when he stopped spinning and looked me in the eye. Pure joy spread from ear to ear; he laid his hand on my chilled cheek. "Prudence Penderhaus, you're beautiful."

"Ha," I laughed, one obnoxious heehaw donkey bark. "I don't know about that, but thank you." Having no clue of his knowledge of the opposite sex, what with his probable seclusion and all, I didn't quite know how to react. Truth be told, no one had ever said those words to me—my mom didn't count.

The dark intensity of his eyes made them hard to look at. His shaggy black hair clung to the sides of his face, dripping water down his cheeks and over those dimples of his. Odd as he was, Cassius Shooster was actually kind of cute. "I'm glad you're happy out here. In the rain." *With me*, I wanted to add but didn't. It seemed both too cheesy and too subtle for his literal interpretations of things.

"I do love the rain." He looked down the street. "Not the thunder." He shook his head. "Where is your house?" he asked, practically boiling over with anticipation.

"The yellow one, three houses down, 23 Marigold Lane, is me." I smiled, but he looked like he didn't really get it. "That's my house number," I added, to be clear.

"Can I see your house?" he asked through his never-ending grin.

So much for baby steps. I wasn't sure that was a good idea. I didn't want him locked up in his house, but I also didn't know his parents and didn't want to basically kidnap their son. I wanted to be a rule breaker, not a lawbreaker. Spending my last months in the slammer wasn't on my bucket list.

I sighed and looked down the street at my house. It was right there. It wasn't like he was running away to Timbuktu. "All right..." I hesitated. "But just for a bit, and then we'll come back here." Responsible babysitter-extraordinaire reared her sensible head. "We'll talk to your dad when he gets home and ask if maybe we can hang out at my house from now on." That sounded reasonable enough to me.

School had been out long enough only the last stragglers of students meandered down Thyme across the street. No one bothered to look our way—which if only one of them had, they'd have seen the hidden boy who did not own a coffin nor was a vampire standing in plain sight. Wet and drunk on freedom.

My wet sweater clung to me, making my thin frame obvious beneath it. I pulled the thick fabric away from my skin in the center, then at each shoulder. On the last tug, I tapped the stupid thing under my arm and sent pain zinging through my body; the sensation brought bile up my throat. The most I could do was close my eyes, drown out the world, and wait for the pain to go away.

According to Doc Harris, tumors like mine were predominantly painless. I'd lucked out and become a statistic within a statistic. My tumor took up shop in a prime nerve location. I had pain, almost constant, and swelling, and limited movement, and all those wonderful things that happen when a deadly intruder encroached on your skinny wing.

"Prudence Penderhaus?" Cassius's voice called to me. His large, wet, cold hand touched my face. "Prudence?"

"I'm fine," I lied through gritted teeth.

"You're lying on the pavement."

It appeared I was. Cold and wet, my baby-giraffe-on-roller-skates body had tumbled down and landed flat. "I'm sorry," I apologized for no reason. "I'll be fine."

My head swam. I'd fainted a few times before that, and all because of the thing taking over my life. Not that it was the direct cause necessarily, more that it was a big-ass ball pressing on nerves and cutting off blood circulation.

I struggled to sit up, avoiding elbow propping all together, and almost lacking the core strength in the end. I'd hit my head when I landed and had a growing knot to prove it. The world was shades of gray, partly due to the rainy weather and partly because of my half-conscious state.

"Are you sick?"

Yes. I didn't know how to tell him that though. His apparent lack of worldly experience made me question his possible reaction to my being ill. If he cared at all. "I'm fine," I lied again.

Without another word, Cassius put his hands in mine and pulled me to my feet. It was the most normal gesture he'd expressed in our short time together. My arm zinged again, I winced and forced my stomach to pick up the slack. I stood on my own two feet and regretted it almost immediately. Knees buckling, I nearly dropped like an acme safe, but the hands of my new friend caught me and held me until I righted myself again.

"You should see a doctor."

I laughed at Captain Obvious and deliberated internally how I would explain it to him—if we were to remain friends, of course. There was always a chance the day of movies and rain would be fleeting, an experience to be recalled fondly as we both moved on with our craptacular lives and nothing more. Grateful I'd made the choice to knock on his door and worried our encounter would end, I wrapped my long arms around his middle and squeezed him as tightly as my stupid arm would allow. Cassius stood there with his arms pinned straight at his sides. When I pressed my face into his chest, he relaxed enough to breathe again. A few breaths later, he finally slinked his surprisingly strong arms around me.

Tears welled at my lashes. I couldn't cry. Not right then, there, with the odd boy in the rain. I'd done more than my fair share of crying in the recent past and had no good reason to be unloading in front of a kid I just met. Unless of course my subconscious knew something I didn't. Maybe it was the knowledge that whatever happened, neither of our lives would be the same after that afternoon in the rain.

"You're a nice boy, Cassius Shooster," I said instead of the million other things on my mind. If nothing else, I wanted him to know that much.

We hugged for a long few minutes, standing in the rain, pretending the world didn't matter. I hoped—not a God-fearing person, prayer wasn't my thing, but at that moment I came close—that was the first of many hugs.

"Cassius Marcel Shooster, what on God's green earth are you doing out here?" a flustered voice called to us. "And who is *this*?"

Cassius quickly let me go and slammed his hands to his sides. His spitting image stood in the driveway wearing a khaki trench coat. Cassius looked at his shoes and not at his dad. *It's not five o'clock yet.*

I panicked, he was early, I wasn't prepared, and I opened my big trap and started talking. "Hi, Mr. Shooster. I'm Prudence Penderhaus. I live down at 23, the yellow house." He stared at me with the same piercing brown eyes as his son. "You see, it's a funny story." I chuckled nervously and continued. "Some ass—*mean* boys from my school threw soda on me, and Cassius was nice enough to let me in and use your sink to wash it off. I was in there"—I pointed to the house—"and the power went out. Cassius was terrified of the storm and—"

He flung his hands in the air and slapped them to his thighs. "This is just preposterous. Cassius, you get inside now, young man."

Cassius gave me one last anxious glance and shuffled

into the house. Not wanting him to feel the wrath of his parents, I took it upon myself to fix everything right up. "Mr. Shooster," I said and stepped toward his car.

"Save it." He put his hand up to stop me. Checking over his shoulder for peepers, he lowered his voice and continued. "Do you know what you've done?" I muttered something unintelligible, but he didn't stop. "That boy has enough to deal with without bringing some girl into the mix."

Some girl? "That boy has spent his entire life trapped in his room." Contempt seeped from my pores.

"His mother decided that was for his own good. He could never survive—"

"School? He's too *scary*?" I wiggled my fingers in the air between us. I didn't care if I sounded like a bitch. Someone needed to stand up for him, and I had nothing better to do with the rest of my life than make sure that happened.

"He has a special set of needs, you see, which are not met at Flintlock High School." He fidgeted with his overcoat.

"I've never seen him. He's lived here with you all my seventeen years? I didn't know he existed. That's downright torture. You haven't protected him from anything. You've kept him from living." I only had a tenth of the knowledge necessary for a valid argument, but I wasn't letting that stop me from making a point.

Mr. Shooster closed the distance between us. "Do you

know what he is? Do you have any idea what your life would be like with him in it?" The idea was ridiculous. Cassius was witty and accepting, unlike other boys his age. Odd, maybe. Strange, sure. But who wanted to be normal, really? Normal was boring and highly overrated. When I didn't answer his silly question, he answered it for me. "His life is filled with necessary routine. A schedule from morning to night. His ticks, obsessions, aversions... his rage, they all run our lives."

"Maybe he wouldn't be so odd if he had some socialization," I said with moxie, talking with my hands more than appropriate for the situation.

He puffed out his chest and planted his hands on his hips. "Asperger's doesn't make room for such things."

"Ass what?" I honestly had no clue what he'd just said.

"Autism, ASD, whatever you want to call it, it's a life ruler. He cannot be out in the world. Cassius has a disability that will forever run his life. He will always be dependent on us. He will never get married or have children. He has no room in his head for things like love, and his sensory sensitivities make affection impossible." He waved his hand as if waxing away the ideas he'd just portrayed. "In the end, he's dangerous and unpredictable. You're a young girl with a whole life ahead of you. Why would you ever want to fill it with the strained relationship my son will bring?"

Because I'm dying. "Your son has more soul than any human I've met, and I've known him all of eight hours."

Some Inspector Gadget wannabe wasn't going to convince me otherwise, no matter how desperate he was. "I don't care what he has. In my opinion, his only disabilities are his parents. You better believe this isn't the last you'll see of me. You and your blind bigotry can suck a duck for all I care." I shot my pointer finger in the air. "Cassius is my friend. End. Of. Story." I poked that single finger in his chest with each word. It was the boldest thing I'd done in my life.

The shocked look on Mr. Shooster's face was more than words could describe. I'd meant every word I'd said and judging by his silent reaction, he wasn't expecting it. Weird I was. Different? Sure. Kind of a loser, I could accept that. But no one would ever say Prudence Penderhaus didn't have gumption.

I turned on my heel and stomped in the puddles down the walk and out the gate. Stealing one last look at the house, I caught Cassius in his window, his large hand pressed against the glass. I wondered how often I'd walked right past him up there. How many rainy days did he look out and watch me walk by? My heart broke at the thought.

I wanted desperately to run up the stairs and drag him out. Beat his parents over the head for hiding him away because he was different. Because he needed extra care. I needed extra care too. No one was hiding me away. I'd be damned if Cassius spent one more day trapped in that life.

The rain picked up, and poured down on my already

drenched head. I made the turn at my walkway, feet slapping the wet pavement. I noticed the expression on my face in the window on the door and feared for anyone who chose to impede my path. I had a mission to accomplish. I had a boy to save. First, I had to research Asperger's.

3

"ASPERGER SYNDROME IS OFTEN CONSIDERED A HIGH-functioning form of autism. It can lead to difficulty interacting socially, repeat behaviors, and clumsiness," I read aloud from my computer screen. "Well, that doesn't seem so bad. Why the hell would his parents lock him away? Who could do that to their own kid?" I shook my head in disgust and scrubbed my spindly fingers down my face. "How bad could it really be?"

Tapping a single finger against my keyboard, I thought of all the horrible possibilities that could come about from Cassius and his Asperger's. I imagined he got stuck in a string of snaps while simultaneously tripping on his own clodhoppers, unable to catch himself because of the snapping, he tumbled ass over teakettle, smashing his lovely face. It seemed extreme, but not outside the realm of possibilities. A number of scenarios played out in my head. Ranging from seven straight hours of increasingly uncomfortable silence to creating a portable fortress of solitude so he could enjoy the world on his terms.

Even in all those possibilities, I couldn't come up with one good reason not to be friends, good friends in fact, with Cassius Shooster.

Staring at the words on the screen, accepting all possibilities, I made up my mind with a poignant nod of my head. "I need a friend—other than Bonnie—and so does he. Starting tomorrow, I will make sure Cassius Shooster knows he has someone who wants to get to know him. Someone who wants to be his friend. Someone who—"

"Who are you talking to?"

I yelped, nearly spinning myself out of my chair. Cassius's face stared at me from just above the windowsill, his dark brown eyes more inquisitive than piercing. I couldn't, for a moment, figure out how in the hell he was peering through my window.

"Myself." I rushed to the window to investigate, screeching on my way, "What are you doing?"

Standing precariously on the porch roof, Cassius held my backpack in one hand and a DVD case in the other. Clumsiness seemed to not apply in his case. He'd managed to climb the rose lattice that crept up the west side of the house and pull himself to the roof. I'd only attempted that feat once, when I was eleven and swore to my mother I was running away right after my dad died.

For the record, I didn't get far.

"I brought you your backpack," he said, lifting it into view.

"I see that." He hadn't made any attempt to come in, just stood there, chin hardly reaching the sill. "Why did you climb my trellis?"

"Because your window is on the second floor." Odd boys had odd ways. Most would have just rung the doorbell.

"But my front door is on the first," I said, a grin plastered on my face.

He looked confused. "But no one knows me." He dropped his voice. "I'm a secret." The thorny truth in his words snagged and stung on their way down.

Pinching my lips between my teeth, I swallowed back sorrow. "Not yet, Cass, but they will." I'd called him Cass without thinking and waited for him to snap at me.

"It's Cassius," he said quickly under his breath. He spoke low, dropping his eyes and his chin, turtling without tucking his head. "Sometimes it's hard for me to understand people." His words came so fast I almost didn't catch them all. "My dad says I'm weird and people won't like me."

Five million exclamation points dotted above my head. "Me too." No one on the planet could understand those words better than Prudence Penderhaus. "Want to come in?"

He didn't respond at first. Bit his cheek, gnawing on

the question. "Yes, I do."

Hesitantly, first weighing all modes of execution, he wrapped impressive hands over the sill. In one heave, he pulled his pushing-seven-feet up to his hip and stuck one long leg through the window, then the other. As seamless as the takeoff had been, the landing was twice as awkward. Lower half in, upper half out, Cassius perched on the sill, carefully planning. I stood, helpless, stuck in a spastic loop of reaching out to help him and stepping back away and giving him space to work. There was no telling if he saw me, because he never acted as though he would have taken the help either way.

Just as the moment was on the verge of becoming too unnerving to bear, he slinked in, belly first, catching his sweater on the lock and pulling it over his face. My eyes widened and my cheeks flushed. Waistband to nipple, pale as the dead, fully exposed. He slid through, a newborn giraffe tumbling from his mother, all limbs.

Cheeks a healthy shade of lobster, I watched him right his hoodie and shake his hair into place. Other than my dad and Angus, I'd never had a boy in my room. I was nearly eighteen; there was no reason I could see to keep up that tradition.

It was truly a full minute before Cassius got himself together. And it was less than a breath after that the reality of it all sunk in. Shock began to take over his face. He'd left his house, his cell, and now was standing in someone else's house. Someone else's room. The idea of that scratched across his face in a series of expressions that finally settled on cautious but interested.

In all of my possibilities, I hadn't actually considered how I, Prudence Penderhaus, painfully average—outside of the red hair and six-feet—and wrenchingly boring, was going to acclimate a young man on the autism spectrum who had spent his life in a prison.

I supposed I could start by not being so average and boring.

"I take it your parents are unaware of your great escape."

He tucked his hands inside his sleeves in a movement that spread from thumbs to shoulders. "They'd be pretty pissed," he said under his breath, laughing at himself and surprising me with his relaxed choice of words.

After staring at his shoes for thirty-seven seconds, he shoved a hand in the pocket of his hoodie and pulled out the DVD case he'd squirreled away. "I brought this for you."

It was the one I'd been coveting when he caught me peeping at his collection. "Wow, thank you." I stared at the case, dragging a finger over its edges. "How did you know?"

"I remember things, things I see."

I finally looked up from the case. "That sounds like it could come in handy," I said, my smile terrifyingly large.

He swallowed back nervousness, looking at me, then away, shuffling those big feet of his. Two snaps in his ear and he was off, talking fast, almost too fast to follow. "Would you help me? Help me—" He stopped, two snaps, back again. "—be a regular human. Because I don't"— two snaps—"know... how to be human."

His words poked at my insides. How could he have learned how to human having never been taught the skills of basic human interaction beyond his absentee mother and questionable father? I wanted to punch both of his parents directly in the face. One good pop to the nose. In truth, I didn't know how to punch, but that wouldn't stop me from plotting the moment in detail.

I mulled over my approach too long, taking the liberty to imagine me punching the Shoosters. Cassius grew impatient, letting out an exasperated sigh when I didn't respond quickly enough.

"Yes," I blurted, panicked. It was simple, but a promise nonetheless. "I've never met anyone like you before." He pulled his bottom lip under his teeth. "Granted, I don't know you that well. Er—at all." I was losing him inch by inch into his hoodie. "First impressions and all, you're definitely not like boys your age." Dismay flashed across his face. He clearly wanted to be just like boys his age. An idea I would fight to the teeth to stop. "That's a good thing," I said, keeping pity from my voice.

He pulled in a deep breath, pressing a hand to his chest. "My mother thanks you. My father thanks you. My sister thanks you. And I thank you," he quoted the infamous James Cagney line—sans dying father.

It didn't surprise me that his repertoire of social interaction came directly from pop culture. With a drunk for a mother and a father who seemed to want nothing more than to hide his son away from the world, the only way he could've learned how to interact would've been from watching it on the television. The fact that *my* social interaction was predominately based on movie quotes was far more concerning. I blamed my father.

I grinned and laid a hand on his shoulder. "You're something else, Cassius Shooster."

"What am I?" he asked, reminding me of the article I'd read and his inability to understand context.

What was he? An odd boy. A weirdo. A freak, like me. "You, my friend, are an enigma. That's what you are." He smiled, proving he'd received some form of education locked away in that house. I sighed. "Do you have to get back home? I mean, they're going to notice you're gone eventually. I don't want you in trouble. I plan on talking to your dad about you and me tomorrow when he's calmed down. I want him to meet my mom, so he knows I'm not some freak." Whatever reasons they'd had for locking him up were stupid, and now that I'd discovered him, they were pointless.

He shook his head, black eyes wide, hair flopping around his head. "My dad said you're trouble for me. He said I don't know how to handle you and I should stay away, or you'll get hurt and I'll go to prison."

"*Prison?*" I shrieked. "What in the fu—" I laughed

out the end of the word, but sadness in my core grew. "Have your parents—*your dad*—taught you about people and stuff? Like girls and school and other kids." His eyes, which had been stuck on me, looked away in shame. "I'm just trying to figure out your life up till now. You don't have to answer anything I ask if you don't want to. Just know that I can't help you if you don't help me." There was so much more to the story than I was getting, and it killed me not knowing.

He shrugged. "My dad taught me everything I know."

That says a lot. "What about school? You should be a senior, right? Getting ready to graduate and all." I held back the mile-long line of questions I had built up in the course of the day.

"I don't go to Flintlock."

"I guessed that."

"Dad teaches me at home, so I stay out of trouble." His words were fast and mumbled over one another in that deep, chest-rumbling tone. "Dad says I'm trouble for the world and it's best I just stay out of it. He says I'm dangerous and the world can't handle me."

"Yeah, your dad says a lot of things." I was getting damn tired of things Dad said. "Look, Cassius, I don't know why your parents feel you can't live a life like any other teen, but I know you can. I looked up Asperger's online and it—"

"What's Asperger's?" His innocence, a key ingredient of what made him up as a human being, both warmed my heart and shattered it.

Are you effing kidding me? "It's something you have." His parents hadn't just hidden him from the world, they'd hidden him from himself. How could he ever come to terms with his own brain if he didn't even know it worked a bit differently than the typical teenage boy?

"Like a disease?"

"No."

"Like cancer."

My lungs sucked in air faster than my brain could catch up. "No." I let the gulp of air out. "Not like cancer."

Lips pursed, I restrained the slew of curses waiting in line on the tip of my tongue. "It's the reason, some of it anyway, that you don't know how to be human." His flat expression said he needed more. "It's something you were born with, something you'll always have, but you can do things to help. You can learn how to cope with the things that bother you, like the thunder, and let yourself be happy in the world. Your parents should have told you this years ago." Google had come through. I stood up a little straighter in the knowledge that I had.

"My parents told me I was strange. Too scary and too strange. Too dangerous." He'd used the word dangerous more than once. I made a mental note to bring that up to his dad because that word was bullshit.

"Actually, Cassius, you're a boy just like all the other boys. You've just got to learn how the world works and how you work in it. It's not that different from any other teenager. You just have some catching up to do."

His chest rose and fell, slowly at first, then one huge heaving breath. "This is preposterous," he shouted and clapped his hands together—Papa Shooster rearing his ugly head.

I flinched and blinked away my shock. "What do you mean?"

"Aha," he scoffed. "Me?" he shrieked and jammed a finger into his chest, bending the tip, turning it purple. "A normal teenage boy. I. Am. Not. Normal." He karate chopped his open palm for each word. "I'm odd. I'm weird. I'm too dangerous for my own good, and I'll never make it out there in the world. They'll lock me up and throw away the key." He pulled the hood of his sweatshirt over his head, hiding his face, avoiding me completely.

"Cass." I touched his shoulder. "Listen, I—"

"Don't touch me!" he screamed and shoved me away. "I'm just a retard." He screeched the last word, clearly imitating his mother.

His footfalls echoed as he stomped toward the window before I could stop him. Terrified he'd hurt himself trying to escape my presence over the roof and down the trellis, I hurried after him, snagging the back of his sweatshirt with one hand as one of his long legs flipped out the window.

"Oh, no you don't," I protested, breathless from trying to hold back his heavy body. "I won't stop you from leaving, but you'll leave out the front door like a nor—

anyone else."

Frantic knocks shook my bedroom door. We both stopped and stared at it.

"Pru, what in the world is going on in there?" my mom thundered from the other side. Before I could answer, she opened the door. Her blue eyes caught us in their beam. A couple of peculiar giants perched oddly over the windowsill, all arms and legs. "I really think I need an explanation."

I stuttered and stammered something that sounded like, "This is Cassius Shooster. He lives down in 17." When she didn't respond, I continued to dig my hole. "He, uh, we met this morning." She blinked. "He was very nice to me and helped me when Morgan and his band of idiots were jerks to me. He was just bringing me back my backpack." I nodded to it.

"Through the window?"

Because my room is on the second floor. "He didn't want to disturb you by ringing the bell." It made absolute sense at the time, but looking back, I could have said something else. Anything else.

Mom stood there, pudgy hand gripping the knob. Her mom brow was set, crooked almost to her hairline. She obviously hadn't believed a word I'd said, leaving me two choices—continue the lie and hope it came around or abandon ship and come out with the truth.

"Prudence's mother," Cassius interrupted, still half hanging out the window. "I've never been outside of my house before."

Mom's expression fell, brows pulling up at the center. At first I would have sworn she wasn't going to believe him, standing there breathing like she was, then she said, "Come in this house, boy. It's time to sort all this out." My mom, God love her, was a little too easygoing at times and had taken for granted my lack of sociability all these years.

Cassius did as he was told and slinked back in, head hanging. Whether it be from shame or some other unknown cause, he refused to look up at my mom. She grabbed him up with fingers pinched to his sleeve and pulled him to the hallway. He dragged his feet the entire way.

Aside from the typical cranky-teenage-girl stuff, I'd never truly pissed my mom off. Stubborn and weird, but never defiant or reckless. Not until the day I'd ditched school, shacked up with a stranger, and uncovered a secret my neighbors had been hiding my entire life.

"Mom," I started to argue but didn't have anything worth saying so I shut myself up.

"Cassius, right?" she asked, and he nodded, looking anywhere but at her. "Where do you go to school?" He shrugged, mostly ignoring her, but she didn't let it go. "I'm not mad. I just want to know more about your life."

"I go to school in my basement." His slow, honest answer burned the back of my throat.

"I see." She pursed her lips and looked at me from the

corner of her eyes. "Cassius, I want you to tell me about your parents. What do they do?"

"My dad is a geneticist and my mom drinks wine on the La-Z-Boy until my dad gets home from MileStone GenTech Incorporated at 5:00 p.m."

I wasn't shocked to learn the peculiar looking man was a mad scientist. Aside from learning his look-alike father's occupation, the information was nearly exact to what he'd already told me, almost word for word. I'd all but confirmed the drunken mom factor when I peered over her already drunk sleeping head at eight that morning, empty bottle in hand.

"Do they know you're here?" He shook his head, waves flopping over his forehead. "When was the last time you were out of the house?" Her face was stone, but her voice held pity.

"When Prudence pulled me out into the rain." *Snap, snap.* "She hugged me, then my dad came home and sent her away." Emotion spilled into his voice. "I've never been anywhere before today," he answered instinctively.

Mom pulled in a long, ragged breath. "Not even to see a doctor?"

Cassius shook his head, slowly tucking it further into his hood.

Mom's face turned an unhealthy shade of pink. "I think it's time we talk to your father," Mom said, tugging him toward the stairs by the sleeve again.

"No, no, no." His words cramped my stomach into

knots and stopped Mom in her tracks. "I don't want that. No roses. No roses, please." He pulled his hood over his head and began a string of mumbling, inaudible rants.

Mom's eyes shifted to me, then back at Cassius. At first she seemed confused, unsure of the boy in her grasp, but a moment later, a wash of understanding hit her. She bit her cheek, searching her brain for a solution. "Where do you store your socks?" she asked, seemingly from left field.

Cassius stopped his rambling and looked at her, brows drawn tight at the center. "In the top right drawer," he said as though she'd just asked the most ludicrous question he'd ever heard.

"Me too," she said with a grin. In one nonsensical question, she'd pulled him right out of an anxiety loop and back into the now. I'd have to ask her later how she did such magic. "Now, I think I can help you and your situation. You just have to trust me. Can you do that?"

His dark eyes shifted to me and back at his feet three or four times before I finally nodded my approval. "Yes," he grumbled.

"Good. Now, let's all go together and figure this out."

He hesitated at the top of the steps, looked back at me, and then slowly clomped down. My heart thudded in my chest. There was no telling what his parents would do. Judging by the reaction I'd received from his dad, it wasn't going to be good. Out the front door and into the night, the three of us headed down the walk. Nerves had taken hold of me and continued to rip apart my gut each step closer we came to 17 Marigold Lane.

His height nearly twice hers, Mom—her face set with determination—towed Cassius by the shirt sleeve along beside her. I took up the rear, gnawing on my mostly chewed nails. My gut told me to stop her. Turn around and call an authority of some sort to come handle the situation. She didn't know what she was doing. What could she do? She taught first grade. She could teach him to add, maybe. He seemed smart enough; I figured he had that one under control. Aside from adding and writing his name on the top of his paper, I couldn't come up with any solid offer my mother could make to his parents to turn them around. That said, I had no idea what would make me think they would have listened to almost-adult Prudence Penderhaus either. Maybe authorities were exactly who should have been involved from minute one.

Clouds in various shades of almost black shifted slowly overhead. Ominous storm clouds covered the night's sky. It was a typical dreary October night in Flintlock, but one couldn't help but feel the oppression—a sinking ceiling, soggy from a leak, in the moments before it burst and fell.

We reached the gate—the final barrier before sudden death. Mom swung it open without hesitation, stomping up each step in her size seven Reeboks. She seemed to have built up steam on our three-house walk up the street. Her knock proved that. Loud and hard, her small fist shook the aging wood door.

The wait for footsteps and locks unlocking seemed

like an eternity. I'd chewed my nail down to the knuckle by the first fumbling lock. Then another, and another. Four in total, each lock unlocked with uncertainty before the door eventually creaked open.

Cassius's look-alike dad stood in the doorway. Even from the back I could see Mom's jaw drop. I'd gotten over that shock, and in a few breaths, so did Mom.

"Cassius," Mr. Shooster shouted. A spindly arm jutted through the crack of the door, light blue dress shirt sleeve rolled haphazardly to the elbow. Mr. Shooster snatched Cassius up by the shirt and yanked him through a crack only wide enough for his slim body to tumble through. "What are you— I am so sorry, ma'am. He shouldn't have been—"

"Sir." Mom cut him off curtly. "You and I need to speak. May we come inside?"

Mr. Shooster stuttered and stammered, seeming for a moment to actually be considering the idea before he eventually exclaimed, "No, you may not." He puffed out his skinny chest, asserting his authority.

Mom smiled sweetly, looked at the pink toes of her sneakers, and scuffed a toe against the grungy old wood. She pursed her lips and took a step forward, closing the distance between them. Craning her neck to meet his eyes, she said through her teeth, "If you don't let me in that damn house, I will call the police and report the blatant neglect that has been going on here." Blatant was a gross exaggeration, possible would have been a better choice of word, but the expression on Mr. Shooster's face said he feared we knew more than we actually did. I bit my cheeks to hide a smile. Cassius pulled his hood tight over his head, watching me from behind his dad. When Mr. Shooster scoffed, Mom finished him off. "I'm sure my old buddy, Elroy Floyd—that's our sheriff, you know— would love to hear from his high school sweetheart." Her threat was solid and sound. I'd never seen that strength. I didn't know she had it in her.

Mr. Shooster blinked over and over again; his voice caught in his throat. I heard a snort from somewhere deep in the house and assumed Mrs. Shooster was snoring away in her drunken stupor. Mr. Shooster looked back over his shoulder into the house. His Adam's apple bobbed around a thick gulp. Cassius's dark eyes darted to his dad and back to me while his father weighed his options. Finally, and with reluctance that oozed from his pores, Mr. Shooster nodded and mumbled something that sounded like an invitation.

Mom didn't wait for him to open the door and pushed past him into the entryway. Her eyes fell over every last ugly rose-covered knickknack in the sitting room guarding any unwanted escapees. I wondered then if Cassius had climbed out his own window to avoid those roses only to scuttle around the real thing on his way up to mine.

"You two go wait over there." She nodded to the other side of the staircase.

Mr. Shooster rubbed his hand nervously over his

forehead, shoving waves of black hair away from his face. "I—I don't think you understand Ms—"

"I don't think *you* understand. Your boy is escaping his home late at night to visit my daughter, normal teenage behavior, but according to him, it's the first time he's left this house. Do you understand the implications of that? That's kidnapping," Mom said with one hand on her hip and a finger pointed in his face.

I craned my neck as far as it would go on my way out of the room until the two were completely out of sight. Cassius and I made our way around the stairs but didn't bother to go farther into the kitchen or living room area, where I knew his mom was likely passed out. Instead, we waited quietly around the back side of the stairs, peering cautiously through the balusters—Mom had forced me for years to dust between those spindly things on account of my equally shaped fingers—and listened to the ass reaming his dad was getting from my mom, a woman who was half his height and twice his width.

"Kidnapping?" Mr. Shooster scoffed and ruffled his hand through his pitch-black hair. "I can't kidnap my own son."

Whether his point was valid or not, Mom bypassed it and went straight for the threat. "The point is, I will be contacting the law tomorrow morning. I expect to see your son out in the open air by the end of the week. I respect your choice of education, homeschooling is always an option, but if there is one T not crossed on your paperwork, I swear to everything you hold dear I will rain down hellfire upon you like you've never seen." Her voice dropped deep and almost growling.

I held my hand over my mouth, stifling nervous laughter. I'd never heard my mom lose her temper. Ever. Demure was her middle name. But there she was standing in a stranger's home threatening hellfire.

Mr. Shooster was quiet for a long minute, shuffling his feet, raking his hair—shuffle, rake, repeat. I shifted my feet, and Cassius pulled his hands inside his sleeves. He wouldn't look at me, but I honestly wasn't trying very hard to make eye contact. We waited, quiet and hidden, for any sound. In the dead silence, a clocked ticked from the room with all the roses and knickknacks by the front door. Cassius closed his eyes and tucked his head deeper into his hood.

"Get out of my home." Mr. Shooster broke the silence and drowned out the clock. "Keep your daughter away from my son."

Shit.

Cassius slammed his head against the balusters, groaning through gritted teeth at his father's revelation. Mr. Shooster's words stung deep in my gut. I hadn't known Cassius but a day, but I knew he deserved better than the life he was given. I wanted to be his friend, dying or not. The idea of that friendship had been ripped from my heart with those seven words. Without another thought, I stuck my slender fingers up his empty sleeve and found his clenched fist, tight and unforgiving; I didn't let it stop me. I wrapped my fingers around his large fist and squeezed, deciding that Cassius Shooster meant more than seven little words.

Mr. Shooster could huff and puff, but my house was brick and nothing would blow it down.

"Pru, let's go," Mom growled at me.

I didn't want to leave him. Who knew what would happen once we were out that door. I looked at him, forcing his dark eyes to meet mine through the shadow of his hood. I squeezed his hand once more and whispered, "I'm here," before finally letting him go.

I felt him reach for me when I turned around, but it was too late. I'd already bounded around the foot of the stairs and into view. Mom was waiting and grabbed me up by the sleeve, dragging me to the door.

I stole one last look over my shoulder at Cassius; his face hardly visible behind the balusters, a metaphorical prison of intricately carved wood bars. My feet stopped, but Mom pulled me along with her. I trusted she wouldn't let the issue rest until she knew it had been taken care of, but I didn't know what could happen in the time between.

Mom pushed me through the doorway. "We'll take care of everything," she promised. Her hand was on the knob when Mr. Shooster called out to her for one last jab.

"Who do you think you are?"

Mom stopped and turned her head slowly. With one blonde brow cocked, she said, "I'm Mrs. Penderhaus. I teach first grade. You haven't seen the last of me." With those classic final words, she slammed the door shut behind her.

4

I COULDN'T STOP THINKING ABOUT CASSIUS. OTHERWISE nondescript, the day passed slowly. Leaving me to watch the clock and daydream about a life I feared I'd never have with a person I couldn't promise would be there regardless of the timeline.

No one cared I'd been out the day before, so no one asked where I'd been. No one but Bonnie. She probably cared, but she wasn't there to ask. It wasn't odd for Bonnie to miss school. Although, missing was a far less accurate description than skipping. To miss school implies you weren't out on purpose.

I had been disappointed when Bonnie didn't come bouncing into second period. Or third. Her smoke spot had been cleaned of smashed butts. She had likely missed—skipped—yesterday too. Bonnie was the only person I cared knew about my current situation, and she wasn't around to hear about it. Situation being Cassius, not my arm. *That* situation could stay silent. I had done something major— *major, major*—and no one knew. As far as Flintlock was concerned, I was still just Prudence Penderhaus, loser, weirdo, freak.

I shoved out the double front doors of Flintlock High, half smirking with the knowledge I knew something none of the lemmings could have possibly fathomed. Two steps down the front stairs, I caught sight of the enemy. Reminding me vaguely of a squatty flying monkey, Morgan shuffled around Brady Miles as he schmoozed his typical congress of meatheads.

I snarled and tucked myself as far into my backpack as I could. Neither of them pried themselves away long enough to notice me. I'd nearly escaped, just a few steps from the front sidewalk.

"Penderhaus," Marlin Sheave, Flintlock's very own future Bill Gates—in the genius sense, not the nerdy white guy sense—called to me from the top of the steps, drawing all attention away from Brady and toward me.

I stopped and looked back at him over my shoulder with annoyed disdain. "Yes, Marlin?" I replied sarcastically, eyeing the sniggering group behind him.

Realizing his mistake, he mouthed the word sorry and trotted down the steps toward me. His perfectly combed curly coif bounced in an ironically large pompadour over his forehead. The polka-dot button-down and tight brown slacks he sported quantified the word hipster for all of Flintlock.

"Where were you yesterday?" he asked, pushing a pair of black-framed glasses up his freckled nose. "And Monday. Prudence Penderhaus out for two days? Someone call the press."

"Out," I answered curtly, not ready to expose Cassius or my secret before we had a game plan for treatment.

"Prudence Penderhaus is never *out*. Spill it," he demanded. His golden skin and freckles always reminded me of Morgan Freeman. Only cuter. And gayer. Well, probably gayer. He hadn't exactly come out, but he wasn't fooling anyone.

"Hellacious cramps," I lied, holding my stomach. He snarled at my exaggerated expression. "Ooh, it was a doozy. Yup. Blood everywhere."

Marlin held up a disgusted hand. "You've painted a vivid picture, Pru." He tucked his books against his chest. "So, I wanted to ask you if you'd consider helping with set design again this year. We have two productions in the works…."

He went on, but I stopped listening. I'd worked backstage crew with him in some aspect every year for every performance; it would've been odd not to participate this year. I knew I couldn't commit to anything without knowing my treatment plan first. It just wouldn't be fair to make promises I knew I couldn't keep.

I recalled for the millionth time that day the boy I'd met and the promise I'd made. You could almost see the peaked roof of his house from the front of the school. As Marlin went on about backdrops and painting schedules, I thought about the boy with dark eyes and floppy hair. "Hey, I'll think about it, okay?"

He bumped his elbow against mine and gave me a prodding nod. Marlin was far from stupid, and just like he wasn't fooling anyone, I wasn't fooling him. Before long, I'd have to come clean and fess up to everything. Now that the wheels were in motion, there would be no hiding Cassius, and a secret like that would certainly blow Flintlock's collective mind. Also, at some point, someone would want me to explain my gaunt appearance and abrupt baldness.

"Well, I gotta run. See ya."

I couldn't commit to Marlin because I'd already committed to Cassius. To keep my promise, Cassius would have to be my main focus as long as I could manage. And treatment. Cassius and treatment.

My abnormally long black-and-white sneakers slapped the pavement on Beaker Street, and I was officially free. A sliver of yellow wood siding peeked from between the trees and rooftops that stood between me and home.

The walk home, usually either a time of short-lived boredom or a sprint for fear of projectiles, began as the former. I stopped only long enough to fish my phone from my backpack and turn it on. It came as no shock that after a solid thirty seconds, no notifications popped onto my screen. Not even Bonnie. I shuffled along, focused on typing out a message to Bonnie that I deleted and rewrote three times. The end result asked if she'd grace me with her presence at school tomorrow. I shoved it in my back pocket and picked up my pace, eager to reach Marigold.

I bit my nail as the October breeze kicked wads of red hair around my face. I'd thought about Cassius more than anything else since the moment I woke up, and the walk home would prove to be no different.

I wanted desperately to run, thin legs pumping frantically, toward his house. I wanted to burst through the door. I wanted to wrap my arms around his waist and drag him from that place and out into the world.

I was halfway through replaying the scene of my mom and Mr. Shooster when I spotted the corner of Marigold from across the street. Red and blue lights rhythmically lit up the front of the old brown house on the corner. A sheriff's officer stood near the front gate and two empty police cars sat on the street out front.

I didn't think before my feet carried me across the street and toward the scene. The echoes of a police radio bounced off houses. My heart thudded in my chest, fluttering painfully hard against my ribs. Images of a bloody and beaten Cassius flashed in my head. Why else would the cops be there? His parents had beaten the life out of him for leaving the house. They'd initially locked him up for a reason, and I didn't see any way they'd let him off without some kind of retaliation.

I screeched to a halt in front of a young female sheriff's

officer standing guard at the gate. She put her hand up as if to silently tell me I'd better stop or else. Panting, I clambered to grab hold of the gate and hold myself still without bursting at the seams.

"I—" I panted. "I know him," I said vaguely. When her confusion was apparent, I added, "Cassius, is he okay? He's my friend."

The look on her face shifted from confusion to shock. "You *know* him?" she asked, as though I was talking about the prince of bloody England.

"Yes, I met him yesterday." My words came out slowly and slightly stunted, emulating my confusion.

When a moment of silence careened into an awkward stare of understanding, the deputy and I both realized neither of us quite grasped the situation.

"Where? Where did you meet Cassius Shooster?" Her posture was relaxed, not matching her words in the slightest.

"Here. Right there on the front porch." I pointed to the steps in question. "He told me he'd never been out of the house. But then he was, when he left and came to my house. And my mom got really pissed off and yelled at his dad and—oh, my God, is he alive?" I stammered and stuttered out each word at a mile a minute.

Her tone shifted, but her face was a wash of stoicism. "Of course he's alive."

I hadn't thought my question was that out on a limb. I wondered if the officer had any idea what was happening in that house. "Oh, well, good." I stopped and thought about why two police cars would be out on the street with a deputy guarding the front gate. "Then… why are you here?" I wanted to ask if that old drunk Mrs. Shooster had finally croaked from liver failure or something, but kept my mouth shut.

"I'm sorry, sweetie, I can't talk about that. I can tell you your friend is fine and we're taking care of things." She looked tough as steel, but her reassuring nature proved she was a human and not an automaton with a badge.

"Listen, that boy isn't like other boys. He's different. His parents had him locked up in that room up there for seventeen years, as far as I know. That's just inhumane. He's probably scared to death in there with those other deputies. Can I see him?" Desperation slipped from my lips, a slug, slippery and slopping to the concrete with a splat.

"No, not right now. Let the boys take care of it." Her sarcastic tone wasn't lost on me, and I felt for her plight but had no room to intermingle it with my own. "You can visit another time."

"But my mom—"

"Miss, please. Just let the sheriff handle this situation. You can come by later to see your friend."

Easy for you to say. "Fine. But he'd better be in there ripping into those parents. Cassius should be out in the world. He should be at school. He should be with *me*." There was that slug again. *Slugulus Eructo.*

I had no solid reason why he should be with me of all people. I didn't have any special skills or tight relationship with him to speak of. It just made sense somehow. Like I knew deep down I was the only one who cared. Me. The dying girl he'd met for a few hours on a Tuesday morning.

The deputy looked away from me and eyed the street, left, then right. She never made eye contact again. She was done listening to me. I stood there for two more left-right rotations, watching her tight chestnut-brown bun slide back and forth over the edge of her collar. It was a bulky thing, likely a tightly wound twist of long thick hair, all bound up and tucked under her cap. A last clutch of femininity knotted up and hidden away behind an androgynous uniform. I applauded her choices and begrudgingly left her to her watch. Whether she was just performing her duties or genuinely unapologetic, it didn't matter. I wasn't going to get anywhere with the tightly wound deputy. I would wait. I didn't have much choice in the matter.

I turned on my heel. One big foot slapped the pavement before a deep voice bellowed my name.

"Penderhaus."

I turned to find the always smiling rosy face of Sheriff Elroy Floyd. He'd lost a few more of his salt and pepper hairs from his head, but it appeared they'd landed safely above his lip. That bushy mustache got thicker every time I saw him.

"Hey, Sheriff." I forced a grin and waved a lengthy

hand awkwardly in his direction. "Is he okay?" I nodded toward the old brown house.

The sheriff looked at the house, then at his feet, then to me. "I can't explain anything right now. I know you're some sort of a friend of his now and your mom and I go way back, so I'll throw you a bone." *Gee, thanks.* "The boy won't be locked up in that house anymore. I can't make any guarantees about visits to the Penderhaus residence, but I can say I will personally be making surprise checks to ensure he's being better taken care of." The sheriff paused for a moment and looked up at the house curiously. Eyeing me slyly from the corner of his eye, he added, "Ya know, I didn't even know the Shoosters had a kid."

"That's no surprise." The statement was both an agreement of poor parenting and the acknowledgment that the whole of Flintlock sheriff's department was dumber than chewing gum while eating Oreo's. Deputy Bunhead currently excluded.

The sheriff grunt-coughed in clueless agreement and kicked at the sidewalk. It was possible he felt ashamed about his oversight. A kid had grown up in his town and he hadn't even known the kid existed. I probably would have felt like an ass too.

I honestly didn't care what Sheriff Floyd thought of the situation. I only had one thing on my mind. "Can I see him?" I practically pleaded, crossing my fingers inside my hoodie pocket.

"Well,"—he looked up again at the house—"that's

their call. I can't force them to allow you access to their son." He planted two sausage hands just under a set of love handles. "I can judge by appearance there hasn't been years of neglect.*" Were your eyes open?* "The boy is fed and clothed, but that aside, your mom asked me to handle this… situation, and that's what I've done. I understand the boy"—he called Cassius the boy as though he had no name—"has some form of mental retardation."

"He's not retarded," I grumbled under my breath.

But he paid no attention to me. "I can see how that could be overwhelming for a set of new parents." He said it as though the Shoosters weren't easily pushing fifty. "I've given them an official warning." The sheriff puffed his chest out and nodded. "The boy—"

"His name is Cassius." I cut him off, but he kept talking.

"—belongs outside in the sunshine. Your mom's right." A growl of thunder roared overhead. The sheriff looked to the dark gray sky, an ironically poetic metaphor for the situation. He sniffed, ruffling his mustache. "Well, better get out of this before I get gnarled by a bolt of lightning. You get home, Prudence." He tipped his head to me and winked. "Tell your mama I said hi."

I curled my lip against the sick in my gut and nodded. He'd always been nice enough, but his perpetual crush on my mom was stomach churning. He'd also pissed me off with his flippant disregard toward "the boy," Cassius Shooster.

I knew it couldn't be easy for him. For any of them. I was a rare individual in the town of Flintlock. Others like me, those who could see Cassius for who he could be, would be few and far between. It wouldn't be long before everyone and their dog knew about Cassius, or thought they did. Was it naive of me to expect each one of them to shut up and behave?

The sheriff got into his police car, turned off the flashing lights, and pulled away. The deputy guarding the gate took one last glance at me and the house before getting into the passenger seat of the second car. Another deputy, a man with cropped blond hair, got into the driver seat without looking at me. Not a one of them glanced in my direction as they passed me, then my house, and to the end of the street, leaving me to stand alone at the foot of that big old brown house.

Thunder tolled again, a final warning to get inside. I pulled my backpack tighter against my shoulders. Cassius had been terrified of the thunder. He'd held me and begged me to stay with him. What was he enduring in that house without me? Looking at his window, I caught a fleeting glimpse of his pale skin and dark hair before the curtain slammed shut again.

He'd been watching. He knew I was there. I wanted more than anything to burst through his gate, stomp up his steps, and beat his front door in. I didn't. Impulse would have to take a backseat to rationale until this situation resolved itself. So I waited. I waited and I hoped that seeing me there would be enough for him to know I wasn't going to give up on him. I waited long enough to feel like a moron standing there staring at an empty window when the rain started to fall a few minutes later. I'd waited, but he never came back to the window.

Home felt empty. For the first time in my life, the storm made me uncomfortable and wary. I suddenly felt the need to peek around every corner and check over my shoulder. I'd lived in that yellow house since the day I came home from the hospital, and not one of those days did I spend afraid of bumps in the night. Or day. Whatever.

Shaking off the heebie-jeebies, I started on my homework. With the events over the last few days—child neglect and the big C—hanging over my head, geometry seemed shallow. Pointless. Shallow and pointless. I slid a set of headphones over my ears and turned the music up to drown out the sound of the storm. Begrudgingly, I put pencil to paper and got to work.

I was two problems away from done when movement caught my eye. My head shot up and my eyes tracked any and all motion, which was mostly nothing. Shadows from blowing trees out front flittered along the walls of the living room, but otherwise all was still. My heart returning to normal function, I let out a shaky breath and tried to refocus.

The tip of my pencil snapped against my notebook

a moment later when a clattering noise penetrated my supposedly noise-cancelling headphones and made me jump. I flipped the headphones off my ears and forced them to focus on sounds inside the house. Only the *trip-trap* of the rain on the window filled the room. I looked out the water-streaked glass, plops of water slapping against it, at the blowing trees. A bright bolt of lightning scratched across the sky, lighting up the room.

"Prudence Penderhaus." Like a scene from a horror movie, someone called my name in the midst of thunder and lightning just before Halloween, and I almost died right there on the couch clutching a ragged math book.

I squealed and dropped my book to the floor, leaping onto the back of the couch in one quick movement. My eyes temporarily flash blind, I blinked at the figure standing in my living room.

"Cassius?" I asked, finally refocusing. "How did you get in here?" I squeaked.

"Your window was open."

"The doorbell," I reminded, my heart still thrumming from fright, and pointed at the entryway. Breathy, I said, "Why are you here?"

He looked out the window, nervously shifting from one foot to the other. "Police came today. They told Dad I have to be able to leave the house *on occasion*."

"I guess my mom wasn't screwing around." My brain caught up to the situation and a thought crossed my mind. "You left your house all by yourself. No backpack to return. No excuse. For the first time. Ever. That's kind of a big deal."

He shrugged. "I never had a reason before." He risked a fleeting glance from under his lashes and met my eyes.

I swallowed and moved the conversation away from me. "Did use your front door this time?"

A solid ten seconds passed before he answered. "There was no specification of how or when I could leave." He skirted around the question.

"Cass…." I didn't want to send him home, but I was concerned, with good reason, his parents would have kittens if they discovered him missing. "You can't just leave without telling them. I don't want to play the devil's advocate here but—"

"The devil isn't real," he interjected with one of his literal interpretations.

A theological argument was not on the agenda, and honestly, I didn't know where I stood on that front, so I let it go. "It's a figure of speech. It means I hate to suddenly side with your rotten parents, but you still have to follow some form of rules." We were quiet for a long stretch. "Right?" I asked, unexpectedly questioning my own validity.

Was I just a boring Goody Two-shoes? Not really. A Goody One-shoe maybe….

I didn't know why I felt it was so important for the Shoosters to like me in some way. I didn't like them; they were absurd. They treated their son like a beast to be hidden away. Quasimodo in his bell tower. An embarrassment not allowed to show his face in public. Sheriff Floyd had said it himself, and I couldn't agree more—we didn't even know they had a kid. And I was starting to realize that was the intention.

He ignored me altogether and produced a DVD case from the pocket of his black hoodie. "I have *Halloween*. The 1978 version, featuring Jamie Lee Curtis," he said.

I didn't want to turn him away. I couldn't. He'd ventured from home not once but twice in a row to find me. For a boy who'd never left home, a boy with so many supposed disabilities, that was sure spectacular. What with my limited lifespan and all, it didn't make any sense to put rules and homework before friendship. In the grand scheme, what would mean more in the end? Friends or quadrilaterals?

"Hit it," I said energetically.

He blinked dark, fanned lashes over equally dark eyes. "Does that mean put on the movie?"

"Yes, it means put on the movie."

There truly was no time like the present anymore. I had to stop thinking in terms of what would happen and start working on the notion of what *could* happen.

Cassius loped awkwardly to the couch and sat as far from me as possible. One long leg crossed over the other away from me. The corners of my mouth turned down, and I slyly sniffed my pits. It was more than a friend zone move. It was a deliberate action to sit as far from me as possible, and it stung in the pit of my stomach.

The opening credits had just transitioned to Judith Meyers in the throes of passion with her beau when a gust of wind and rain followed Mom through the front door. She shut it quickly behind her and stood for a moment, dripping water onto the mat at her feet. Blonde hair clung to her cheeks, and mascara was just making its way under her eyes.

"It is pouring," Mom said, exaggerating each syllable.

"Hey, Mom," I said, and Cassius turned his head away from her but kept an uneasy eye from under his lashes.

"Hi, Pru." She walked into the living room and finally caught sight of the boy sitting on the other end of the couch. "Oh," she exclaimed, more than just a little surprised. "Well, hi, Cassius." A smile spread across her face, but it just missed her eyes. "I didn't expect—" She cut herself short and changed it up. "I'm glad to see you. How's your dad?" she asked as though she didn't care, when I knew she really did. Unraveling a red knit scarf from her neck, she pulled off her drenched outer layer and hung it on a rack near the door.

"He's enraged," Cassius said honestly.

"Well"—Mom sighed and pulled her shoes off with a toe at each heel—"that's just too bad." Mom was also speaking honestly. I wondered if that was good or bad when it came to Cassius and his apparent ability, or rather inability, to follow subtleties.

Cassius looked at Mom with both dark eyes. They

twinkled, reflecting light like water on an oil slick, and from his quiet mouth came a laugh I hadn't known he possessed. His large hands slapped against his knees and wrapped around his middle as he laughed. I stared at first, unsure of the situation, but with laughter as infectious as his, it didn't take long to catch. I laughed along with him. And after a solid few seconds, Mom chuckled too.

"Aw, Cass, that was your first laugh," I said through sore cheeks. My eyes welled and surely glistened with pride. In only a day of semi-freedom, the sullen boy had let out a belly laugh. His parents could get boned.

"I have laughed many times before, Prudence." His smiling face returned to its indifferent norm.

I glanced away from him, embarrassed. "I'm sorry, I just thought…. It was your first big laugh with *me*." I shrugged. "I like it." I added the last bit without thinking. I had liked his laugh, but the words sounded stupid coming out of my mouth.

Cassius, still and silent, stared at me. His dark eyes didn't focus on mine usually—well, as usually as one can imagine in a matter of a day—so the moment quickly became intense. With eyes so dark they looked like pools of shiny tar amidst thick fanned lashes, it was easy to fall in and stay there.

"Well," Mom spoke quietly and mostly to herself, clearly uncomfortable with the situation, "I'll fix something up for dinner."

Mom's words broke our stare, and Cassius looked

away from me. "Uh, thanks," he mumbled out of one side of his mouth.

I watched Cassius from the corner of my eye. He stared intently at the screen, mouthing many of the lines as they were spoken. I wanted to ask him who had taught him manners and how to brush his teeth and put on clothes. His mom seemed useless, but I had no clue when that started. Mr. Shooster was a big science-type guy according to Cassius, but did that mean he taught his son to be a science guy too? Had imprisonment in his house for his entire life meant he was all alone to fend for himself? My calculations pointed to no. While I didn't ask him those questions at that moment sitting alone on my couch, I tallied them up and stored them for later. I wanted to know everything there was to know about Cassius Shooster before I croaked, and as I sat there, I formulated the plan for how to make that happen.

Mom clanked around in the kitchen, whipping up something that was beginning to smell like spaghetti. Cassius hadn't taken his eyes off the screen. The storm outside raged on, and I began to wonder if I would need to draft plans for an ark.

"So," I began. "How does it feel to be free?" I wasn't able to keep my mouth shut with the cause of all my curiosity sitting right next to me. Er, a whole cushion and a few inches away.

He shrugged. "I'm sitting in a house watching movies. It doesn't feel all that different." He snapped his fingers a few times. "I get to watch my favorite movie with my favorite person. That's different," he mumbled.

I couldn't keep the ridiculous smile off my face. Looking away from him, I hid my blush. I wouldn't exactly call myself a dating expert—okay, novice—but if I had to put money down, I would have said, in his odd Cassius way, he was flirting with me.

"What are your plans now that you can leave your house on occasion?"

"I don't know. Maybe get a bike, or something."

"A bike?" I chuckled. Would I have to teach him to ride it? "Okay, we can see about a bike." I stopped for a minute and carefully thought over my next words. "Cassius," I started gently. "Do you know why your parents kept you inside all these years?" I tried to put it as plainly as I could.

He looked down at his hands, letting too much time pass for comfort. "Because…." He stopped long enough I thought he wasn't going to finish his sentence. "Because that's where I belong."

"You can't really think that's true? Cassius, come on. You are the first person I've ever met that treated me like I was a human, no questions asked. Don't get me wrong, toots, Bonnie and Marlin are the cat's meow, but you're aces, baby." I pulled off a shitty version of James Cagney at the end there to lighten things up. And because I'm weird.

"That's because you *are* human, Prudence. Or, are

you an alien?" He did his voice up like a space robot and laughed at his joke.

"Hello. I'm the Doctor," I said in the crappiest English accent this side of Kevin Costner.

"Doctor who?" he asked and sucked all the wind from my geeky sails.

I felt oddly deflated. Even in the company of someone with less social skills than me, I'd managed to look like a reject. "You know... Time Lord. From Gallifrey. Like the show."

Cassius jumped to his feet and bent over me threateningly. "You are an enemy of the Daleks! You must be destroyed!" He'd changed his robot voice to mimic that of the infamous tin can villains. Which also sounded robotic. But more Dalek than robot. It was just different. 'Kay?

"Can we call a truce?" I asked, smiling from ear to ear at our unexpected and beloved bonding moment.

"Exterminate. Exterminate," he repeated in his not-so-robot-mostly-Dalek voice. Using his index finger, he swirled it over my head and face with a buzzing sound, threatening to poke me with it. "Human female detected."

My stomach ached from laughter. Cassius's finger still whirled around over my head, but he'd stopped talking. A major milestone in geekery, we'd successfully discovered a mutual fondness for the madman in the blue police box and hadn't even meant to. Sooner or later, we'd have found each other based solely on our viewing preferences.

If he ever escaped his prison. If I ever escaped mine.

"You're a…," I started without thinking, meeting his eyes unintentionally. "Pretty cool dude." *Smooth as silk, Prudence Penderhaus, smooth as silk.*

He sat beside me. Close. Very close. "I'm going to say thank you, because I'm sure that was meant as a compliment. However, I'd like to admit in advance that I suck at listening." He drew in a long breath. "I am also terrible at talking."

"Well, me too. I'd assume you haven't talked all that much, so it's to be expected."

"Expectations. Those will be the death of me." His ominous tone turned my stomach.

His dark eyes burrowed into mine. He hadn't stood or made any attempt to move away from me. His close proximity brought nervous butterflies to life in my gut. The moment, a tiny spec on the timeline of human existence, dragged on for an eternity. I wanted nothing more than to crawl inside that mysterious head of his and pull out every bit of information he had hidden away in there. I desperately needed to know what he was thinking. What he needed from me. He made me want to fight to survive, if only to see what the future held for us. Me and my clandestine boy.

Jamie Lee was whimpering in a closet with a wire hanger as her only defense when something banged loudly against the front door. I jumped, and Cassius's head shot toward the noise. Hoping it was just a branch *thwapping* against the house, I waited in silence for more. When two distinct raps rattled the door, I knew someone was out there and wanted in. Or more accurately, wanted someone to come out.

"Do your parents know you're here?" Mom whispered angrily as she hustled from the kitchen to the door. I hoped she had a plan, because at that moment, I was fairly useless.

The door was hardly open an inch when the bellowing voice of Mr. Shooster outbid the rain for volume. "Mrs. Penderhaus, I thought I made myself clear." Cassius stood, pulled his hood over his face, and sank back into the couch. "I'd like my son, and I'd like this to be the first and last time I stand on your front porch."

"I can arrange that," Mom said with surprising snark. "Cass, honey, your dad is here." She called him Cass and he didn't correct her. Either he didn't care or something else was blocking that from his mind.

He didn't budge. Only the quick movement of his chest rising and falling with each anxious breath indicated he was alive inside that hood. I nudged at his leg with my foot, too scared to lean across the couch and touch him in any other way for fear his dad would see me and fly into a fit of rage.

"Hey, your dad's here," I said quietly, so as to not alert anyone of my participation.

"Cassius, son, now it's time you come home. You know you're not supposed to be down here bothering the Penderhaus ladies."

"He's no bother," Mom reassured, still blocking the doorway with her stocky frame.

"Cassius Shooster, come out here now. It's time to go home," he said in a tone far angrier than the previous.

"He's more than welcome to stay for dinner." Mom's continued hindrance appeared to piss Mr. Shooster off more than he could stand, because a moment later, he shoved past Mom and was through the door, snatching his son up by the arm.

"Excuse me," Mom growled at him, in shock over his antics. "Douchebag," she said under her breath. He ignored her completely.

"Now, I said you are not to come down here. Sheriff Floyd can't make me allow that, and he knows it. Get up off this couch and get home. Your mother is worried sick."

I jumped from my seat. "Oh, I'll bet she is," I said, folding my arms over my chest, almost squeezing a little too tight. "Or is she just stuck in a perpetual hangover and without her punching bag?"

Mr. Shooster snarled at me.

Mom had scurried into the living room after Mr. Shooster, ready to usher him right back out. He grabbed Cassius by the arm and turned quickly to drag him out, nearly running right over the top of her.

"Don't you barge into my house, Shooster. I'll call

Elroy Floyd again." She wagged a thick finger at him.

"Not necessary. I have what I came for."

Mr. Shooster stormed out of the house, dragging Cassius behind him. Panicked, he looked back at me over his shoulder. His hood fell back from his face and exposed an expression red from fury. Stumbling over big feet, Cassius struggled against the pull of his father but didn't bother physically overpowering him, which I thought he might be able to do. Thin or not, Cassius was a seventeen-ish-year-old boy; he surely had some stamina over his similarly built but aging father.

"We'll see you soon, sweetie," Mom said with an annoyed smile as they hurried out the door. "Goodnight."

I stood in the living room, my lips pursed, nearly white from rage. Life was short. Too damn short for such absurd antics. Impulse won the war with rationale and I bolted for the door. Thoughtlessly shoving Mom out of the way, I didn't stop until I hit the end of our walkway.

"Cassius," I called out into the rainy night. "See you tomorrow." I didn't know if that was true or not, but I had to say *something*.

If he and I were characters in a movie, I would have yelled something more along the lines of "I love you," or "don't forget about me." Alas, real life had no room for things of that magnitude and nothing—rarely—ever happened like it did in the movies.

Soaked from the rain, I turned on a sad heel and loped toward the house. Cassius never answered or even attempted to let me know he'd heard me. Instead, he disappeared into the sheets of rain with his dad. Two tall, thin, dark figures making their way through the stormy night to their ironically creepy house, where one of them was being held against his will.

Maybe a movie wasn't such an inaccurate description.

5

"DUDE, PENDERHAUS, IS IT TRUE?" RUFUS ALABASTER
asked, his beefy, freckled arm draped over my shoulder
as I walked up the front steps to Flintlock High School.
There hadn't been one single year he and I hadn't shared
at least one teacher. Ever. But I was pretty certain that
was the first time he'd spoken directly to me since fourth
grade.

"Is what true?" I shrugged out from under his heavy
arm.

"Oh, come on. You don't have to bullshit me. I mean,
come on, Pru, it's *me*," he said, but his narcissistic
name-drop held little weight. Bonding over a common
redheaded trait, Rufus and I had never been anything
more than the two gingers of Flintlock. "Your mom broke
into that creepy house on the corner and uncovered a dead
body," he confessed with a fist pump.

The air in my lungs escaped in a rush, leaving me woozy, lost for words. "What?" I shook my head and blinked my eyes. "What?" I stammered *what* about six more times, but he talked over me.

"Everyone is talking about it." My head shook uncontrollably.

"How…" I bumbled.

"Your mom is *so* cool!"

The information may have been skewed—mostly wrong—but it had reached Rufus *the tank* Alabaster in a little over twenty-four hours. Who else knew something, *anything* about Cassius Shooster? What lies were spreading like a virus through Flintlock? I knew this would come, it really was inevitable, but I hadn't actually prepared my brain for Mom discovering dead bodies.

"Shut up, Rufus," I breathed, "you're an idiot."

I didn't wait around for his rebuttal and hurried up the steps. Rufus pointed at me as I walked away, an enamored grin plastered across his face. I ignored it and left him standing alone with his single college-ruled notebook and half-chewed pencil.

I climbed the stairs, avoiding the knowing eyes of my peers. Just as I was beginning to create a scenario in which somehow my mother became Bones momentarily, I was halted by a gaggle of girls with what I called greasy chicken lips.

I was almost past them when one called out to me. "Oh. My. God. Prudence, right?" My eyebrows lifted in dread, and a tiny whimpering noise came from my throat. "What was it like inside?"

I should have kept walking. Should have ignored them all and gone home. Instead, I stopped and said, "What?" I really needed cue cards or something.

They crowded around me. A circle of overly glossed lemmings staring up at me through incredibly long false lashes. "Inside that old house on Marigold. You went inside, right? What was in there? Like devil stuff. Like, Satan worship stuff?" I didn't answer. My eyes darted from one girl to another. Their shiny lips, coated one too many times, glistening in the muted light, distracted me. "There was vampire stuff. I knew it," the head girl exclaimed. I didn't know her name but was pretty sure she was a sophomore. They all were. Probably.

The girls glommed onto each other again without another question and moved away from me like a single-celled organism. Locked in astonishment, I could do nothing other than blink and try not to drool with my mouth wide open.

Dead bodies, Satan, vampires, breaking and entering, Flintlock High had seen far too much CW network programming.

"What in the—" I started to myself.

"Tell me she did it, tell me." Bonnie's face was suddenly an inch from mine. In the five-foot-four sense. An inch from my chest? Her small hands gripped my shoulders. I didn't say anything for an entire second, so she shook me wildly. "What. Is. Going. On?"

"I have no idea," I admitted, head still swimming in half-truths. "What's happening here, Bon?"

"Apparently, you and your mom kicked down the door of that house on the corner to save some boy. Everyone is saying your mom sucker punched the kid's dad and broke his nose. The sheriff is calling your mother a hero. Your mother. A hero."

While she hadn't punched anyone, sadly, she had in her own way bullied her way into their home and saved Cassius from whatever his life had been. Well, in theory anyway. "Not exactly."

"Not exactly. What does that mean? Not exactly." She threw her hands in the air and let them fall dramatically.

"She didn't punch anyone. And no one kicked in a door. And despite word on the street, no dead body was found. And while I'm on that subject, neither was Satan in any aspect or relation. What is wrong with people?"

"Well," she said with a deep breath, as was customary. "You know Clarabelle Floyd is the sheriff's daughter. Well, over dinner last night, Sheriff spills everything. The fight, the boy, everything. This is big news for Flintlock, Pru. Big. And you, my dear, are a major player."

Damage control. Danger. Danger. "Bonnie, this isn't big. It's hardly news." When in doubt, downplay, walk away. "I was on my way to school the day before yesterday, and I met a boy—"

"*You?* Met a boy?"

I nodded. "Yes, keep up. I found out his parents had been keeping him locked up in his house because he's—" The bell rang and cut me off abruptly. Saved. "Time's up."

"Shit." She looked up, as if to look at the bell itself. "You will finish this story at the earliest possible moment." I would, of course, but it would be as unsensational as I could make it. "I gotta pee first. I'll be right there. Cover for me."

I rolled my eyes and watched Bonnie run in the direction of the bathrooms. She knew she wasn't peeing. I knew she wasn't peeing, but she also knew I'd bust her balls for smoking. I was no prude, but a beer at the well was quite different from loading your body with cancer agents. Cancer sucked.

Making my way to class, I kept my head low, narrowly avoiding further idiocy. In class, I flopped my army green bag to the floor by my feet with a huff. Even though I'd known most everyone since kindergarten, I hadn't heard my name being said—or more appropriately whispered—more times in my life.

Stares came from the corners of every eye in the room. Students leaned in close to each other in order to more covertly spread whatever rumor their clique had accepted as truth. Everyone was talking to each other, and they were all talking about me. Prudence Penderhaus. The most boring, ordinary wallflower, weirdo walking the halls of Flintlock High. And it was all bullshit.

Mr. Kincaid came into the room as the final bell rang

but didn't stop the chatter. In fact, his face looked flushed, and the thin flap of hair that swooped from one side of his shiny head to the other appeared in disarray. Shaped more like a turnip than a human being, Mr. Kincaid shuffled his miniature legs around his desk and fussed with meaningless papers and things. It took only a moment for me to realize he wasn't looking at me. Avoiding in fact. Even he knew some version of what I'd been up to in my two days *out*.

A twinge of pain rocked my bicep, and I squeezed my eyes shut. That stupid thing needed to go. *Take the whole damn arm with it*, I thought. It was possible. Likely, in fact. The invader's size, placement, and stage combined with my age determined my fate, and that wasn't looking good.

When I opened my eyes, everyone was staring at me—both eyes, directly at me. Effort had been made by most to turn in their seat for a better view. With the pain in my arm and the sudden onset of defiance coursing through my body, I couldn't stop the adrenaline from forcing itself on me.

"Hey," I shouted and leapt to my feet. Everyone turned away from me in unison, rattling desks and sending pencils rolling onto the ground. "What in the hell is going on here?" I asked, my voice raised octaves above classroom appropriate.

"Miss Penderhaus, well, uh—" Mr. Kincaid stuttered out in his unwarranted Foghorn Leghorn intonation. He'd grown up in Flintlock, as far as I knew, which I must point out is nowhere near Kentucky, or any other southern state, for that matter. He was in the middle of bumbling out something more when the classroom door opened and explained everything.

I was standing when he came in. My tall, lean form loomed over the heads of seated students. In one swift sweep, without hesitation, his pitch-dark eyes locked on to mine. Terror streaked across his face, though it was mostly hidden behind a veil of wavy black hair. I wanted to go to him, hold his hand deep in his sleeve, and make sure he was okay. I didn't of course, because that would have been weird even for me. So I waited and watched.

"Cassius Shooster, welcome to, uh, Flintlock." Mr. Kincaid welcomed him to town instead of school, addressing Cassius but not looking at him directly. "Class, Cassius is new, so let's make sure, uh, we show him how things are done here."

Cassius refused to look at anyone but me. Standing there with his hands pulled into his sleeves, looking for all intents and purposes like your standard disconnected seventeen-year-old boy, one could easily assume that was exactly what he was. I knew better. I knew he was so much more.

Our dumpy, textbook-horrendous, principal, Ms.— *no comment*—Ratzass, nudged her hefty body through the door and stood next to Cassius. "Well," she huffed and looked around her as though something other than her girth was making her out of breath, "I see you're acquainted. Go on and take a seat now." She spoke to him as though he were an imbecile. An idiot. A feral child not worthy of her crappy school. I wanted to shriek in her face and tell her he just didn't know any better and to shut her fat trap, but I didn't. I just stood there like an asshole. "Miss Penderhaus, is there something we can do for you?" Her patronizing tone brought giggles and gasps from the peanut gallery.

I stuttered and shook myself back to attention. I was indeed the only one standing, second row from the right all the way in the back. "No, I'm... sorry." I whispered the last and slid quickly into my seat.

The only empty desks in the room were one row to the right and one up from me and right smack dab to the left of me. Cassius had two choices; my stomach fluttered with anticipation. He would sit next to me. He had to. He didn't know anyone else, why would he sit somewhere else?

I watched him shuffle cumbersomely through the desks toward me. His sneakers squeaked awkwardly along the floor, and he tucked his head further into his hood. Most of the class hadn't even really gotten a look at him yet between his hair and hood. They all wanted to. No one even bothered to hide it. Curious eyes watched him from every row, some turned around completely to see him make his way toward the back. I sat up straighter and let an anticipatory smile turn up the corners of my mouth.

One row over and one up, he stopped, looked away from me, and slid into the seat. My jaw fell to the desk. What was he thinking? I was right there with an open seat next to me, and he didn't sit there. Most of the class watched him, but from the corner of my eye, I noticed some watching me. Catching my reaction, many of them began to piece together a puzzle they thought they'd had figured out.

A scandal in Flintlock. Someone call Lifetime.

"If you would, uh, please remove your hood, Mr. Shooster," Mr. Kincaid stammered from the front of the room. He looked to Ms. Ratzass, and the two turned their backs to us in unison and began whispering.

Cassius sighed heavily from his one-over-one-up spot. He did what he was told and slid the black hood off his head. Dark hair fell over his forehead. He didn't bother to fix it, instead using it as a veil to further hide his face. I'd grown to appreciate the pale skin and dark eyes he had hidden behind that hair, and I wanted to see it. Screw everyone else and their pointless, vapid curiosity, I *needed* to see his face.

The ache in my gut outbid my arm for the moment and I sat, wallowing in the sadness Cassius's snub had left in my core. What had changed in half a day?

Homeroom would be over in less than an hour, and he couldn't hide from me during passing time. I wouldn't let him. No time for debauchery. No time for bullshit. No time for letting it go. I'd force a friendship on him if I had to. Then I'd regret it, stew in my own self-pity, only to ultimately apologize profusely in the end because of who I am as a person. A milk-toast person.

Mr. Kincaid rambled on about Spain or something of the sort, his thick mustache wiggling about under his nose; a caterpillar nesting on his upper lip. I watched the clock. Those three stupid hands moved sluggishly around their axis. Cassius hadn't so much as glanced at me over his shoulder. The room was still; most everyone watched Cassius, many of them putting together rumors about me and the sudden appearance of a new kid. I'd spent my entire school career being invisible. That was all about to change, thanks to my own bizarre curiosity. Well, maybe the big, fat ball of death clinging to my bicep had a hand in it too—with the dying-anyway-courage and all. At the very least I wasn't the cancer girl. I'd take odd boy rescuer over dead girl walking any day.

The bell rang while I stared at the side of Cassius's head. His eyes had been focused on the back of the head in front of him. He hadn't written anything. Hadn't pulled out a pencil or paper. Just sat there and endured it until it was over. His eyes shot up to the box high on the wall emitting the sound. He turned his head to look at the offender, his dark hair fell back over the side of his face, exposing a dark splotch around his left eye. Purple and red mottling encompassed the cheekbone under it. A gasp escaped before I could catch it. He certainly hadn't left my house with that shiner. My gut writhed with anger and the sick churning pang of guilt. Maybe cancer girl would have been better.

Cassius didn't wait for me. He slipped his lean body from the desk and quickly filed out of the room with the other students. He stood a head taller than all but one, me. His dark head sticking out over the top of the crowd made him hard to miss. I shoved my notebook into my bag as I skirted out the door behind him.

I caught sight of him up ahead, shuffling along beside his peers like he was walking through a dream, which wasn't too far off from those he shuffled with. To anyone not paying attention, he blended well with the population of FHS, but I knew better. Even in a short few days I'd figured out he had a steadfast personal bubble and noise issues. Both of which were currently being violated. His hands were pulled high up in his sleeves, making him look like an amputee. I could tell just by the set of his broad shoulders he wasn't coping well, but instead of clamping his hands over his ears or snapping a thousand times, he did his best to avoid touching or looking at anyone. Having been locked away from society for his entire life, it was a wonder Cassius Shooster wasn't some wild jungle boy scaling the walls and flinging his poop.

My long legs carried me down the hall, passing through small groups of chatting people, all of whom were looking—in some way—at Cassius. I kept my eyes focused on him. When I was close enough to almost reach out and touch him, I called out.

"Cass," I said, and my voice echoed through the halls,

bouncing off the unused lockers that lined the hallway.

Cassius stopped, turned, and looked over his shoulder. So did everyone else. All eyes were on him... and *me*. Heads moved in unison from Cassius to me and back again. As he flipped his hood over his head, he raised his hand to his ear. *Snap, snap*. It was an odd gesture as far as teenage boys went and wasn't lost on the gawking crowd. Silence spread peanut-butter thick through the people-filled space. I cautiously eyed those around me, silently pleading with the powers that be to make this moment go away and hoping like hell no one was judging the weirdo snapping his fingers.

"It's Cassius," he growled his name; a furious crunchy candy shell with despair in the gooey center.

A unified gasp went over the crowd. Everyone looked at me, desperately awaiting my response. "Can we talk?" I asked, moving in to close the chasm between us.

"You *are* talking." I couldn't tell if he was being rude or naïve. Both equally bothered me in completely different ways.

The crowd closed in on us. No one hid the fact that they were listening, leaning in close to better hear our totally public breakdown of communication. Cassius clenched his jaw, muscles working over words he didn't want to say, or couldn't find, then turned his back and walked away from me. I huffed—thoroughly sick of the day and it wasn't even second period—and sped toward him, catching up in just a few long strides.

"Somewhere else," I said through gritted teeth, grabbing him up by his sleeve like my mom had and dragging him with me.

The millisecond we cleared the crowded area, the whispers began. I cringed at the thought of what they might've been saying. What lies they could be concocting. Dreading the idea that over the course of our more private conversation, I will have gotten pregnant, had an abortion, obtained a nasty coke addiction, and gone to rehab, I decided to keep it within eyeshot of at least a few corroborating witnesses.

Parked ten feet from the theater entrance, I whispered, "What is going on?" He didn't answer. His eyes looked everywhere but at me. "Cassius…" I let my anger with the situation slip out in the form of his name hissed through clenched teeth. "What is going on?" He pursed his lips, chewing again on something unsaid. Twenty-seven seconds. I counted. "What happened to your face?" Instinctively, I reached to touch his shiner.

Cassius jerked away dramatically. "Hands down," he demanded.

My chest rose quickly under the burden of a gasp. "Cass…." I hadn't expected his reaction. "Talk to me. I'm worried about you."

He swallowed hard, jaw working overtime. Then, in one jumbled mess of words, it finally burst from his lips. "You did this to me." I literally stumbled back a step, heart officially ripped from my chest. "I left the house for you. I came to *you*." His typical baritone squeaked at the end. "Then I got this." He pointed to his injury. "And now I have to be here." His black eyes looked around the hallway with disdain.

My head shook uncontrollably; back, forth, back… "I'm—I'm—I don't…," I stuttered, frantically hunting for the right thing to say. "Cassius, what can I do?" I settled on those words out of necessity.

"You can never talk to me again. How about that?" My insides seared, his words acid on my soft tender bits.

"But—" I stopped myself, tears dangling precariously from my lashes. I felt the sudden pressure of everyone's eyes on me. The handful of students who frequented that span of hallway had doubled, all dying with curiosity. I stepped in closer and whispered, "Cassius… I… I just wanted you to be happy."

Expressionless, he stopped moving, stopped shifting his weight from foot to foot, no more fidgeting, stone still. If I'd stared any harder, I would have burrowed a hole in his forehead. I stared at Cassius and he stared at my feet, giving zero clue as to what he could have possibly been thinking. I wouldn't have even ventured a guess. I didn't have to be his best friend forever to understand Cassius Shooster was complicated.

His face, mostly shadowed by his hood, shifted to resolve. "My brain can't be happy." I could assume with reason those were his dad's words being spewed at me.

"That's a lie and you know it." I didn't waste any

time playing nice. He tried to keep his face mostly hidden from me. He failed. Anger swept over his face. "Now, I'm sorry you got hurt, that is not what I wanted, but this is better." I pointed both fingers to the ground at our feet. "I promise. Life is better than... than whatever that was you were living."

Cassius took in a long, deep breath and leaned in close enough for me to smell his laundry soap. Those standing behind us surely anticipated a climactic kiss. "You have no clue what you've done," he growled into my face, then turned and stormed away.

My chest heaved with the threat of a sob on the brink. The bell shrieked overhead. *Time's up. Move along.* Silence. No one moved. Everyone waited, watching me.

I turned and met fifty faces. All eyes and big O mouths. "What?" I screamed at the crowd. "What the hell are you all looking at? Huh? Poor Prudence Penderhaus, always the friggin' loser." I sent an elbow into the locker behind me, and it rattled back with the muted echo of my rage.

As I stormed through the hall toward the double doors that led to the front steps, groups of students watched me carefully from their peripheral vision. Hissing whispers floated through the air. The hiss of degradation. Never in my life had I ever spoken up for myself. Not to that degree, anyhow. I'd honestly never seen the point in engaging with those people. It felt good. Damn good.

Feet from the door, a crooked smile pulled one corner of my mouth upward. *Screw it*, I thought. *You've got one life, better get on with it. No time for whiners. No time for lemmings. No time for bullshit.*

Letting my long spindly arms fly above my head, I shouted without turning around, "Suck it, Flintlock High." The middle finger on each hand jutted up from my two clenched fists, aimed at the whispering douchebags behind me. There were a few specific people I had in mind that deserved a one-on-one reaming. I'd save that for another day. With one long leg and big foot, I kicked the front doors open dramatically and strolled right out without looking back.

Two steps from the top of the stairs, my gut sank. What had I done? That incident would surely land me in Ratzass's office. My grades were good, not the best Flintlock had to offer, but better than most. I'd never been in any trouble. Never made waves. They'd let me off with a warning. Right?

Hands gripped my shoulders from behind and practically knocked me down the steps with their weight. "Penderhaus," a familiar voice echoed in my swimming head. "I didn't know you had it in you," Bonnie said, hanging off my shoulders like a baby monkey. I prayed she didn't go for the piggyback; there was no way I could manage her weight and my arm in the same space and time.

After a few seconds of allowing the blood to flow back to my head, I was able to speak again. "Bonnie, hey" was all I could muster.

"Hey." She laughed and circled her arm around my waist. Standing at an average eighteen-year-old-girl height, her head hardly cleared my boobs. "You have *got* to tell me about this new boy."

Now you're ready to talk? "I believe I've tried. Multiple times." She'd recently been crowned the queen of absent—in both the school and social life category.

"Yeah, sorry, kid...." In typical Bonnie fashion, she gave no explanation and no intention to at any point in the future.

"I've texted you like twenty times. Where have you been?"

I hadn't been paying attention when we stepped off the last step and onto the sidewalk. I'd ditched. Officially, 100 percent ditched school. Not just didn't go because I was shacked up with the weird kid in the spook house on Marigold. Walked right off the property without a hitch. It was no wonder Bonnie did it all the time. It had been too easy.

She laughed, one loud bark. "Where I've been is nothing compared to what my little Prudence has been up to. Spill it," she demanded.

Her mention of my situation brought about the sudden realization I'd left school and in doing so left Cassius behind.

My feet stopped, refusing to move another inch. "I can't, Bon." Shaking my head, I took a step backward.

"Don't be a chicken. One foot in front of the other. C'mon now." She pulled at my arm as though I were blind.

"No, really. I can't go." I took another step back.

"You're not going to get busted. You'll be fine." Her vapid reassurance reminded me of how I must've sounded to Cassius. Never mind those shark fins, jump on in, the water is fine.

"Bonnie, I can't leave him behind. He needs me," I proclaimed knowing full well he'd told me to stay out of his life.

Bonnie folded her arms over her chest. "Dude, it's just a guy. He'll be there tomorrow."

She didn't get it. She would never get it. "You don't understand." I stood at the foot of the steps to the high school, whining like a child.

"Why don't you explain it to me, then?"

I wanted to. I really did. Even the stuff about my arm—though not nearly as much that. But I didn't have the time. I had to find him. I had to fix it.

"He doesn't know what to do." I turned and left her standing on the sidewalk. "He doesn't know how to be human," I hollered over my shoulder as I bounded back up the stairs.

The tardy bell rang the second I put my hand on the door. I'd just flipped off half the student body. Going back into that place only minutes after seemed a little… flaky. I didn't know the rules about those sorts of things and had no clue how to act now that I'd let 'er rip.

"What's your plan, Penderhaus?" Bonnie called from the foot of the steps.

My hand trembled on the door handle. If I opened that door and barreled back in, I would face sure embarrassment. If I turned back and left with Bonnie, I'd be leaving behind an innocent not prepared for the wilds of high school.

"Bonnie," I called over my shoulder, "meet me at the spot after school. I have someone I want you to meet."

"Must be pretty special," she said. I could hear the smile in her voice.

Must be, I thought and pulled the door open with all my might. It flung wide and brought with it a gust that flipped papers away from their stapled spots on the wall. I hadn't a clue as to where he might be, but the school was small and, as far as senior classes went, there weren't many options.

My big feet slapped the slick floor as I made my way to the office. The least I could do was check with Marlene, the adorable, and rightfully unapologetic, overweight sweetheart who ran the office. She and I had clicked on day one. Twenty years older than me, she knew just how cruel high school could be—for the fat and the skinny.

"Hi, Prudence, why aren't you in class?" she asked when I pushed through the office door.

"I need to know where Cassius Shooster is right now."

She hesitated and stammered, her thick cheeks jiggled a bit. "Well, why?"

"Uh...." I wasn't prepared with what to say and before I knew it, everything was spilling out. "He's my neighbor, and I know him, and I know he's not ready for school and—"

"Whoa, slow down." She thought on it for a moment. "He's the boy on Marigold." She puckered her lips and clicked her tongue, pondering my speedy words. "And you know him?" she asked, surprised.

"I'm the reason he's here," I admitted. "I just want to know he's okay." I paused. "Please."

Marlene looked around the office, likely looking out for Ms. Ratzass. One plump hand dug through her thick dark brown bun and pulled out a pencil. She clicked some stuff into her computer and jotted the information down. "I didn't give you this." She smiled and handed me the slip of paper she'd scrawled on. "Go get 'em," she whispered.

I nodded, smiled, and leaned my slender body over the counter, planting a grateful kiss on her forehead. She giggled and shooed me on my way. I grabbed a gummy bear from her jar on my way out. "You're a peach, Ms. Wilco."

My yellow sticky note read, *English, second period.* I could only assume it meant Jerry, our English-four teacher and friend. He emphasized his laid-back approach to leadership by insisting we call him Jerry and keep his home number on file "just in case we're ever in trouble." He was a cool guy, but his beard was beginning to get out of control.

Jerry's room was forty-nine south. South meaning south hall, one of the four main hallways that made up Flintlock High. Most junior and senior classes were in south hall. North was almost all freshman and sophomore classes, and east housed metal shop and the media lab. West was taken up mostly by the theater and an art class. The gym and cafeteria were out of the cross halls and stood as their own buildings on the property.

Class had been in for almost five minutes and I was running through the halls clutching a sticky note on a frantic hunt for a boy no one knew existed until this morning. I hadn't thought about my arm or impending doom—aside from the occasional zing of pain—since I'd met Cassius. As if I were just an average American teenager on an unexpected adventure. I think they called that a placebo.

I skidded around the corner, my sneakers squeaking a few times on my way. Forty-nine south, English-four. I skidded to a stop and grabbed the knob. Without thinking, I flung the door open and stumbled in with the grace of a giraffe on roller skates. My shoe squeaked once, catching on the shiny wood floor, I tottered and stopped hard. My bag slung off my shoulder and down my arm—the good one. Everyone stared at me, but I didn't bother to return the favor. My eyes quickly scanned the faces in the room until I caught his. He'd made it. I let out a sigh of relief.

"Prudence, can I help you?" Jerry's tender tone came with a lilt of surprise.

"Uh…." Nervous laughter bubbled up my throat and pointed at Cassius. "Just, uh, checking on my buddy, Cassius." Jerry looked at Cassius and back to me, expression all eyebrows, a thick sandy beard censoring the rest of his face. "He's new and doesn't know—" I stopped myself. No one else needed to know Cassius couldn't human. "Well… I'll be going now."

I gave Cassius a look, nodding, hoping with all I had that he understood I meant I'd be waiting for him, keeping an eye, proving how much I cared. Completely ignoring his demand that I leave his life forever.

"Goodbye, Prudence," Jerry said. "See you this afternoon."

"Hm, yeah." I chuckled, all nerves and anxiety. "Bye." I waved, turned, and slammed my shoulder into the doorjamb. The bad one.

An oomph bounced out of my chest and echoed back at me. The class hummed with stifled laughter. Any other classroom would have erupted in a show of finger pointing and dramatic hilarity, but Jerry kept a tight rein on bullying. I stumbled around the door as I opened it wider, an embarrassed chuckle escaping before I could stop it. I was mostly out of the door when Morgan Pennington broke the cardinal rule of room forty-nine.

"Way to go, Lurch," he yelled to me from the back of the room.

I stopped, cringed, and looked over my shoulder. Not at Morgan, but Cassius. I hadn't even considered it before it happened, but the very last thing I wanted Cassius to witness was the perpetual bullying of me. In the moment, I wasn't certain if it was because I didn't want his first view of the world to be assholes, or because I didn't want him to see me for the pathetic creature I was.

"Hey, no trash talking, Morgan." Jerry tried, bless his hippy heart, but he was no match for the crowd.

Morgan's lemmings laughed and nudged each other with pride. Cassius sat motionless, frozen in a state of jaw-clenching torment. He wanted out of the situation more than it appeared. I sucked in air through pursed lips. A desperate attempt to stop myself from blowing up into either tears or obscenities. As the seconds ticked, the latter was winning by a mile.

"Lurch," some of the other students repeated, laughing as though they'd never heard the name before in all the years he'd been calling me that.

A bang rattled up from somewhere in the back. My eyes shot to Cass.

"Shut up," Cassius grumbled. No one listened.

Jerry tried in his positive reinforcement kind of way to calm the room, but it did nothing. His timid voice was almost completely drowned out by the snorting of little piggies in the back row. They had their punching bag and nothing short of Ratzass was going to stop them.

Cassius seethed. Chest rising over panting breaths. Anger boiled up to his wavy locks. "Shut up," he said in a tone almost as useless as Jerry's. Still no one cared.

When the moment had run its course, when it looked like the classroom would just be a cage for the uncivilized apes, Cassius stood. His lanky body nearly tipped over in his desk in the process. "Did you not hear me?" he shouted. "Shut up!" His bellow—a near replica of Arnold's *Kindergarten Cop*—echoed through the room, and everyone fell silent. Cassius's hood still shadowed most of his face, but I could see his eyes, round and black with anger. Shock kept my feet planted but instinctively my arms reached for him, fear for what he'd do next fueling the movement.

The classroom now quiet, Jerry's voice could finally be heard. "Cassius, friend, thank you, but please relax and take a seat."

"I will do nothing of the sort." His fast cadence and odd manner of speaking brought confused faces to the tittering morons. "This…"—he looked around for a long minute at all the faces pointed in his direction—"this is preposterous." He repeatedly shook his head back and forth, shaking away the world around him. "I don't belong here." *Snap, snap*, his fingers clicked near his head. It was more than just two snaps. It was a production of movement that started at his elbow and ended in a flick of not just his fingers but his entire hand.

Morgan had been cautiously scowling at Cassius, and it seemed he was going to ignore him outright, until, without warning, Cassius stood miles over the top of him. In an honest fight, I didn't know who would win, but looking at them together, it was clear Morgan would have to learn to climb.

Starting at his feet first, Morgan looked up at Cassius, glaring, but anyone with eyes could see a thread of fear stitched across Morgan's face. It wasn't just the height difference, Cassius was new and clearly different—odd, strange, weird—something to be feared in a town like Flintlock. Not to mention his connection with 17 Marigold Lane, the creep house.

I was honestly surprised he didn't already have more of a following from the Salvatore-Cullen fan club of Flintlock. It was a legit club that met twice a week to discuss all things brooding and sparkly. A new pale mystery man at school was right up their alley. That coffin in his house must've been his vampire lair. Or some stupid shit like that.

"Cass," I said, calm, collected, and still standing at the door.

He didn't move at first, I almost thought he was going to pretend he didn't hear me, but he finally looked over his shoulder to me, then back to Morgan. Tension spread across his shoulders. Broader than I'd ever noticed, his back and arms flexed under his classic black hoodie. Time had slowed, nearly stopped. Locked in a standoff, Morgan and Cassius glared at each other, hackles up, teeth bared.

Cass, come on. Walk away, I silently begged him, sending my thoughts torpedoing into his brain. I took one step away from the door, then another. By the third step, my torpedo thoughts had hit. Cassius stood up straight, turned his back on Morgan and his cronies, and met my eyes. I nodded; an approving smirk tugged my mouth up at the corners. My breath puffed out when he started shuffling toward me. He was two rows away from me when all hell broke loose.

"Ha," Morgan said, looking around at his friends to save face. "The freak's a Lurch lover." I shook my head. *Don't say it, Pennington. Don't you do it.* "Mr. and Mrs. Lurch."

And there it is, I thought. My nightmare.

There was no time to stop it from happening. In a blink, Cassius left me standing there, jaw on the floor, cleared the two-desk space between them and wrapped his two oversized hands around Morgan's shirt. In two solid yanks, he pulled Morgan's hefty body from his desk, sending the thing clattering to the floor. Broad shoulders or no, I would have never guessed Cassius had that sort of strength. Judging by Morgan's face, neither did he.

"Stop," I called out, sounding a little like Willy Wonka warning the naughty children against their crappy behavior. Morgan deserved to get pummeled. As long as Cassius didn't get expelled on his first day of school, which seemed to be on his agenda.

Morgan was on his back, Cassius crouched over the top of him. Although I'd expected it, Cass didn't throw a punch. Not one. He gripped Morgan by the collar, already pale fists white with tension. Cassius's face only an inch or two from Morgan's, he spoke through gritted teeth.

"Shut. Up. Imbecile." Cassius released Morgan's collar with force, shoving him hard against the floor.

Cassius stood, a giant unfolding from the bottom up, tall and broad. One slick movement and he flipped his hood off his head, exposing his face. The shiner that encompassed his eye was a stark contrast to the translucency of his skin. His black eyes threatened the faces that stared at him. My heart thudded hard against my rib cage as fear began to make itself at home. All I could do was stand there and watch my perfectly imperfect plan backfire in my face.

"Cass, brother—"

"Get your hands off me, you damn dirty ape," Cassius said, and shoved Jerry's hand off his shoulder. He turned to stare at Jerry. "You are *not* my brother."

"Whoa, it's cool, Cassius," Jerry said, holding his hands up in surrender.

Cassius turned hard and headed for the door. And me. Every set of eyes in the room were locked on him. That Thursday, second period English, would soon become a legend in Flintlock. Multiple versions of events that would likely include Cassius baring a knife or Morgan rescuing me from the freak in room forty-nine.

"Ca—" I started but stopped short when his dense shoulder slammed me into the door on his way out. He stormed right past me as everyone watched Mr. Lurch proving once and for all he was certainly *not* a Lurch lover. Even Jerry couldn't believe his eyes. Not a one of them had any idea the boy they called a freak had an absolutely valid reason for behaving like a madman. Me. His reason was pretty much me.

I took a second to snarl at Morgan, still sitting on the floor, eyes wide, breath thready, then sliding out the door before it closed on me.

"Hey," I called after him, letting the door slam shut behind me. Cassius didn't turn back. Didn't even acknowledge my existence. The girl he watched walk by his house every day for however long. The smack of my sneakers on the floor echoed, cutting the silence. "Cassius, wait." I'd caught up to him and snatched him up by the arm. Which seemed to be his natural handhold.

"Stop. Stop touching me." He wouldn't look at me, but also didn't try to pull away.

I puffed out my chest and held my ground. "No."

"I said, yes. Hands down."

I tightened my grip on his sweater and grabbed his arm with my other hand. "Not on your life." He could get pissed off all he wanted; I wasn't letting him be alone again. Self-pity be damned. For both of us.

"What is wrong with you?" he asked in a tone that was all too familiar. I'd been asked that question my entire life by my peers. And certain staff members in the Flintlock school district.

"What's wrong with *me*?" I asked, defenses high. "I could ask you the same question. I'm not the one pummeling people in the middle of a classroom. What were you thinking?"

"That guy is a jerk." His honesty made me smile, but as far as Flintlock was concerned, Morgan Pennington shit gold.

"That is not untrue, but you can't just go beating people up in class. It's just not done."

"Why?"

"Because it's not. There are rules here."

"Where?"

"Here at school."

He huffed at my stupidity. "Where are the rules? I'd like to read them."

"Uh," I stammered and thought the question over. "Well, ha, you know—" The following few seconds were taken up by me making awkward noises with my mouth and flapping my hands against my thighs. "I don't have them on me, or anything. They're just known. We just know."

"Rules should be posted. How does anyone know when they're breaking a rule if they aren't posted?"

Damn logic. Of course he wouldn't know. Though the rules were neatly packed into a legalese forty-page booklet, he had a point. Who the hell reads those things anyway? "You know... you're right. It makes no sense. And, unfortunately, the concept is not sanctioned to school. Life, as a whole, makes no sense." I thought for a moment. "I'm sorry I forced you into a world you don't understand," I apologized, regret vining from my heart down to my toes. Pity party, my house, four o'clock.

We were quiet too long. A place of comfort for him, quiet. It'd been a few minutes at least since the great battle of room forty-nine and no one came to take him away. Jerry must not have called the office. Maybe he trusted me to handle the situation. Maybe he knew more about Cassius than I assumed. Even though we should have been in class, in the office, or leaving the country, we just stood there; my hands still clutched to his sleeves. Standing alone in the hallway during class time for no real reason made our simple, heartfelt conversation a daring protest to conformity. Or something like that.

"Hey, losers," Bonnie called from the corner of the main hall. "Ready to blow this Popsicle stand?"

I hadn't been ready to ditch school the first time, but there was little that could force me to stay in that moment. I looked at Cassius, who appeared to be confused by her sudden presence. I didn't blame him; Bonnie was good for that sort of thing. "So, are you in for getting the hell outta here?" I asked, eyes on his impressive feet, suddenly feeling coy. I was, aside from Bonnie yards away, alone in the hall with a boy thinking about ditching school. A daring first for Prudence Penderhaus.

Three deep breaths in and out, Cassius stared at my mouth. "Prudence…" I was beginning to appreciate my own name the more he said it. "I'm having a hard time understanding what you're saying."

Thankful for his honesty, I clarified. "I'm going to leave with Bonnie, and I want you to come with me."

"Where?"

"Somewhere way cooler than here." My answer was truthful. The spot, as we lovingly called it, was the only sanctuary outside of home for the black sheep of Flintlock.

Two breaths. In. Out. "Okay."

"Okay."

I reached out, without asking, and took him by the hand, which was clenched in his sleeve. Cassius didn't fight me as I towed him along behind me. Two steps from the corner, the voice of hell called us home.

"Penderhaus!" Ms. Ratzass bellowed from the far end of the hall.

"Book it!" Bonnie demanded and took off toward the doors.

My sneakers squeaked against the waxed floor as I tore off into a sprint. "Run," I shouted at Cassius, my voice echoed down the hall. He followed my directive, but it was clear the boy had never had the chance to break out into an all-out leg pumping run in his life.

Through the doors we burst and into the dreary daylight. Ms. Ratzass's wobbly little legs scurried along behind us just before the doors shut us out. Not one of us looked back. One by one we bounded down the stairs.

The doors burst open. "Penderhaus, I'm calling your mother!" she screamed, her shrill sent a flock of birds flittering from the nearby tree.

Shit. I looked over my shoulder. She would most definitely be calling my mom. I just wasn't sure how much I cared. In the grand scheme of it, who would? The hobbit-looking woman standing at the top of the stairs grew smaller and smaller as I ran in the opposite direction.

6

THE SPOT—A WOODED GROVE STRADDLING THE COUNTY line—hid away the miscreants that called it their sanctuary. We hadn't discovered it, and we'd likely not be the last Flintlock students to hide out there. Bonnie and I had been shown the way my freshman year by a few seniors who, looking back now, were the reflection of who we'd eventually become. We hadn't yet found a set of outcast freshmen to take under our rebellious—*I'm getting there*—wings and show them the ropes. But the year was young and opportunities abounded.

It's a fifteen-minute walk from school to the spot. And as we discovered, only an eight-minute run. Cassius had been silent during our journey, which I was understanding was a norm for him. It wasn't until we finally slowed to a panting stop in the center of a clearing of trees that he spoke.

"We're in the woods." His voice calm for having just ran a mile.

Bonnie scoffed. "Yeah." Her condescending tone was lost on Cassius, but I picked it up right away and shot her a threatening glance. In her defense, she didn't know. Just like the rest of Flintlock, she was ignorant to things not slapping her in the face.

"Cass," I said, and he didn't correct me. "You can relax. No one will screw with you here." I spread my arms wide. "This is our sanctuary."

I reassured him the best I could and hoped it wasn't in vain. I honestly had no idea what I was doing with him and whether my attempts at socialization would eventually be a good or bad thing—our current situation notwithstanding. But I had to believe that anything was better than what he had. He was just about ready to be an adult, or so I assumed, not knowing his actual birthday, and it was high time he ventured out and saw what the world had to offer. I also realized I could do well by taking my own advice.

"Sanctuary," he repeated.

"Yup." I rocked forward on my toes and back again, hands tucked into my back pockets.

His dark eyes scanned the trees, branches, every last yellow leaf clinging to its branch. Birds sang, squirrels scurried up trunks and into their burrows. And Cassius watched it all with new eyes. So many new sounds, new sights, to take in and find a place for them in his brain.

Cassius watched the world, taking it all in, and I watched him with equal curiosity. With his hood pulled tight over his head, eyes never finding mine, it was difficult to gauge his reaction to our adventure. For all I knew, he was dying inside. I wished I could climb into his head and dig around to see what was what. It would certainly make things easier.

"What do you think?"

Bonnie's sandy blonde brows tucked in at the center. I would have to sit her down and explain everything when Cassius wasn't there. I refused to talk about him like he wasn't standing right there like his father had.

"It's crinkly."

"Crinkly?"

He nodded; his mop of hair bounced around his forehead. "Yes."

"Cass…" I wanted to laugh, it was silly, but I stopped it at a grin. "What does crinkly mean?"

He breathed, thinking, chewing his cheek. Both hands raised to his ears, and I waited for the snaps. His tell. But they didn't come. Instead, he ran both hands over his ears, a cat preening, wiping away the crinkle. "The trees are crinkly." He reached out and dragged his fingertips down the cracked bark of the trunk. A squirrel scampered across a bough above his head. His eyes shot up to find the sound. A crinkle of tiny claws over tree skin.

"Squirrels. Their nails scratch the bark when they run. It helps keep them from falling off." I swallowed, reaching out the feel the crinkly tree with him. "It sounds crinkly," I agreed.

Dark eyes finally found mine. The new crinkly world still shined in them. Shimmered. A beacon beckoning me in. "Prudence…" He started, then let it go. His brow set, so serious, so stoic and yet so completely lost. A lighthouse without a keeper.

Bonnie pulled out a cigarette from her shoulder bag. "You know, Cassius—" She lit her smoke. "—you really should lighten up."

Cassius broke our stare. His eyes dimmed, drunk with new experience. "Lighten up with a cigarette," he said and reached out to take one of her smokes. She pinched hers between her lips to free both hands and pulled out one for him.

What the hell was Bonnie thinking? I watched Cassius take it, put the white cancer stick between his lips and do his best with her lighter.

"No," I shouted and karate chopped the white stick from his lips. "What are you *thinking*?" I asked Bonnie.

Stunned at my reaction, Bonnie stepped back. "The kid wants a smoke. B.F.D." She really didn't understand. He didn't either. And, in a way, neither did I. In a world of ignorance, misunderstandings ruled.

I threw my hands in the air. "He doesn't even know what a smoke is," I scolded, my own ignorance shining through.

Cassius's thin black brows scowled. "Do you think

I'm an idiot?" Cassius asked, his tone sharp and pointy, snagged on my tender nerves.

I huffed. "Well, no, but…." I hadn't meant offense, I really hadn't. "I just want to keep you safe."

Bonnie chortled and Cassius argued, "I know what cigarettes are, Prudence."

"Well, ha," I scoffed and stumbled over my words. Of course he did. His pre-1980 video collection alone would have given him that knowledge. "You've been locked away in that house so long, I don't really know what you know of the world." My defenses riled up and I did my best to squash them down.

"What?" Bonnie said, her smoldering cigarette bounced between her lips.

Closing my eyes, I took a deep breath and thought about what I would say regarding the delicate situation. I wouldn't talk about him like he wasn't there. I wouldn't. Bonnie had secondhand knowledge, and it was time I cleared things up.

Letting out a long sigh, I began. "I met Cassius a few days ago while I was walking to school. He lives on my street. Come to find out, his parents hadn't allowed him out of the house. Ever." That was easier than I'd thought.

"So it's true."

"Most of it. Probably."

"This is like… some Lifetime original movie shit." She'd hit the nail on the head with that statement.

"That's what I said."

"What's a Lifetime original movie?"

Clearly Cassius's video collection ended at the VHS and DVD. It wasn't a surprise he'd never been exposed to cable television.

"It's a TV network that makes cheesy plot-driven films with B-list actors and poor dialogue."

He nodded, then thought twice about it. "Prudence, I do not agree with this lifetime. Our dialogue is intriguing and heartfelt." He paused and added. "One for the ages."

I blushed, Bonnie caught it and wiggled her brows at me. "Agreed." I went on, doing my best to hide my reddened cheeks. "Morgan *effing* Pennington nailed me with a Big Gulp Tuesday morning."

"Savages in this town," Cassius quoted.

"Word," Bonnie agreed.

"I decided to ask the folks at 17 to use their bathroom."

"Ooh, adventurous."

Bonnie joked, but she wasn't wrong. It wasn't just a step for Prudence Penderhaus. It was a major leap for Flintlock in general. "I know. So, low and behold, there's Cassius at the door." I grinned at him and he looked at his feet.

"As it turns out, the Shoosters had been holding Cassius up in the house his entire life—"

"That explains a lot." She glanced at Cassius. "Sorry." He shrugged.

"So, Mom"—she called my mom *Mom* since she really didn't have one of her own—"flipped a lid and called

Sheriff Floyd who has obviously forced the Shoosters to enroll him in school. And here we are today."

"At the spot, breaking the law, ditching school on his first day; seems like you're doing a great job keeping him safe, Pru. Maybe his parents were just worried about bad influences." She laughed it off as a joke, too, but there was truth there. I wasn't doing a very good job introducing Cassius Shooster to the world.

"Actually," he said, "my parents were worried I'd hurt someone, like I hurt Andrew."

If we'd had a soundtrack, curious, foreboding music would have begun as I turned slowly to look at Bonnie. *Who the hell is Andrew?* I opened my mouth to ask just that when a familiar asshole bellowed through the clearing.

"Penderhaus," Morgan sneered. "You're so predictable. Of course you'd run away to Loser Woods." No one had ever called it that before, and even he had to admit it was a lame nickname. He'd really missed a golden opportunity with Sherweird Forrest. But that was what separated us, wit and a mostly formed cerebral cortex.

Four-letter words played over and over in my mind— some louder than others. "What do you want, Morgan?" I asked through my teeth.

He held his meaty hands in the air, a faux surrender. "Just wanted to talk to my new buddy." Morgan clasped his paw on Cassius's shoulder and gave it a shake. Pennington wore a smile, but it was as fake as his mother's tan.

Cassius's brows dropped, hanging over his heavy-lidded eyes. "Don't touch me," he grumbled.

"What's wrong, guy? We're friends, right?"

Cassius looked at me for answers. "No, Morgan, he's not your friend. Assholes don't have friends." I realized the second it left my lips that my words would be flipped and dipped and turned around right back at me, Prudence *friendless* Penderhaus.

"Obviously," Morgan jeered. His cheeks shoved his beady eyes into half-moons when he laughed and looked at the cronies flanking him. As if I hadn't literally handed him that one. "Cass," Morgan said, and Cassius's face contorted.

"It's *Cassius*," I grumbled.

Morgan ignored me completely. No surprise. "I think you and I got off to a bad start." His meaty arm draped over Cassius's shoulder. Like a midget in a wrestling match, Morgan standing a good six inches shorter than Cassius. "A misunderstanding." Morgan patted Cassius's stomach. "It's all good, right, bro?"

Speaking without his lips moving, he replied through his teeth, "You're not my brother."

"Sure we are." Morgan's condescending tone was obvious enough to me, but I didn't know if Cassius understood the intent behind the words. "Look, me and the guys are heading out to the well later tonight to chase some brews. Why don't you come along with us?" Morgan spread a plastic smile across his face and squeezed the shoulder he struggled to reach. Cassius tolerated Morgan's touch as though he were trying to prevent a hulking green beastie bursting from his skin. Aggravation twisted Cassius's face into a bow. "Just us guys."

Cassius looked at me. Black pools, endless, full of everything and nothing at the same time. I swallowed hard. Cassius at the well, alone with Morgan and his band of idiots, was a worst possible scenario. It just could not happen. I shook my head. "Don't" was all I could squeak out before Morgan sealed the deal.

"You want to fit in, right? Me and my boys can show you everything there is to know about how to be a *man* in Flintlock." Cassius's dark eyes shifted away from me and toward Morgan at his shoulder. "What do you say?" Cassius was quiet for what felt like a full minute, eyeing me, then Morgan and back again. "C'mon, you don't want to hang out with a bunch of *girls* all day, do you?"

He said girls as though we weren't even that. Trash. He meant trash. "Bite me, Pennington," Bonnie added, smoke bobbing between her lips.

Morgan sneered at her, then stood on his toes to reach Cassius's ear for a whisper, coming in short at least an inch. "Take it from someone who knows. Penderhaus is a freak. You're better off ditching her now before it's too late." He leaned in closer, pulling Cassius to him, and whispered through the side of his mouth. "Two words. Social. Suicide."

I heard everything he said, which had probably been

the point. After so many years hearing his bullshit, it didn't bother me anymore. What bothered me was the look on Cassius's face. As though he were falling for everything Morgan was feeding him. As if he were just seeing me for what I was. A loser freak. Naïve and vulnerable, Cassius didn't stand a chance with the likes of Morgan and the morons. Sounded like a shitty cover band. And still a better name than *Loser Woods*.

Cassius nodded. "Tonight?" he asked.

"No," I breathed.

"Yeah. You, me, Brady, and the rest. A guys' night."

Brows pulled, desperately pleading with him to say no, all I could do was shake my head.

"Where is the well?" Cassius asked, refusing to look at me.

"Don't worry about it. I'll come pick you up. You're in the spook house on the corner of Marigold, right?"

I cringed. I'd intentionally avoided using that phrase.

"Spook house?" Cassius asked.

"Shut up, Morgan," I growled. He shooed me with a beefy hand.

"Oh, ha," Morgan stumbled over his words. "Yeah, you know, your house is kinda creepy looking, so some of the guys started calling it the spook house a while back. We didn't know anyone even lived there."

That was a lie. Everyone knew *someone* lived there, most just didn't know who exactly. And no one ever suspected a kid was growing up in that house right alongside us. A spook house it was called, among other things, as long as I could remember. No one ever corrected it, so no one ever suspected it was wrong. Dead wrong. I'd been in that house. It was no scarier than my own house or any other on that side of town. They were old, it came with the territory. The unfortunate aspect of 17 Marigold Lane was that the odd boy who suddenly emerged from the scariest house in town would surely be viewed with the same terrified contempt as his house. His natural propensity for oddness wouldn't help that fact.

"Shouldn't you be in class, Morgan?" Bonnie asked, leaned against her favorite stump. "Football does still require a C average, right?"

"I could ask you the same question. Weren't you a senior last year too, Templeton?"

"I'm a delinquent. What's your excuse? Had to cut out early to see your mommy?" Everyone knew Morgan was a mama's boy. No one made a fuss about it since his mother was the head of everything: PTA, Women's Club, bake sales, charity events, you name it, his mother was in charge.

"Humph," Morgan scoffed. His band of morons stood behind him. Each looked like a mob movie henchman. I waited for one of them to smash a fist into his palm. "Shut your fat mouth, *trash*."

If there was anything Bonnie hated, it was being called fat. Trash didn't seem to bother her anymore.

"Go tell your mother to come shut it for me." She flicked her tongue at him between the V of her fingers. Morgan dropped his arm from Cassius's shoulder and made a move toward Bonnie. He stopped short, eyes widening for a moment before dropping into a Clint Eastwood squint. A glint of something metal caught my eye, and I noticed the blade Bonnie held low in her hand. "Want to see what trash can do to that face of yours, rich boy?" she threatened, never lifting the knife above her waist.

Normally, I'd have stopped her. Taken the knife from her and told her to walk away. But not today. I wanted Morgan to leave. Scampering away with his tail between his legs, Bonnie could take credit for that one.

"Get out of here, Morgan," I demanded and nodded toward the tree line.

Morgan squinted his heavy-rimmed eyelids around baby poop-colored eyes. Bonnie didn't move. Not even a twitch. I loved Bonnie and knew she was better than most made her out to be, but I wouldn't want to be stuck in a dark alley with her unless I was on her team.

"Let's get outta here," Morgan said to his goons. "See you tonight, Cass." He patted Cassius on the back and shot one last glance at Bonnie over his shoulder before disappearing into the woods.

"It's Cassius," he corrected under his breath.

Bonnie lit another cigarette. Cassius dropped his head, his hair falling over his forehead. I didn't breathe, waiting for thirty-two ounces of cola to come through the trees, crashing into the side of my head. Once the rustling was far enough away, and we knew they were gone, my heart started beating again.

I spun around and pointed at Bonnie. "What the hell is *that*?"

"Like it?" She held it up for inspection, the new shiny metal glinting in the light. "Dad picked it up last week in Marysville on a job. Thought I could use it for protection."

"Against who? Street thugs? This is Flintlock, the only criminals in this town are—" *your family*, I wanted to say but stopped myself. She knew it to be true; I didn't need to remind her. "What the hell were you thinking, pulling a knife on Morgan? Do you want the whole town to know about it? Just wait until his mom finds out. You'll be—"

She cut me off.

"Just because your life is perfect doesn't mean mine is something to look down at, Penderhaus." Bonnie huffed and shoved her smokes and knife back into her bag. "You know, for someone with no friends, you sure are quick to judge others." She slung her bag across her body. "Look out for yourself, boy. People in this town aren't what they seem." She slapped him once on the back before leaving the spot in the opposite direction of Morgan and the morons.

Perfect? In less than a week, I'd learned I was dying, met a boy and subsequently destroyed said boy's life, and possibly alienated my best friend. Not to mention the years I'd spent as Lurch, Penderhaus the flick freak, the loser with no friends and no dad. Life was perfect. Yeah, sure.

"Are you okay?" I asked Cassius.

"I want to go home," he said in a tone that scared me.

"Are you mad?"

"Yes, and I want to go home. Now."

With all that had happened over the course of the morning, I wasn't really sure where I stood with my new friend—or my old, for that matter. I wanted to ask him if it was me he was angry with. If he still wanted me out of his life. Judging by his tone, the way he turned his body away from me, the answer to both would be yes. I wasn't ready to hear that. I wanted to pretend just a little bit longer.

"Let's go."

He walked two feet behind me through the trees, around the pond, and back onto Thyme, where he moved to walk in the gutter a foot to the left, and a foot behind me. He'd measured in his own head, of that I was sure. Why, I didn't know. And really, I didn't care. It was a Cassius thing.

There were still a few hours left of school, and rightfully that was where we should've been. I didn't bother to explain that to Cassius. He'd had a shitty morning and mostly on my account. Far be it from me to make matters worse. With his dad at work until five o'clock and Mommy Dearest sacked out watching trashy television, no one would know he was home early anyhow. Ms. Ratzass had likely called my mom, and I would probably be in some form of trouble when I got home, regardless of the time, so it didn't really matter anyway. In the end, Cassius was still not ready to leave the house and I was still dying. I hadn't made anything better for anyone.

Did *anything* really matter?

7

"WHAT IN THE HOLY HELL WERE YOU THINKING?" MOM bellowed. Her slippers scuffed against the floor as she paced back and forth in the living room—soggy shoes drying on the mat in the entryway.

I opened my mouth to talk, but the clock on the mantel chimed five times and forced me to wait it out in order to be heard. "Mom, I was thinking about my friend." Whose father was probably walking through the front door of the spook house as we spoke.

"Oh, your *friend*? Bonnie has been nothing but trouble since sixth grade. After that stunt she pulled last year, I can't believe they let her back a second year." Bonnie was a second-year senior with a rap sheet; Mom had a point, no matter how irrelevant. "Why you're still friends with her, I'll never—"

"Not Bonnie," I huffed. "Cassius."

She stopped and stared at me. "Oh."

"He showed up at school today out of the blue. Pissed." I accentuated the word with my hands. "He was mad that Sheriff Floyd made him go to school. Mad at me." Sadness filled my heart, but I refused to let it take over. "And mad at you. Then he proceeded to fist fight with Morgan in the middle of second period English."

Mom let out one loud burst of laughter. "Cassius Shooster got into a *fight* with Morgan Pennington?"

I nodded, realizing quickly I'd exaggerated, which wouldn't help Cassius at all. "Okay, maybe more of a scuffle. Or a skirmish." I nodded again.

"Who won?"

"Well...." I thought on it. Not being a fist fight aficionado, I made my best assumption. "I guess Cassius." Mom smiled with what seemed like pride, but it fell quickly when the ramifications of his actions set in. "He didn't understand any of it, and eventually Ms. Ratzass chased him, and me, off campus." I wasn't a bad kid, I didn't lie or sneak, but I knew to leave in just enough truth to make it believable without revealing your whole hand. "I had to follow him, Mom. I had to keep him safe." I'd left out a lot of the story, mostly my screwups, but who really needed every detail? "Bonnie just happened to be there. Thankfully she was, because later Morgan showed up at the spot and tried to convince Cassius everything was fine and they were good buddies." Okay, that's enough. "And then she pulled a knife." Too much, abort. Abort! "I knew he was full of it, but Cassius... I don't know." Save yourself! "They convinced him to go to *the well* tonight."

She knew the implications of Cassius at the well and thankfully let Bonnie and her knife go. "The well?" she asked, a hint of worry in her voice.

Mom knew what went down at the well. Everyone who'd gone to high school in Flintlock at any point since the twenties knew the well. It was, and had always been, a place where kids went to be kids. Drink beer, make out, and take part in general shenanigans. The severity of partying had increased over the years; regardless, many new generations had been seeded at the well, including my father. Anyone who is anyone partied at the well. Your girl, Prudence, had never been and didn't plan to.

"Yup. I tried to tell Cassius it was a bad idea, but in the end, he was fuming and just wanted to go home. Refused to speak to me; his face... so angry." I flung my head back, grumbling a frustrated growl toward the ceiling. "It's all my fault, Mom. I just wanted him to have a normal life. And now look." Hello, self-pity. Oh, I see you brought guilt with you this time.

"Honey, there's only so much you can do for people before they have to start helping themselves. Give him time, he'll come around." Her tone didn't match her words, as if she didn't really believe it either.

The notion of time wrenched my gut. Time was the one thing I didn't have on my side. The thing that had motivated my meeting Cassius in the first place was the thing that would—probably—eventually take me away from him. It had been selfish of me to bring a boy out into a world I couldn't promise to be in. I was young and otherwise healthy, the doctor had said. I had a good fighting chance of survival. Fighting was all I had left to do. Fight for Cassius and his place in the world. Fight for my life and a chance to live it out. Fight to be a good person until my last dying breath.

"I don't have time. I never did," I said sullenly and, in full teen fashion, stomped off to my room.

My door slammed harder than I'd intended, and I cringed at the sound. I wasn't actually angry with my mom, and she didn't deserve my tantrum. In all actuality, I hadn't really given myself time to cope with the life I had ahead of me, and there was a good chance the feelings I had welling up inside of me would sooner or later boil over and spew out in a volcanic eruption of grief and regret. Cassius had been a means of distraction. A final good deed. One last shot at doing something spectacular. Never had I imagined this would be the outcome of knocking on the door of the spook house.

Give him time, Mom had said. Time to do what? Time to fester in his anger and grow to hate me? Time for his parents to wind the noose a little tighter? I didn't know him, not really, but I wanted to. Oh, how I wanted to. Odd he was. Strange, even. But it only intrigued me. Cassius Shooster wasn't like anyone else in Flintlock, and for that, he was extraordinary.

I flopped onto my bed and stared at the ceiling. Closing my eyes, I thought of Cassius. His dark, mysterious eyes, intense in their passive way, seemed all-knowing. Like a window into a fiery soul hiding behind a timid boy. So innocent in nature, he was a sitting duck for people to take advantage of him. Even I, in a way, had used him for my own needs. My need to feel alive and daring had brought me to him, and my desire to feel worthy made me stay.

"How do I fix this?" I asked myself.

The silent bubble of my room burst with the rumbling sound of an old engine. I jumped from my bed to look out the window that faced Beaker Street—the one I'd looked out of every day for most of my life, past Mrs. Carroway's white craftsman and the now empty blue gingerbread beyond that, right at the side of the spook house. Headlights reflected off the wet asphalt down the street. A car horn honked, and moments later, heavy car doors slammed shut. The engine revved and the headlights grew brighter. My stomach sank as the car made its way down the street and into view. Brady Miles's primer-spotted American muscle passed my house.

It was almost fully dark out, cloud coverage dimmed what little daylight was left, leaving my street a few shades from pitch-black. The headlights had made it difficult to see into the windshield but once they passed, I could make out five heads through the back window. One stuck up taller than all the rest. Cassius was in that car. If I was ever going to make sure Cassius never got hurt again, I had to protect him from whatever bullshit Morgan and Brady had in mind.

"Damn it," I shouted and slammed my opened hands against the window. "Crap. Crap. Crap"

Frantically, I looked around my room for a plan. What the hell did a plan look like? I didn't find anything, obviously, so I did the only thing I could do. Called for backup.

The phone rang. And rang. "Ugh, come on," I begged the empty line.

"This is Bonnie, you know what to do," her voicemail said.

"Bonnie, look, I'm sorry. I need your help. Morgan has Cassius. Meet me at the well ASAP. Bye."

I took the stairs two at a time and slid on the rug at the bottom. Narrowly keeping my butt from hitting the floor, I caught myself with one hand on the corner of the wall and snatched Mom's car keys off the peg with the other. My arm zinged with pain, but adrenaline helped me ignore it.

"Going to save Cassius. Love you," I called out as the door shut behind me.

I didn't drive often—rarely would be accurate—but I had my license and knew I could pull it off in case of an emergency. I shoved the key into the ignition. The glow plug light clicked on, letting me know I had to wait for the old engine to warm up. After a moment, Mom's ancient diesel Mercedes roared to life and puffed exhaust from the pipe.

In that time, Mom had processed what I'd said, left her spot on the couch, and flew from the front door. "Prudence," she screamed, hardly audible over the sound of the engine.

I waved once and hurriedly backed down the driveway, leaving Mom standing there with her hands over her mouth. I felt bad, really I did, but I didn't have time to wait around for help or explain my antics. Cassius didn't have time. Lord only knew what Morgan was up to, and I couldn't trust Cassius to make decisions that required far more life experience than he possessed.

I screeched around the corner of Marigold and Temperance and headed toward the south edge of town.

The well, an actual stone well that had sat about a mile inside the county line since the turn of the century, had been dried up for years and served no purpose other than a landmark for immorality. I'd only ever been there the one time Bonnie and I ventured out alone one afternoon to check it out. We couldn't see the appeal so never made any attempt to go back. We were fringe people, she and I. We didn't get invited to things, and we didn't care to try. Outcasts to the core, we were perfectly content making our home at the spot, a knock-off version of the well discovered by our outcast ancestors some time in the distant sixties.

Temperance dead-ended at Main, which gave two choices. Right, into town and where the shops and businesses took up residency. Left, out of town to the south where Flintlock met Marysville. I hardly slowed before making the left away from Flintlock and the hypocrisy it held. Supposedly the pillar of community and family, the town was more a cesspool of assholes and gaping chasms between social classes. No different than most small towns, but Flintlock had its own special brand of small-town nepotism.

Main curved sharply to the right about a mile down and became Highway 7. This desolate span of road stretched on for ten miles before it met up with the main highway that connected the dozen or so towns in a hundred-mile stretch.

I was only minutes behind them, but the Benz was a tank and didn't take the potholes well, and Highway 7 was riddled with them. I had to slow down a bit or go flying all over the road Mr. Toad style. At that pace, I'd never catch up to them before they made it to the well. In a weird way, I trusted Brady to not be a complete tool; Morgan had always been the instigator. He was notoriously rowdy and regularly ended up in some testosterone-riddled skirmish. My phone rang in my pocket. Taking my chances, I reached in and fished it out.

"Yeah?" I answered.

"What the hell is going on?" Mom screeched, hardly

audible over the rumble of the engine, squeaking springs, rattling bolts, and sudden patter of rain against the windshield.

My sinking heart leveed my foot off the gas pedal as though I had an internal pulley system. *Shit.* I'd expected Bonnie. "Can't talk right now, driving." I hung up without taking my eyes off the road. It wasn't until my foot regained control over the pedal I realized it had taken her a while to call. What had she been doing during the almost ten-minute gap?

That stretch of road was always dark. There wouldn't be a streetlight until Highway 7 met the blinking yellow signal that guarded the T-crossing at 52E—the mainest main highway until you hit the interstate. The sky above blackened with sunset and cloud coverage. Massive plops of rain hit the windshield. Rain was not my friend, being a rookie driver and emotional and all that. It took me a horrifying nearly-blind-with-tears moment to find the wipers.

"Shit," I exclaimed, squinting through the downpour.

I knew I'd recall the turnoff when I saw it, but seeing it was quickly becoming an issue. The slower I drove, the heavier the rain beat against the glass. Each plop pelting the heavy steel roof was its own gunshot until it sounded like someone was car surfing with a Tommy Gun.

Panic set in with the thought that not only would I not make it in time, but I'd likely kill myself in the process. This was thirteen on the worst-case list. Right above taking literally the phrase *blow your socks off* and an incident with a leaf blower I didn't want to get into.

Tears welled in my eyes for whatever reason—pick one. Whether the pity was for myself or my innocent friend, or the overall situation, it sank deep into my gut, defeat pulling me to the side of the road.

In through the nose. Out through the mouth. I breathed, slow and steady, convincing myself it wasn't that bad. At least it wasn't number one. What was the worst that could happen?

Morgan wasn't a murderer or anything like that—probably. Cassius wouldn't *die* in the time it took me to find him. Social embarrassment was not out of the question—likely, in fact—along with any other stupid prank or humiliating hazing Morgan could think up in that thick skull of his.

"Yes," I hissed and fist pumped when I caught sight of the old oak and an ancient wooden sign that read in aging white letters, "The Well. Nothing to See Here, Officer." A senior prank turned landmark sometime in the youth of my parents' generation.

I turned right onto the dirt road that was more of a mud bog, praying the Benz didn't get stuck. If my memory was correct, the well itself stood about a half mile up the road. The tank bumped along the pothole-pocked path, splashing into every puddle like a little kid in rain boots.

Just about the moment I started to worry I'd made a

wrong turn, my headlights fell over the back of Brady's car. To the left, a mass of shadows. I turned the wheel to aim my lights at the old stack of stones that once served as a water source for the original Flintlock residents.

"No," I gasped, flung open the door, and left the engine running.

My feet slapped into thick muddy puddles as I ran toward the well and the boy who I'd come to save. Dangling backward over the edge of the stone circle from two clenched fists at his collar, a hundred feet above the bottom, Morgan cried out for me.

"Penderhaus, get your freak off me before he kills me." His voice, shrill with fear, was little match for the rain and my car.

"Cassius!" I shouted over the downpour and the sound of my engine. *This* was number one.

I took off into a full sprint toward them, slipped in the mud, and I fell hard on my butt. There, in the mud with me, were Morgan's two goons and Brady Miles. All three seemingly knocked unconscious—or, perhaps, they were taking a nap—lay there motionless and silent. My heart tumbled to my muddy shoes. What had he done?

Morgan struggled against Cassius's grip, but it seemed to be no use. His feet kicked against the outside of the stone circle, more than a yard above the ground, trying for leverage. If he fought too hard, he risked pulling himself from Cassius's grip and falling anyway. The strength I'd seen that morning in class was nothing compared to what

Cassius was demonstrating in that moment. Morgan was a beefy, stocky inside linebacker, weighing in at a hefty 210 pounds, and Cass held him over the well like he was a bag of apples. *Dangerous*, Mr. Shooster's warning played over in my head. Had he really taken out those three all-state jocks by himself? Maybe Edward Cullen wasn't too far off.

My boats slid in the mud, sinking an inch deep, before catching traction. "Cassius," I pleaded, wrapping my hand around his arm. "You're going to kill him." I didn't know that for sure, but one slip and Morgan would have been careening down a hundred-foot well.

"So what? I told you I'm dangerous. I told you the world is not safe with me in it." His typical baritone had dropped into a rumbling growl. But it wasn't just anger, it was despair, and in that, wrapped in a Snuggie making itself at home, was resolve. As if this was all he could ever be, so he might as well be it.

I stood in stunned silence. This wasn't the boy I'd met. The awkward, strange boy who loved movies and hated thunder. This was rage. This wasn't just Morgan, this was his entire life, his parents, the world, me, every wrong thing that had ever happened to him. Plain and simple. Cassius Shooster wasn't dangerous. He was a victim and he was fighting back.

"This isn't you." My voice sounded distant, my pleas hardly making a dent in the decibel level. "You're better than this."

Cassius huffed once through his nose, an angry bull shooting raindrops from the tip of it. The muscles in his jaw flexed, chewing on my words. Seconds felt like minutes waiting for him to respond.

His shoulders, all angles and sharp edges, rose and fell with each huffing breath. Black strips of hair clung to his forehead and cheeks. He didn't let go, but his shoulders rounded.

"Let him go and I'll take you out of here."

He swallowed, sending his Adam's apple bobbing in his throat.

Heavy drops of Pacific Northwest rain pelted the roof of the Benz, a constant hollow *ting* I wished would just stop. I was drenched. Cassius was drenched. All the dirt had turned to mud long ago and the area surrounding the well was quickly becoming a bog. The Swamps of Sadness prepared to forever swallow us whole.

"Please," I begged, pulling in a shaking breath in defiance of tears teetering on the edge.

Cassius's dark eyes slid to the corners to look at my mouth, which I pinched between my teeth. His hands, still clenched around Morgan's collar, began to relax. I nodded. *Yes. Yes. Please just let him go.*

In that moment, the goons began to awake from their slumber. *No. No. No.* One after the other they sat up, shook the stupid from their heads, and finally found Cassius and Morgan in the mess of mud and rain. The smallest of them, and the first to fully regain consciousness, recognized his chances, and scurried from the ground, quickly running down the road away from the calamity. Brady Miles and henchman number two scrambled from the ground, slipping and sliding until finally finding their footing. Brady, the largest of them all, richest, most likely to belong to the Illuminati, and everything sports, made his way toward us. The other flanked to my left. The two would attack Cassius soon enough, and when they did, there would be nothing I could do to stop it. I was no match for two big dudes, no matter how tough I tried to be about life and death and all things in between.

I put my hands up in surrender, as if that would help anything at all. Whispering to Cassius, I said, "We need to go now."

They'd been silent but not enough. Cassius tightened his grip, knowing soon enough someone would come and shove him right into that well if he didn't have a hostage to take down with him.

"No," he said through his teeth. "He deserves to be punished."

"He doesn't deserve to *die*."

Cassius looked at me. Both of his eyes on both of my eyes. His black hair plastered to his face; rain dripped over long lashes. "He said you were a *freak*. He said you should just jump down this well and end your pathetic life. And that I should go with you. He said I was a freak. He said I was a monster locked up in my house because my parents hated me. Hated me because I was a mistake."

Well, what a shithead.

I looked at Morgan, craning my neck to even my head with his. Terrified, vulnerable, two-thirds of his body hanging over the edge of the well, the landmark of his youth and social standing threatening to be his demise. There was a sense of irony no one could pass up, and I wished I had a camera to commemorate the moment.

"Those are pretty shitty things to say, Pennington." Morgan begged me with his eyes to stop Cassius. "Maybe people should think about their words before they spurt from their lips like diarrhea."

Movement from the corner of my eye caught my attention. Brady and his goon were right on top of us and ready to make a move. They knew just as I did that all Cassius had to do was let go and Morgan would fall to his death.

Brady, clearly the more clever of the group, had snuck up behind Cassius. I saw his plan play out, and if my thinking was the same as his thinking, he was going to pull Cassius backward, effectively removing his boyfriend— in the homophobic sense—from imminent danger. The other, whose name I didn't know or care to know, had fetched a crowbar from Brady's car and held it above his head.

My heart thudded painfully in my chest. I'd wanted to feel alive, so I rang a forbidden doorbell, symbolically checking that off my before-I-die list. Standing in the rain in the middle of a street brawl certainly deserved a bucket list checkmark of its own.

Seconds felt like minutes. The rain, the headlights, my swimming head, all brought the scene to life in flashes, in strobes of color and streaks of water. There was no time to move. Hardly time to think. I was forming a plan of attack when a roaring engine emerged from nowhere, blinding us with one bright headlight.

Mud slung over my arms and face. Brady and the other guy jumped away from the mudslinging tires and plopped back to their butts. I hoped the swamp swallowed them whole.

I blinked away dirt and water. The rain pouring on us outlined a shape in the beam of my headlights. A motorcycle sat, engine idling, beside Brady's car. The rider's curvy legs were topped with heavy black boots. She pulled her helmet from her head, curly blonde hair spilled out, instantly falling prey to the downpour.

"Hey, losers," Bonnie said. "What's the hullabaloo?"

I blinked at her again and again. Her timing had been incredible. Miraculous even. And though her sudden appearance had sent Brady and the other guy stumbling to the ground, Cassius was mostly unfazed. Morgan didn't move, of course, that would have been stupid, but his whimpers had grown loud enough to hear over the engines and rain.

"Wow, Pennington, got yourself into some shit, didn't you?" she joked, and I didn't know if she was aware of the danger and just didn't care. If I'm honest, I almost didn't.

In fact, the only person I cared about in that situation was Cassius.

"Bon, wow, you've got some timing."

Brady stood, shook mud from his hair like a dog, and stalked toward us.

"Clearly there's a situation here." My tone was light, but I was literally dying inside. I coped with strenuous situations with sarcasm and lighthearted humor. Sue me.

"Brady, back off, I'll handle it." I held up a hand, but Brady had his sites locked on Cassius. "You're just making it worse, please." I'd never thought I'd say please to Brady Miles for anything. Ever. Yet there I was.

"Miles, dude, just chill out," Bonnie urged, plopping her helmet onto the handlebars as she shoved the kickstand into the soft mud.

Brady didn't acknowledge Bonnie. His broad shoulders seemed bigger, bulkier, stronger, better meant for hunting saber tooth tigers than hurling footballs.

"Cass," I hissed, "You have to let him go. Brady is coming, and he's really buff. I can't stop him. You're going to get hurt. Or *dead*."

Lights and sirens broke through the rain and tension.

My eyes went wide. "Or arrested."

"Oh, that's my cue." Bonnie sat back down on her bike as though she planned to cut out before the cops made it up the muddy drive.

The first sheriff's car skidded to a stop beside mine, blocking Bonnie in before she could even think about putting her helmet back on. Before I could blink, Sheriff Floyd flopped out. Gun in hand, aimed directly at Cassius, he called out over the rain, "Let him go, son. I don't want to shoot you."

Shoot?

"Elroy, you can't be serious?" my mom scolded him from the passenger seat of his car.

"Get back in the car, Frankie." His focus didn't move from Cassius. "Come on now, son. We all know he didn't do anything." *How in the hell could you know that?* "If you don't let him go, I'll have to arrest you. You want to go to jail?"

"Cass, he's serious," I whispered. "Shut up, Floyd," I shouted over the grumbling engines. He'd shoot Cassius. I knew that in my gut. If given a choice between the spook house freak and Flintlock's golden child, Cassius would lose every time, regardless of Morgan's inherent douchebaggery.

Cassius didn't seem to be listening to anything the sheriff said. "Cass, it's time to let him go," I said softly and laid a hand on his solid arm. The tensed muscle flexed under his hoodie, and I finally felt a portion of what was going through him. Like a dog protecting his beloved owner, Cassius had acted on instinct, and now I stared into the face of pure adrenaline. I let out a breath and moved my hand to his face. Running my thumb over his jaw, I pulled his face to look at mine. "Let's go home," I prompted and the tension in his jaw loosened.

"Something really bad is going to happen if you don't walk away." I stunted each word with a full stop at the end.

One finger at a time, Cassius unclasped his hands. He paid no mind to the distance Morgan's little legs were from the ground. When he suddenly let him go, Morgan teetered dangerously on the edge of the stone circle—everyone watching gasped, waiting for him to fall—before righting himself and falling to his knees in the mud. Cassius stood over the top of Morgan, glaring down at him, and flipped his hood over his head.

Boots splashed through the mud and flapped it all over me. Brown speckles dotted my arms, lost in a sea of freckles, and quickly washed away with rain. An officer pulled Morgan from the ground and out of view. Another deputy charged Cassius, missing me by an inch, taking him to the ground with a sloppy thud. A sharp gasp burst from my chest when they hit. Three more officers crowded around, each holding a limb as though he were a wild beast and they were awaiting the tranquilizer.

My hands clamped over my mouth, I watched in horror as four Flintlock deputies manhandled Cassius into a pair of cuffs. He fought against the bodies that piled on top of him, and with good reason. Unarmed and surrendering, he had no reason to be assaulted. A freak must be handled accordingly, and small-town justice knew exactly how to handle that.

"Cassius," I screamed, "stop fighting. Just let them

take you in. We'll be right behind you. Don't be scared."
The look on his face proved my words meant nothing.
"Cass, you're making it worse. They're going to hurt you
if you don't just hold still and let them put you in the car."
It was useless. He was lost in his own head and nothing
short of time and patience was going to get him out.

Two bulky officers hefted Cassius to his feet and
dragged him toward the police car. I couldn't do anything
but watch. The group sloshed in the mud; the rain had
let up to a drizzle. Bonnie leaned on her bike, watching
vigilantly over the boy she didn't quite understand.
More than anything else in Flintlock, Bonnie hated cops.
Especially Elroy Floyd. She'd had her fair share of issues
with Flintlock's finest and she knew exactly how thin that
blue line was. So she watched, likely taking note of use
of force and the like. The one thing you could almost set
a clock by was the ability for underdogs to stick together.

"Elroy," Mom shouted as she slammed the passenger
door. She tromped around the car, toward her old flame.
"You let that boy go. You hear me?"

"Now, you listen here, woman." My mom fumed, but
he ignored her. "That boy is a danger. Always has been."
My eyes shot to the sheriff when I heard it. How had a
boy he'd only just met *always* been dangerous? Had the
Shoosters gotten to the sheriff? Did he know more than he
was willing to let on?

Sheriff Floyd tucked his gun back into its holster and
walked away from the car, and Mom, to meet Cassius as

the officers shoved him into the other car. Elroy leaned down into the door, thick arm resting on the roof, to talk to Cass, whose face I couldn't see. At that distance, with all those engines humming, it was impossible to hear what he said, but it was probably something unnecessary and cruel.

"Pru." Mom's voice pulled me away from Cassius and the sheriff. "Are you okay?"

I nodded. "Yeah. Yeah, I'm fine. Just soaked and worried." Her blue eyes shifted to Elroy and Cassius inside the cruiser.

"He'll be okay," she said about Cassius with the same half-hearted tone she'd had earlier.

"This is all my fault." A flood of emotions bubbled up my throat. "All of it."

"We'll fix it. Okay?" Her words didn't match the tone in which she said them. "We'll fix it together." I doubted that completely.

Bonnie watched an officer to my left talking with Morgan and Brady. The officer patted Morgan on the shoulder, and he dramatically rubbed his neck acting as though he'd been hanging over the well by his throat and not his collar.

What a shithead.

Brady shook rain from his hair like a dog, with a charming grin he used on sophomore girls. The officer laughed. They chummed it up like nothing had happened, like it was all a damn joke. They were acting like Morgan was an innocent bystander and Cassius was some fiend out for blood. Brady, Morgan, the whole of Flintlock sheriff's department were behaving as though Cassius was nothing more than a beast on a rampage and poor Morgan just got caught in the fray.

I saw red. And it wasn't my hair.

My nostrils flared, and I grunted deep in my chest, a bull preparing to burst from the chute. Someone slammed the car door shut behind me like a shot from a starting gun, and it sent me sprinting toward Morgan the cowardly douchebag. I was quick and unexpected; they didn't even see me coming.

I pounced on Morgan, easily taking him to the ground in the slick mud. I'd honestly been lucky I hadn't skidded out on takeoff. Rain poured down on us as I threw awkward, unpracticed punches into his face. I'd never hit anyone before and didn't know what I was doing, but in my flailing my knuckles connected with something that cracked loudly over the rain. Blood seeped from his nose, intermingling with the rain and running down the sides of his face in a muted shade of pink. I'd gotten in more than a dozen unhindered swings before hands wrapped around my spindly arms and pulled me away.

I winced, gagging with pain from the officer's hand gripping my arm. I fought against his hold, but it only made things worse. The officer wrapped one arm around my waist when I refused to stop wriggling, dragging me away from the scene.

"Come on, girl. Give it up," a different officer said condescendingly, acting as though I had been no threat. Ask Morgan's nose.

I kicked my long legs frantically through empty air. "That son of a bitch is a liar," I screamed. "He coaxed Cassius here and told him to kill himself. Told him I should kill myself and he should follow me down that well. *He's* the monster!" I jabbed a finger toward Morgan.

I fought harder than Cassius had against the police, yet no one took me to the ground and cuffed me. I wasn't the freak from the spook house on Marigold. I was Prudence Penderhaus, a nobody. A nonthreat. Instead of locking me up in the back of a cop car, I was being carted away like a piece of luggage.

"Now, Prudence, calm down," Sheriff Floyd said through his mustache, tugging his service belt, which was permanently stuck under his paunchy belly. "We'll get to the bottom of this." He feigned reassurance.

The officer dropped me down in front of the sheriff's car. I stood up straight, fixed my shirt with an irritated tug, and shot the officer a death glare. "Like hell you will," I said to Sheriff Floyd. "I want Morgan arrested."

The sheriff scoffed. "For what?"

"For threatening me and Cassius."

"Honey, that's not how it works. Now—"

"Then arrest me too." I stepped closer to him, jutting my chin in his direction. "It's only fair. I attacked Morgan. That's assault. Arrest me."

"Prudence, you're just riled up. The jail is no place for—"

Nearly knocking the mustache right from under his nose, my slap stung Sheriff Floyd's ego even more than his face. "Arrest me," I demanded.

He couldn't argue with that. I'd assaulted a police officer. *The sheriff.* If he didn't arrest me, the Shoosters would have a case in court over police bias. Elroy Floyd glared at me, and then his eyes shifted over all of the other officers watching him, waiting for him to make a move.

The shock on Sheriff Floyd's face was nothing compared to the look on my mother's. An odd mix of astonishment and pride washed over her. It'd taken nearly all of my childhood, but I was finally living up to my redhead stereotype. Someone would soon be calling me a firecracker.

I'd taken five or six heaving breaths staring at the sheriff before an officer had me in cuffs and was shoving me into the back of a police car. I smiled the whole way.

Cassius sat eerily still in the car next to mine and watched me through the rain-streaked windows, expressionless. I wished I could talk to him. I leaned my forehead against it, and my clammy skin squeaked against the glass. Cassius's black eyes stayed locked on mine. My breath fogged the glass, then sucked it back in again, hiding him for a moment, then bringing him back again. Always the same still, stoic, odd boy.

The sympathetic female officer I'd met out in front of

Cassius's house and her partner got into the cruiser, and a moment later, Cassius was moving out of view. I watched him until I couldn't possibly see him anymore.

My gut sank with fear for Cassius. Most of the deputies had once been the Bradys and Morgans of Flintlock High. Good ol' boys for life; Cassius didn't stand a chance on his own. His only saving grace in my mind was the female officer in his car. I knew my mom would be right behind us in the Benz, and surely someone would call Cassius's parents. Who, let's face it, were unpredictable in their punishment tactics. The likelihood of his coming out of the evening unscathed was dwindling with each new epiphany. He wasn't safe at home, he wasn't safe at school, not even with the police. The only person he had on his side was about to stick one foot in the grave trying to keep from it. How was that poor kid supposed to manage his new life? It was obvious Cassius needed more help adjusting than I'd been prepared for. Without support, he'd fail. Epically.

Two officers got into the front seat, slammed the doors, didn't buckle, and backed into a two-point turnaround. The seat was hard, plastic, cupped into a butt shape. My boney cheeks slammed against the unforgiving plastic with each sloppy pothole. The officer in the passenger seat looked slyly over his shoulder, a half smirk pulled his eye into a dubious squint.

Thanks. Jerk. If that was the treatment I was getting, what could be happening to the freak in the car ahead of us? My heart skipped twice in a row before catching up in an all-out sprint. I was the one who'd slapped their head cheese, maybe I'd get it worse. Maybe it was payback for slapping the shit out of their precious sheriff. Maybe.

A bright light filled the cab of the car. I turned as best I could to look out the back window at the single headlight pulling up behind us. Bonnie swerved to the left and passed us. She roared off ahead, catching up to the taillights in the distance. There she stayed all the way back to town.

I smiled inside. No matter what happened, Cassius would have me as long as I was on this earth, and I'd have Bonnie. We'd protect each other, as best we could, until we couldn't anymore.

Eventually I'd have to come clean and tell them my fate. Eventually, I'd need them too. That could wait just a little while longer. We had an assault rap to beat, a town to change, and an odd boy to acclimate.

8

THE ANCIENT CELL DOOR CREAKED AND THEN CLANGED
shut, locking me in. I'd stumbled once when the officer
shoved me in. He'd uncuffed me first, which was lucky for
us both because with my flailing arms ad counterbalance,
I'd have surely tumbled right on my face. I turned to face
him, my lip snarled, and kicked the rusting metal. Loose
on its hinges, the old door rattled back at me.

The two-cell room was one long cage split into two
with a walkway around the front and one side. Think
Mayberry, without Sheriff Andy and Deputy Fife. And
the drunk guy sleeping it off in his own personal cell.
Mayberry forty years later. Mayberry, the aftermath. That
was the cell I was trapped in.

A circus animal in a cage; the sensation of being locked
up ate at my insides. Freedom is almost always taken for

granted, and I was no exception.

"Calm down now, girlie," the deputy said over his shoulder as he walked the length of the cells. "Your mom will be here to spring you soon enough."

He pushed through the double door just as I shouted, "You bet your ass she will." The threat was meaningless, a waste of my own breath, but speaking it out loud helped. Just a little.

Slamming my open hand against the metal bars one last time, I used the momentum to shove myself backward and onto the cot against the far wall—just a few feet behind me. My scrawny butt landed, and metal clanged again, this time from the steel shelf that housed a thin mattress. It hurt, and even though I was alone, I refused to let it show on my face.

"Hey," a woman called from the double doors on the other side of the second cell. "You're never going to get anywhere with that lunkhead." It was the female officer, her hair still up in that painful-looking bun. She made her way around the corner and toward my cell. "Too stupid to tie his own shoes." Her brows dropped, heavy over brown eyes.

"That doesn't surprise me." I sat forward, hands braced against the edge of the shelf bed, eager to ask, "Where's Cassius?" He should have been there already. And with only one other cell in the tiny old sheriff's station, there wasn't any other place he should have been.

Her eyes darted to the double doors, then back to me.

"Watch yourself." I stood and moved toward the front of the cell. She leaned closer to the bars and dropped her voice. "Nothing here is right."

That's the understatement of the century. "What do you mean?" She moved away from my cell as though we hadn't just been talking. "What's not right?" The officer's tight bun slid over her stiff collar, back and forth, as she looked at me, then the door again. She watched the door and moved back down the way she came. "Hey, wait, what am I missing?"

Commotion caught my attention. Those scuffed doors flung open. Two deputies led the pack of four men and one odd boy. Mostly hidden by the beefy officers, I had to contort my body to see him. His head hung limply as the men in uniform practically carried him through the double doors that led in from the lobby of the police station. Black hair fell over his forehead, hiding his eyes from me.

I wrenched my neck to keep my eyes on him. His legs, two wobbly noodles, could hardly support his own weight. What had those bastards done to him?

The cell door next to mine flung open, slamming into the bars of my cell, rattling rusting metal. The officers hoisted Cassius's cumbersome body through the door and onto the cot. He lay lifeless, hardly able to support his own head.

Blood pumped through my veins at warp speed. My heart worked overtime under the heavy thumb of adrenaline.

"What'd you do, you sons of bitches? Huh?" I clutched white-knuckle fists around the bars; I rattled and shook and practically scaled the things screaming at the brutes. "Cass," I called out to him. "Cassius," I whimpered, face pressed against the bars.

"He's taking a little nap," said a portly officer with a head like a pack of hot dogs. They all laughed and slammed his cell door, leaving him lying there limp.

The men strutted out the double doors, apathetic to the battered boy in their lockup. The female officer, who according to her badge was named Phillips, eyed us cautiously until the men left the room, then followed them out. There was that thin blue line I was talking about.

The moment we were alone, I scurried to the back of the cell, sliding to my knees in front of the bars that separated us. I sat still, stone silent, watching his chest, waiting to see movement. My racing heart was on lap 267 when Cassius finally pulled in a ragged breath.

"Oh, thank the maker."

He needed medical help, that I was sure. But more than that, I couldn't tell from my view of the side of his head. In desperation, I checked to see if I could fit between the bars. Everything but the head. I wanted to scream, and cuss, and shout, and tear that rotten old place from its hinges. Who would come? Who would help us back there? I had to get us both out of that place. At any cost. Cassius Shooter had single-handedly kick-started my protective instinct into overdrive.

My thin arm slid easily between the bars and into the cell next to mine. I ran my hand over Cassius's dark, wet hair. He breathed heavily but was otherwise out cold.

"Cass." My voice was weak, pathetic. "Wake up." I ran my hand harder over his head to wake him up. "Come on, I need you to wake up. Please." Frustrated tears burned the edges of my eyes, and I wiped them away before they became a thing. "Just sit up and look at me." I shook his head and a tiny sound came from his throat. "Cassius, you have to wake up."

His head moved, and he groaned. I let my breath go and closed my eyes, pressing my forehead against the bars. A moment later, he lifted himself up on his elbow. His breaths were haggard, tired, done with it all. Cassius finally sat up, lanky limbs flopping haphazardly off the edge of the bed shelf. Two breaths. Head hanging. Hair in a dripping veil over his face. He shook his head, sending drops of rain from his hair and onto my face. With his eyes closed, he leaned his head back against the cinderblock wall. Black wavy locks fell from his face, revealing his already black eye and a freshly busted nose. My sharp gasp caught his attention and his dark eyes met mine. Two breaths. Three. My speeding heart kept its pace waiting for Cassius to open his mouth and say something. Anything.

Cassius pulled in one deep breath. "The first night's the toughest, no doubt about it," he quoted Red. A classic quote I could recite back and forth, but he brought to it a defeatist tone only outdone by the great Morgan Freeman.

"Nothing left but all the time in the world to think about it." He skipped a bunch from the iconic scene, but it all made sense to me either way.

"I doubt we'll have to tunnel out. But that was an impressive Morgan Freeman." I kneeled on the concrete floor with my forehead pressed against the bars, I'd likely have a bar-shaped indent on my head. "What'd they do to your face?" My voice sounded far away.

"Pfft." He pushed air loudly through his pursed lips with a half scoff, half snort. "It doesn't matter." He swiped blood and dirt from his face, smearing it into a mustache under his nose.

"It matters to me," I said, keeping serious despite his comical dirtstache.

Silence filled the space between us. He was good at that, taking up space with his stoicism. It hung thick in the air, thick enough to cuddle up in. If it weren't for my natural propensity to solve things, we could have sat comfortably in that silence forever.

"I slapped the sheriff," I said quietly, breaking the silence. Sounding like a reggae song, I fought the urge to finish the lyric. "Got thrown in the clink." He still didn't say a word. "Hey, cellie," I called to him in an old-timey gangster impersonation that was awful and should have never happened.

"This is not funny," he spat through gritted teeth. "This is outlandish. Absolutely outlandish."

"I can't disagree with you there." It was outlandish.

And preposterous. And whatever other thing Cassius would deem it. "I'm joking, but I'm not. It's funny because if it's not, then it's devastating, and that I just can't deal with." He breathed; his eyes focused on his dirty hands. "What the hell happened with Morgan?" His jaw flexed. "Did he threaten you? Did he attack you?" He swallowed. "He didn't *only* tell you to off yourself. There was something else... something more than that, right?" *Dangerous*. He couldn't be. There had to have been some other antecedent. Had to have been.

Cassius didn't move. Cogs worked overtime in his head, unknown thoughts played out in his expression, but that was where it ended. Shallow breaths hardly detectable under his hoodie. His lids lowered over those dark eyes of his until they were little slits. Three, maybe four, more breaths and he finally said, "I'm dangerous, remember? You should have never let me out."

"Bullshit." He turned quickly to look at me. "I'm sorry, but I don't buy it." I sat back on my heels. "Not for one second." He scoffed. "Cass... ius, you are so much more than the weird kid in the spook house. You're..." What was he? Odd. Mysterious. Quiet. "Emotional. Which is a good thing. Most guys your age are definitely not." He sighed, laying his head against the wall. More than anything, I think Cassius Shooster just wanted to be like most guys his age. He didn't know yet how overrated conformity really was. "You're sweet. And kind. And clever. And you get me, which is enigmatic in and of itself. You are anything but dangerous."

"Ha." He laughed once. "You're the only person who believes that."

"Believe me or not, I don't care. That's the truth."

Black hair clung to the mauve cinderblock wall when Cassius turned his head to look at me without lifting it. His black eye had turned a healthy shade of dark purple, blood and mud dried under his nose. It wasn't often Cassius looked me straight in the eye, rare in fact, but when he did, the universe opened up and swallowed me whole.

The double doors swung open, banging against the wall and jarring me back to Earth. Sheriff Floyd, followed by my mom and the porky deputy, barreled through. If I judged by my mother's expression, we were about to be hauled off in front of a firing squad. Elroy Floyd, on the other hand, grinned under his mustache. He wasn't happy, he was smug.

"Let my daughter out of that cage right now, Elroy." Mom stamped her foot and pointed to my cell. "You better open that one too. He's coming with me." My brows rose in shock.

"Now, I told you I couldn't promise that. I'll need to contact his parents."

"You haven't bothered to call his parents yet?" I hissed. "This boy has a medical condition and needs tending to immediately."

The sheriff scoffed. "Medical condition."

"What medical condition?" Mom asked.

"Broken nose." *Maybe*, but I didn't add that part. "Probably internal injuries too, from your piece-of-shit hooligan deputies. Where the hell do you get off?"

Mom shot me a look that said *shut the hell up, stupid.* "Elroy, let them go or I'll be calling a lawyer and filing a suit against the city."

"Don't go making threats you won't come through on, Francine."

Mom stepped closer to the sheriff. She puffed her chest out and tilted her head to look up at his barely five-foot-ten frame. She glared into his eyes with a look that sent chills down my spine. "Dare me."

"All right, all right"—he waved his hands in surrender—"I'll let him out of the cell, but I can't send him home with you. There are charges here, and his parents may need to post bail."

"You're *charging* him?" The sheriff nodded once. "Then charge me too. You have to. You either charge us both or you let us go." I stood strong, just like my mother.

"He attacked four boys, put three of them down and held the other over a hundred-foot well. I can't just let that slide, and you know it." He wriggled his mustache.

"Those buffoons put themselves down slipping in the mud trying to tackle me," Cassius grumbled almost inaudibly, flipping his drenched hood over his head. *Snap, snap*.

"I knew it!" I exclaimed, jutting a Eureka finger

in the air. There had been no way he had done that by himself. "Self-defense, Floyd. Self-de-friggin'-fense." I smiled smugly at the sheriff, who, in true fashion, ignored me.

"Ladies, we have to wait for his parents. Now, I'll hold off on charges until we can get Morgan in here tomorrow with a statement. Either way, we have a few questions for the boy before he can go home."

"His name is Cassius, not *the boy*, and he needs medical treatment before he can answer any questions."

"I didn't know you passed the bar exam, Penderhaus," the fat deputy mouthed off. I recognized his face finally. He'd gained a solid fifty pounds, but he had most certainly been a varsity something or other my freshman year.

"I didn't know you made it through the academy, random guy whose name I don't know, which kind of makes me feel superior to you in a weird way," I said, and everyone looked at me, the oddest girl they'd seen in real life. "Cut the shit, Elroy," I said, and Mom's eyes went wide. I wanted to apologize to her for cussing but didn't want to lower my hand in front of the sheriff. "You can talk to him tomorrow just like Morgan. Besides, do you really think the Shoosters are going to let him sit here for hours answering questions like that?" From what I knew, they were a secretive bunch and the likelihood of that was slim.

"Did someone call the parents?" Sheriff Floyd asked over his shoulder. The fat cop hesitated to respond, so the sheriff shot him a look, and he took off into the lobby.

Sheriff Floyd guided Mom to a desk in the far corner where she leaned her butt, exhausted. Elroy clamped a hand on her shoulder, massaging, touching too much and too long. I glowered at him. He turned his back to me, blocking Mom completely.

Chubs poked his head back in the door a moment later. "Sir, Heego called when they got here." He turned his potato of a head and sneered at me. "Don't worry, Penderhaus, your boyfriend's parents will be here soon to rescue him." He laughed.

"Can it, Porkchop," I said in an insult feat of immeasurable proportions. Porkchop's grin fell at my insult and he glowered at me.

"We'll wait on the parents." The sheriff nodded and ruffled his thick mustache under his nose.

"Then I'll wait too," I said, folding my arms over my body.

"Pru, let's just go home," Mom said, shooting the sheriff a look. "We can check on Cass tomorrow."

"Mom," I whined.

Sheriff Floyd opened my cell and Mom stepped in to retrieve her defiant daughter. "Prudence, he'll be fine. Let's just go," she urged.

How could she just leave him there? "No." I pulled my arm from her grip. "I'm staying."

"You'd do well to listen to your mother, girl," Sheriff Floyd said.

"You'd do best to call off your goons before I call an authority higher than you and let them know all about how a poor, disabled boy was brutally beaten by your officers. How 'bout that?" I felt a new sense of purpose as I stood there, taller than the sheriff by more than an inch, looking down on him. Cassius needed protecting from more than just his parents. He needed a safety seat from the entirety of Flintlock.

"Now you listen here, girl—"

"And stop calling me girl, you misogynistic Neanderthal." The sheriff looked at me as though he wasn't quite sure he'd understood what I'd just said. I smiled smugly inside but didn't let it hit my face. "I'm staying and there's not a damn thing you can do about it." I folded my arms over my chest one last time in a show of defiance and looked down my nose at the sheriff, who shook his head and chuckled gruffly.

"Have it your way, girly."

A few moments later, I fumed outside the police station having been carefully escorted out by my arms and legs by Porkchop and another officer. Pacing like a beast in a cage, I glared through the big window out front at the double doors that hid the only reason I was still standing there. They could kick me out of the building, maybe, but they couldn't kick me off a public sidewalk. I'd stand there until my feet rotted off my body.

Mom came through the double doors not too long later, angry and all fired up. Before Cassius Shooster,

Francine Penderhaus would have never been caught dead boiled over with anger in front of a police station. Ever. Then again, until I met Cassius, I wouldn't have either. Apparently, there was just something about him that made us want to fight tooth and nail for his cause. For me, I knew, in addition to the growing affinity I had for the boy, it had something to do with my impending death, but for Mom, I could only assume it was the need to protect another child the way she couldn't protect me.

Her eyes met mine as she made her way across the lobby toward the front door. I felt the daggers shoot from her eyes and whizz past my head.

"You've really done it now," she said, the second the front door opened.

"*I've* done it? All I've done is try to protect an innocent. He doesn't get it, any of it. He knows how to talk and read and all that, but he's never had to people before."

"People?"

"Be a person. Live in the world. In his words, be a human being. He doesn't get the nuances, Mom. He doesn't get the rules because they're not posted. He doesn't even get me most of the time." I poked myself in the chest with the tips of all my fingers. "We're lucky he lasted this long. With Morgan and all those assholes— sorry, but they are—egging him on all day it's no wonder he flew off the handle like that. Morgan deserved every second of what he got, and in the end, I only wish I'd been there longer to watch him squirm." The look on her face mimicked the surprise I felt in my own core at how callous I sounded. "What Cassius did was for me, too, Mom. I can't just let him sit there all alone. Did you see his face?"

She nodded. "I did. One of those looked a bit older than the rest."

"Yeah, I don't think his parents were too happy about his visit last night. Don't you see? Those bastards are the ones to blame here. Not allowing their child to understand the world was the worst thing they could have done. Calling him dangerous." I shook my head. "Ha! There's not one dangerous hair on his head. Cassius Shooster is a pure soul in need of guidance, that's it." I didn't know this for certain, of course, but I truly felt in my gut Cassius Shooster was not dangerous. *"Dangerous."* I rolled my eyes, shook my head, and planted my hands on my hips. "Some people."

"Pru." Mom's voice was soft, sympathetic, cushioning the blow of what she was about to say next. "I think there's more than we know here."

"I was thinking the same thing. It's like there's a broader conspiracy. And I'm almost positive Sheriff Floyd is hiding something."

"I want you to give yourself some space from Cassius. Okay?" *What?* "Just for the night until we can figure this all out."

I blinked over and over again, not completely understanding what my mother, the protector, had just said.

"What? Are you serious?" I shook my head hard and fast. "No. No. Nuh-uh. Not gonna happen. You and I were his only allies, and now you're going to abandon him too?" I couldn't stop my head from shaking. "I can't believe this. I can't believe you. Don't you trust me to make the right choices for me?"

"Yes, but—"

"Yes, but nothing. I've never been in trouble for anything, ever, and now months before I become an adult, you want to pull in my reins? Because I'm finally passionate about something?"

"No, because the reason you're passionate about this might not be so obvious to you. Pru, honey, you've just had a huge shock, and I feel like you're not thinking with your head. I know it's scary, but you're really going to be fine."

"What a lie! You know that's not true." She'd heard what the doctor said just like I did, and *going to be fine* wasn't in there anywhere. "And so what, I'm dying, Mom, *dying*, and if this is how I want to live my last year, then so be it. Cassius is—"

"Have you told him?" she asked intuitively.

I swallowed hard. I hadn't, and I still wasn't sure how to. "Not yet. Everything's been moving so fast, I really haven't been sure how to slip it in there."

"Have you thought about what that might do to him? Have you considered how selfish you're being?"

Selfish? Me? "Everything I've done has been for him."

Except ringing his rapping on his door in the morning, that was for me. And if I were to be honest with myself, sure, the dying factor had played a role in motivating my more daring adventures, but really, if it weren't for Cassius, I wouldn't have the need for any of it. I'd likely have been locked away in my room like always watching movies and doing a whole lot of nothing until I finally croaked.

"What do you think is going to happen when he gets attached to you and suddenly you're gone?"

She said those words with an unexpected sense of detachment from me, talking about me being gone as though I'd left for the store. "I can only hope I've helped him enough that his life is better for it."

"Is this really better for anyone?" She held her hand in the direction of the police station.

My head still shaking, I looked away from her, hiding tears and forcing them back down. I steadied my breathing until they went away and I could speak without bawling. "Mom—"

"There she is, the skank who took my son," a surly voice slurred.

"Excuse me?" Mom asked, snarling at the woman stumbling toward us.

"You heard me," the woman hissed.

"That's enough," Mr. Shooster said, taking the woman by the arm. Having only ever seen the top of her scraggly brown hair, I could only assume the drunk woman being escorted by Cassius's dad was Mother Shooster.

"Oh, look who it is. Mommy Dearest."

"Prudence," Mom scolded.

I ignored her and stepped in the path of Ma and Pa Shooster. "Did you know you let your son leave the house with someone who was intentionally trying to hurt him? Really observant parents you are."

"You're the one who wanted him out." Mrs. Shooster flipped her hand sloppily through the air. "You let him loose and look what happened. Did he kill someone?" She looked up at Mr. Shooster, snarling angrily, as though she were talking about a mean ole mangy dog on his last strike before the pound.

"He protected himself. He protected me."

"Oh, pfft"—she blew air through her lips—"protected *you*? He doesn't even know what that means. The little shit doesn't know what anything means."

My stomach churned, sickened by the sound of her voice and those words. "You're an awful, evil person. You don't deserve a son like Cassius."

She snorted, leaning closer to me. "You're right, I don't. I want the real one."

"Stop it." Mr. Shooster tugged her by the arm toward the police station.

"You sure you want to take her drunk ass into a police station? I mean, she's obviously soused. Maybe they'll lock her up in the clink where she belongs." Aside from her vicious feelings toward her son, the scene was comical. A drunk woman willingly walking into a police station, passing judgment on everyone around her. "I'll be watching everything you do, Mr. and Mrs. Shooster," I added contemptuously before the door closed behind them.

Looking through the window, I waited for Cassius to emerge from behind the double doors. I swore to myself that if I saw one more mark on his body, the sheriff would have one pissed-off redhead on his ass until one of us died.

Mr. Shooster seemed to do all the talking with Doris, the boxed redhead behind the front desk. After a few minutes of waiting, my boy shoved through the double doors. His face was hard, angry, all angles and shadows. Under it all, a layer of sorrow. Hood covering his head, he snapped almost uncontrollably near his ear, hand shoved inside his hood so as to not muffle the sound he needed. I wanted to scoop him up and take him home with me where everything would be okay. For a while, anyway.

Mr. Shooster didn't say a word to his son, only pulled him along by his sweater sleeve like he'd done before. Mrs. Shooster snarled and, with red-streaked eyes, glared a hole through Cassius. Her mouth moved, but I couldn't hear the words through the glass. The sheriff stood behind Cassius, smiling and nodding, agreeing with whatever she said. She jutted out a finger and poked it into her son's chest over and over again while she talked.

"Don't touch him," I whispered.

"Let's go, Pru," Mom said, pulling on my good arm.

"No." I didn't bother looking at her. She could leave if

she wanted to; I wasn't going anywhere as long as I could still see him.

The sheriff had Mr. Shooster sign something and sent them out the door with a pat on the back. Catching sight of me, Sheriff Floyd shook his head and pointed an authoritative finger in my direction, as if telling me to stay out of it. I grinned, snarling a bit on the edges, shook my head, and gave him a finger of my own.

"Not on your life, bud."

The door opened and the three spilled out into the wet night. Mrs. Shooster hissed something at Cassius that I couldn't make out, and he dropped his head to his chest, hiding from her in his hood.

"Cass," I called to him, and his head shot up to find me. "Are you okay?"

"Prudence—" He started, his dark eyes begging for help, but his atrocious mother cut him off.

"Leave him alone. He's done with you and all of this," she hissed.

Mr. Shooster stepped closer to me. "I warned you about him. He's not fit for this world. It's just not safe." He turned and started to walk away.

"Then put him somewhere," I shouted without thinking. "If he's so dangerous, why isn't he in a hospital where he can get help?" No one turned or acknowledged me in any way.

"Back to the hole," Mother Shooster threatened, shoving Cassius toward their car.

They shuffled to their tan Volvo, dragging Cassius by both arms. As I stood there, watching my odd boy be hauled away to his fate, cool drops of rain fell on my shoulders. I sniffed back tears as the car backed out from its spot and pulled away. Cassius turned over the back seat to look at me. I waved one big sweeping wing above my head and put everything I wanted to say into it. He needed to know I wasn't giving up. As long as I was alive, he wouldn't be alone.

"Prudence, it's time to go home." Rain fell in plops and flattened Mom's blonde hair to her head. "We can't do anymore. They're his parents, Pru. They know him better than you do."

The taillights of the Volvo disappeared down Main Street. Slowly, eyes first, I turned to look Mom dead in the face. "The hole?" I said, looking down at her.

Mom shook her head, turned, and walked toward to the car without another word. What had happened to the fiery woman who'd stormed into the foyer of the spook house? Had Sheriff Floyd gotten to her too?

Mrs. Shooster's words rumbled in my gut. The hole. I'd been in that house. There was certainly no coffin in the living room, but was there a dungeon? An oubliette? A bottomless pit of punishment? Cassius Shooster had been ignored, allowed an existence I was coming to understand had been less than satisfying, and I was expected to just walk away and let him be? Death at my door or not, Prudence Penderhaus was just not that girl. It may have taken a handshake from the grim reaper to realize, but I was most certainly not the girl who allowed things left undone.

9

MOM HADN'T SAID A WORD ON THE WAY HOME. NOT EVEN
when I stomped up the stairs with my muddy sneakers
still on. All of which I had been fine with. I didn't need
her help. And I sure as heck didn't need her in the middle
of the fray, reporting back to Elroy Floyd my every move.

Rain pelted my window as I lay in the darkened silence
thinking of my odd boy. As minutes morphed into hours, I
played scenarios over in my head of Cassius miraculously
having a phone or some way to contact him. I thought, if
only I could sneak up to his room, I could take him my
tablet. He could hide it from his parents, and we could stay
in contact. If he had a way to contact someone, anyone.
It didn't even have to be me. Maybe if he'd had access
to communication with the outside world, he could have
saved himself ages ago. Instead of sleeping, which my
body and brain desperately needed, I thought of a million

ways I could change his life if only I had the power. Which I clearly didn't.

Desperate for any connection with Cassius Shooster, I gave up on sleep altogether and looked up autism symptoms and treatments. Many of the symptoms didn't fit Cassius, most of which seemed to be referring to younger kids and those with a more severe case. From what I could sum up, Cassius was high-functioning and completely capable of living a normal life. Had he had the proper interventions and education growing up, he could've been on his way to college. I didn't know what the hell his dad was talking about, saying he'd never live a normal life with me. Or anyone. His parents were in the dark ages, and because of that, my odd boy had been locked away in his tower, waiting for the damsel in Converse high tops to rescue him.

"If he hadn't been locked away in the hole three houses down, he'd have been tossed into an institution and left to rot," I said to myself.

I wanted to know who'd diagnosed Cassius in the first place, and what resources his parents had been given. I honestly didn't know anything about the spectrum, but I learned enough in an hour of Internet surfing to understand the Shoosters were off their tree to think Cassius was anything but an adorably odd boy.

Mom knocked on my door and made me jump. "Are you ready?"

A glance at the clock said I'd pulled an all-nighter.

"Crap." When had the sun come up? "Not yet," I chimed from beneath my covers.

I'd been distracted by Cassius for days, lost a night of sleep, and completely forgot about my doctor's appointment. Cassius was a worthy distraction. I was happy to be thinking about something that wasn't me. I wanted to focus on him and only him. I didn't want to think about doctors and hospitals and treatment options and all that. I just wanted to obsess over boys like all the other senior girls—and one boy, but he's not *out* yet, so I won't open that closet door for him.

I pulled on a pair of jeans and slipped into my sneakers. Brushing the red rat's nest on my head, I stared at myself in the mirror. I'd aged five years in a week. The bags under my eyes would surely give away my lack of sleep, and knowing my mother, she'd assume I was up all night worrying over my appointment when in reality, I hadn't thought about it all week.

"We better get on the road if we're going to make it in time," Mom called from her room.

"I don't really care," I whispered to myself around my toothbrush.

She poked her head into the bathroom. "Ready?"

"Let's do it." I smiled tightly and refused to meet her eyes in the mirror.

Her brows pulled together in the center. "Didn't sleep a wink." She made it a statement and grabbed me by the chin to inspect my face.

"I'm fine. Let's go." I jerked my chin from her grip and shoved past her. I didn't want to be a dick to my mom, but I really didn't want her sympathy.

Not yet.

Mud caked the fenders of the old Benz. An instant reminder of the night before. My stomach tightened and I looked down the street. From the driveway, most of Cassius's house could be seen. Past Mrs. Carroway's fern garden, beyond Mr. Horowitz's abandoned gingerbread cottage, stood the creepiest house in Flintlock. It was all I could do to not peel out into a full sprint toward the corner of Marigold and Thyme and knock on the door of 17.

"Pru?" Mom called me from one of my many scenarios. "Let's go."

We sat in awkward silence, Mom and I. The hour drive was a tedious repetition of tree lines and shrubbery. Only patches of morning fog broke up the monotony. I was scheduled to see a surgeon about my removal treatment— or something. My oncologist hoped they could remove my tumor without damaging the bone and leave minimal scarring. I didn't give a crap about scars. I just wanted it out. I'd ignored the pain—which sitting in the car with my mom I realized had gotten a bit worse—that entire week thanks to my Cassius obsession. No better drug than distraction.

The hospital was cold, as they tend to be, and smelled

of cleanser. And the afterbirth of a sneeze. People milled around the waiting room, waiting for whatever they were there for. Most were likely waiting on someone to come out of surgery. The likelihood of one of those millers being disappointed before the day was out seemed high. I wanted to hug them all and at the same time scream at them, shake them around, and tell them to suck it up. Life happens while we're all milling around waiting. I refused to mill. I'd milled my whole damn life. Finally, in what could've been the last moments of it, my milling days were over.

"Pender... huss?" A nurse clumsily called my name.

"Penderhaus," I corrected, and got a poke in the ribs from Mom. The sensation made me jerk and sent a shock of pain through my arm. I winced and Mom caught it. Not wanting to see her face, I walked past the nurse and into a wide hallway lined with doors.

"This way, please," the nurse sang, walking quickly down the hallway.

She took us to a room with a desk and a few chairs. Charts of the human body hung beside framed certificates from some medical school I didn't care much about. We took a seat, and Mom nervously crossed her thick legs as best she could.

"I'm just going to take some quick vitals. Okay?" The nurse was young and to me seemed fresh out of school. She stuck a thermometer in my ear for a few seconds until it beeped and wrote down whatever it said in the folder she held. "Can you relax your arm so I can take your blood pressure?" Without warning, she grabbed my arm and tried to wrap the black cuff around it.

The pain brought bile up my throat. I jerked my arm away and cradled it against my chest. "Are you screwed in the head?"

"I'm sorry," Mom apologized on my behalf to the nurse. "You'll have to take it on the other side. She's got a…" She trailed off and mumbled, "…in that arm."

Clearly embarrassed, the nurse shuffled around to my other arm. "I'm sorry," she whispered. She took my pulse and blood pressure in silence. "The doctor will be in shortly," she said when she was finished and closed the door.

"Prudence," Mom snapped at me. "What is wrong with you?"

"The cow jerked on my arm. Doesn't it say in my chart somewhere that I have a big honkin' *tumor* in here?" No sleep, legitimate boy stress, and the forced confrontation of my demise had me on edge. I just wanted to be at school so I could keep an eye on him. If he was even there.

A soft knock and the door opened. A conventionally attractive woman stood in the doorway. "Hi there," she said with a smile that met her eyes. She wore a white coat and a stethoscope, letting the world know she was a doctor. "Miss Penderhaus?" she asked and stuck her hand out to shake mine.

I took it apprehensively, and she shook my hand.

"You're my surgeon?" I asked in disbelief.

She smiled, and her sparkling blue eyes crinkled at the edges, showing she was a bit older than she looked at first glance. "Yes. Hard to believe?"

I nodded. "You're really pretty."

"Pretty girls can be doctors too." She laughed and sat behind the desk. "Prove them all wrong, right?" she joked, and it lightened my mood a teeny tiny bit. I could totally get behind that statement, since it'd recently become my motto. "Now, down to business." She opened my chart and glanced over the pages. We waited in bated silence for too long. My heart began to pound as the seconds ticked on. Nothing good comes from a doctor who takes her time with the news. "Hmm, all right. Your oncologist explained to you the complexity of the growth?"

"He did," Mom said.

"Excellent, don't want to do that twice, so we'll skip over that. Okay with everyone?" We nodded. I appreciated not having to hear it again. "As you know, I am a surgical oncologist and can only remark on your surgical treatment. Your doctor and I work closely together to manage your treatment, but your oncologist is your first stop on the tour for all other questions and concerns regarding your treatment." We nodded again, still waiting for my doom. "We feel it is in your best interest to first surgically remove as much, if not all, of the tumor before beginning chemotherapy." Mom caught her breath, trying not to cry. We hadn't really discussed any of that, and the word hung heavy in the room. "Looking over your chart, I feel surgery is the best option and would like to offer my reassurance that you're in good hands. Survival rate for a healthy young girl like yourself is high even at this stage in the game. Don't get me wrong, you've got quite a road ahead of you, but the odds are ever in your favor."

I hadn't offered myself up as tribute to the cancer reaping, but the quote rang true for a moment. Whether she meant it that way or not, I felt like Katniss and she, my Effie, came to escort me to my death with a smile on her beautiful face.

Mom's heavy breaths begged me to break the silence. "When is this surgery going to take place? And what are our chances you'll be able to take it all?"

"We'll want to schedule your surgery in the next week or two. We want you nice and healthy, so be sure to take your vitamins and try to get plenty of sleep in the time being." Yeah, right. "Looking at your MRI isn't the same as getting in there with my two hands and eyes, but I feel there's a good chance I can get the majority, if not all. The goal is to keep as much of the bone and lymph as possible."

"Cut the damn thing off. Just get it out of me." I meant what I said. I hadn't really had much to live for when I'd first gotten the news, but after my conversation with Mom about Cassius, I knew I had to stick around as long as I possibly could. I wanted to live for him. How sad was that? What a pathetic loser I was to have nothing in my life worth living for before someone told me I was dying.

"Well, Miss Penderhaus, that's exactly what we're trying to avoid and accomplish."

"You mean… she might have to lose her arm?" Mom's voice was shrill with tears on the verge of spilling.

"We're not even considering that at this point, so please don't worry." She looked at me and changed the subject. "How's your pain? I see you're guarding that arm."

"Your nurse wrenched it and damn near killed me." I had no patience for anything at that moment and wanted nothing more than to be at school with Cassius. "I'll be fine. I just want to go to school. Can we go now?"

"You're still in school? Excellent. That's what we like to hear. Just be sure you take it easy, get plenty of sleep, and don't forget to eat. You'd be surprised how quickly your body can turn against you when you're neglectful to it." She smiled, charming and radiant; it was no wonder she went into medicine, she certainly had an excellent bedside manner. "Have a boyfriend waiting to hear the good news?"

"He's not my boyfriend," I said too quickly. "I mean, he's a boy and he's my friend, but he's not my boyfriend. He's just a good friend that needs me." All the words came out far too quickly. Even I didn't buy them.

"That's good you've got someone you're close to. Just make sure he's giving back what he's taking. You'll be needing him soon too. Someone has to grab you Frappuccino and hold your books open for you."

Her smile practically lit up the room.

"He's not really the take-care-of-others type."

She pulled her eyebrows in. "That's too bad. You'll have to show him how it's done."

She was right, of course; that was my end goal. But her implications that Cassius and I had a heavier relationship than we did had me on the defensive. "He's a boy with Asperger's," I spat out. "He's not a boyfriend, and he's not a caretaker."

The pretty doctor stared at me, quiet, her expression soft. She tilted her head to the side slightly. "That boy has all the potential in the world to be both of those things, and better than most boys out there, if you give him a chance."

Butterflies set flight in my stomach. The idea seemed ridiculous to my brain, but my gut, you know, that spot that tells you to run or stay, had other ideas. I hadn't considered Cassius a potential boyfriend because in my head he didn't have the capacity. In my head, he was innocent, naïve, like a child and would never have those types of needs or wants. Was he even into girls? And relationships aside, how would he take care of me? He could hardly take care of himself, let alone me. No. That was just stupid. I couldn't date Cassius Shooster, nor could I ever expect *him* to look after *me*.

I pinched my lips between my teeth. "Can we go?" I asked, not wanting to talk about Cassius or any misconceptions I may have had about him.

Her eyes lowered as she nodded once. "Yes." I was acting like a toddler whose blankie was in the wash, and she was taking it all in stride. "I just need your mother to sign a few things and schedule your surgery date. I have these here for you to look over when you're ready." She handed me a stack of papers with bold printed headlines. "You'll need to know how to take care of yourself if you're so sure you won't have help." A genuine, kind smile pushed crinkles around her eyes, and I suddenly wanted to punch her. Cassius had no reason to take care of me, nor did he see me as his girlfriend or anything of the sort. As far as I knew, at that very moment, he saw me as the idiot who'd destroyed his life.

10

THE BENZ RUMBLED UNDER MY BUTT AS THE TREE LINE flew past. I'd demanded Mom take me to school and make it snappy. No sleep was no *bueno* for the likes of Prudence Penderhaus. No sleep and no Cassius and no promise of the future makes Pru a cranky girl.

"Prudence, I'm not very happy about how you acted in there." I grumbled something inaudible under my breath. "I don't care what you're dealing with right now, it's not fair to those just trying to take care of you."

I scoffed. "What? Like you?" If sarcasm could walk, it would be wearing my sneakers. Mom's glare seared holes into the side of my head. "Sorry."

She huffed. "I'm not fighting with you today, Prudence."

Then stop talking.

"But you need to know that I'm also not going to let

you act like this. I know you're scared. I'm scared too—"

"I'm not scared." It was a lie. I was scared. But less for myself and more for the boy I feared was in the hole and not third period.

"You don't have to play tough with me."

"I'm *not*. I just want to get to school."

Mom didn't say anything until she craned the Benz right at the T-intersection, leaving the highway and entering Flintlock city limits. "You need to let that boy be, Prudence."

I think actual steam shot out my ears. "Over my dead body." Figuratively and literally.

"Prudence, you're sick. You need taking care of. You need pampering. You don't need to be out there worried over some boy who has enough of his own problems."

"When did you go to the dark side? Was it before or after Sheriff Floyd and the well?" My eyes, Eastwood slits, locked onto her, but she refused to look at me.

"Dark side," she scoffed. "I'm on your side. Even if you're not." Such a mom.

"I'm on the side of righteousness." I'd never said that before. I'd never even thought that before. But it was as true and pure as my red hair. "I'm on the side of Cassius and others like him. He needs an ally. And clearly that person is me."

The turn from Main to Thyme was fast approaching. I'd be at school in minutes and the conversation would be over. My foot tapped the floorboard, legs anxious to run far and fast.

"I want you to think for one second about why that boy was kept away from the public. Please."

"I don't need a second, I know why. Because his parents are insane. You thought that too until Elroy *fucking* Floyd got to you."

"Language," she hissed. "And Elroy didn't *get to me*. I didn't stop to think either. I wanted to help him too and I did, and now my part in this is done. His parents know him better than we do, Prudence. And Sheriff Floyd is his ally. Elroy wouldn't allow the abuse of a child. He just wouldn't." As long as the abuse was from his own deputies, that was okay. Clearly. "You have to trust in adults, Pru. Sometimes they really do know best. They really do." She rambled, convincing herself more than she was me. Whether she actually believed whatever bullshit Elroy Floyd had fed her, I didn't know or care. I wasn't buying it.

Mom pulled the Benz against the wrong curb on Thyme in front of the school. I didn't wait for her to say bye. I'd unbuckled my belt the second we passed the football field, ready to leap from the vehicle. The steel door slammed, echoing off the building.

My backpack, slung over my good shoulder, smacked against my back as I took the stairs two at a time. I'd missed the first half of the day, and most everyone was mingling around on the front steps for lunch. Morgan and Brady took up space in their usual spot, surrounded by their usual lemmings. Brady ignored my presence as usual, but Morgan glared at me. His nose had a white strip across the bridge, under his eyes tinged purple. I slowed down just long enough to let him see my smug grin before yanking the door open.

I knew Bonnie wouldn't be caught dead on the front steps with the rest of them, so I hurriedly slinked behind the building to her smoke spot next to the gardener's shed. The offensive cloud of smoke let me know she was right where I knew she'd be.

"Hey," I said, breathless, and she dropped her smoke and stomped on it swiftly.

"Damn it, Penderhaus." She grimaced at the smashed butt on the ground. "That was my last one."

"I'm crying inside. Where's Cassius?"

She was still fretting over her cancer stick. "What? That guy? He's not here."

"That *guy*? Yeah, that one whose ass you helped keep out of the sling last night. What do you mean he's not here?" Worst-case scenario number ten unfolding in front of my very eyes.

"I haven't seen him today. Why?" She wiggled her eyebrows at me.

I rolled my eyes. "Why does everyone assume he's my boyfriend?" I threw my hands up in aggravation.

"I never said boyfriend, but since we're on the subject, what's your obsession?" Since we were in junior high, I'd never expressed an interest in any

Flintlock boy, ever. Bonnie had every reason to question my motives. "Prudence Penderhaus, it's about damn time you have a crush. I thought I'd never see that day. But if it's not like that, then what is it?" She scowled at her crooked cigarette. "Why this guy?"

"Because…." I wasn't ready to let my cancer cat out of the bag quite yet, so in a panic, I said, "I do like him. Okay? Jeez. He's really nice and likes the same stuff I like."

She smiled wide. "And he's totally into you."

"Shut up. You have no idea what you're talking about."

"Like hell I don't. The kid has it hard for you. He kicked Morgan's ass for *you*. He left school on his first day for *you*. He opened his front door for *you*. Hello,"—she *thunked* her hand against my forehead—"McFly. I don't know the kid, sure, but I've seen enough to know he's not just some kid who lived in the spook house. And you're not just worried about how the new kid is adjusting."

He had opened his door for me, but I hadn't necessarily thought about it like that. I had to have been one of very few people that ever knocked on it in the first place. Not to mention, he'd seen me walking by probably a million times before that.

"He just doesn't have the mindset for girls." I didn't really know that for certain, but I assumed being locked away in his house his entire life had to have stunted him socially and that had to mean girls and the like.

"He's a seventeen-year-old boy, right?" I nodded.

"He has a mindset for girls. You, in particular, it seems."

I rolled my eyes. The idea was ridiculous. Cassius Shooster was a kindred spirit. A familiar weirdo. An odd duck just like me. But that was it. He didn't like me. Not like that. Right?

"I hope he's okay." I shifted the conversation out of the uncomfortable and into the realistic.

"What happened last night? Did my good buddies at the Flintlock police station treat you well? I tried to keep up in the rain but lost them when they turned into the covered parking behind the jail." She plucked the smashed cigarette from the ground and worked it in her fingers to straighten it out again.

"No. They beat the shit out of him and threw him in a cell."

Her expression changed, and she looked up at me. "Please tell me you were in a jail cell for at least a minute and a half?"

"Yes."

She laughed, throwing her head back. "Yes. Oh, that's awesome. I'm really sad I missed that."

Leave it to Bonnie to make light of any situation.

"Anyway, they didn't charge him, yet, but when his parents came to pick him up, they made it clear he was in deep shit. His drunk mother called me a skank—"

"*You*?"

"Yes. And told him he was going back in *the hole*." I shuddered at the thought, and the feeling of helplessness

I'd felt standing there in the rain watching him disappear into the night washed over me again. "What the hell did that mean?"

"Shit," she said, her bent cigarette bounced between her lips. "Pru, that's heavy. You think they're... *abusive*?"

I blinked at her. "They've kept him locked away in his house for seventeen-ish years. Trained him to believe he was dangerous, and he couldn't be out in the world because of it. If that's not abuse, I don't know what is."

"No wonder you're so obsessed. You can't buy this kind of drama. Hey, at least you're getting out of that room and living a little. I thought you'd waste away up there in your very own Barnes and Blockbuster." She laughed.

"Ha, that's all I want to do right now, trust me." I wanted to add, with Cassius, but I didn't. It seemed stupid and would only prove points I'd been trying to avoid all day.

We stood in silence; only the sound of her flicking the flint on her lighter could be heard between us. With my hands on my hips, I looked around. My eyes eventually fell on the dark wood siding of Cassius's house, hardly visible but for the peaks of the roof. I bit at my thumbnail, lost in thought.

They could be doing anything to him in that house. The black eye he'd come to school with proved that. How many black eyes had he had that no one had seen? How many days had he spent in the hole? How many times had he watched me walk past that house, begging me to just look up?

"I'll keep lookout," Bonnie said, her crooked, mashed cigarette pressed between her lips.

"Should *I* be the lookout?" I didn't think twice about the proposed mission.

"The porch railing is high enough for a tall person— you—to easily reach the eave of the awning and pull themselves up. Which window is his?"

"Last two on the right side."

Bonnie smiled around her smoldering, comically bent cigarette. I loved her dearly, but the poor thing stank most of the time. "Come on, Romeo. We've got to break some yonder windows, or some shit." She slapped me on the back again and brought pain to my arm.

I winced, and she passed me without looking back. "*Romeo and Juliet* was a tragedy," I said quietly as she walked away.

Bonnie never so much as glanced over her shoulder as she made her way around the front of the school and crossed the street toward Marigold Lane. I followed, more than curiosity tugging me along.

I had to make sure he was okay. Wishing I had my tablet with me to fulfill one of many plans I'd concocted, I stood at the foot of his house staring at the window that might as well had been miles away. In theory, Bonnie's plan was flawless. Mr. Shooster was, as usual, gone until 5:00 p.m., and surely Mommy Dearest was soused on the La-Z-Boy watching trashy television. I could easily reach the awning and pull myself up. If I had full use of my arm.

"What if he doesn't want to see me?" I stalled.

"What if he does?"

"What if I fall?"

"What if you don't?"

"When did you become an optimist?"

"When you needed a kick in the ass to do something legendary." She hugged an arm around my waist. "Up there in that room is a boy *you*, all by yourself, brought out into the light of day. Sure, things didn't work out well, but does that mean you give up and leave him there? Nope. That means you didn't try hard enough to dig up all the shit he's buried under. Get up there and dig."

I can't, I wanted to say. But the look on her face held more determination than I'd ever seen in her. Bonnie wasn't a motivational speaker unless it involved coaxing a beer down my gullet, which hadn't ended well. Although, after my diagnosis, I was more than willing to give that a second try.

My heart banged around in my chest. What in the hell was I thinking? I felt my head nod, but I hadn't done it consciously. The irrationality inside, stemming from impending doom, seemed to be taking over my consciousness.

"All right. All right. All right," I caught myself repeating softly as I snuck up the driveway.

"I'll be right here." Bonnie leaned against the wrought-iron fence that circled the front yard.

Swallowing hard, I choked back the nerves bubbling up my gut. I placed my foot on the edge of the railing around the porch. Judging by my height, the eave on the house wouldn't have been more than half a foot above my head once I was balanced on the railing with both feet. All I had to do was reach out and pull.

I let out a long, calming breath and thought about Cassius's dark features. His pale skin, ridiculously sun-deprived, contrasted his dark eyes in a way that made him look more like a Tim Burton character than a high school boy. Might as well have had a set of scissor hands. He was peculiar, and I liked it. And even though I wanted more than anything to, I liked that I didn't know what was going on in his head. He wasn't like a high school guy, just like I wasn't like a high school girl. We were, us two, odd companions, very much meant for each other.

I reached my long arms above my head and gripped the edge of the awning easily. In my mind, I swore to myself I was strong and tough and perfectly capable of hoisting my body up to his window in the name of love. Or something like that. I thought about my dad and how strong he'd been. How daring and determined. How much like him I was in every other way. I could do it. He'd be proud of every moment I'd spent doing something for someone else. It was the last motivation I needed to force my body into a gravity-defying feat. Gripping tight with my fingers, I pulled and my arm seared. The tumor had taken over the soft tissues in my bicep, muscles, and tendons, and had begun to wrap itself around the bone. Soon enough it would be gone, but in that moment, it screamed at me, a battle cry that ripped through my soul. It wouldn't go without a fight. Neither would I.

Releasing a grunt from the depths of my gut, I pulled my long, lean body upward. My gangly legs kicked around in the open air for a few moments before my knees finally found their footing on the ramshackle roof, which was in desperate need of repair. I sat still on my hands and knees on the porch roof, fearful I'd fall right through, terrified I'd vomit from the pain. I heard a faint *yes* from Bonnie down below. Her cheer fueled me further, and I scurried to the window to complete my mission. The pain in my arm brought tears to my eyes and bile to my throat.

I didn't know how to go about it, so I just knocked on the window as though it was a door. Nothing happened for a long while. The curtains were closed and impossibly thick. I tapped my fingers on the sill and thought on my next move.

"I don't think he's in there," I whispered loudly from my perch down to Bonnie.

She didn't say a word, just shoved her phone back into her bag and nonchalantly opened the front gate. I watched as my best friend strolled up the walkway I'd been so terrified to walk up only days before. She knew, just as everyone else in Flintlock, the stories about the house. They'd been around since we were kids, and probably before that too. She didn't seem to care as I had.

Though I'd pretty much debunked the suburban legend, 17 Marigold Lane was still frigging scary. Nothing short of jail time and a coat of paint was going to change that. Even then, legends were hard to break.

I sat and stared as she boldly walked up to the porch, and I wished someday I could find my own inner badass. Without a thought, she knocked on the door. Knocking again a few moments later, she and I waited. I couldn't see her, but the echoes of her final knock could be heard through the window where I sat.

"Hey," she whispered from right under me. Carefully, I made my way to the edge and looked over. "You'll have to go in. There's no answer, but I can hear sound. Someone's home."

"What? No way. That's all the sheriff needs on me, breaking and entering."

She looked up at me and planted her hands on her hips. "The hole?"

I pinched my lips between my teeth. Bonnie was right. I'd gone there for a reason, and that reason was still somewhere in the house. "Fine. You stay right there."

"Yeah, go." She shooed me off.

New courage built inside me. It was the grown-up version of what had forced me up the steps to knock on the door I perched above. Courage and stupidity and determination had me breaking and entering, trespassing, and who knew how many other felonies and misdemeanors I was about to commit.

My first few tries to open the window were fruitless. After the fifth shove, and almost giving up entirely, it slid open. The screen, like my own window at home, had never really existed so was of no consequence. I popped my head in, parting the curtains with my face.

"Cassius?" I called, hardly above a whisper. "Cass?" My words sounded more like a long hiss than actual words.

Thick black curtains kept the room in shadows. Even the light that peeped through around my head was muted from the perpetual clouds overhead.

I grumbled in frustration and decided to slip in as quietly as possible. One leg at a time, I stepped over the sill and into his room. Feeling lucky for my long legs, I silently congratulated myself for not knocking over a lamp or something of the sort on the desk under the window with my baby giraffe-like grace.

"What the—" I flung back the curtain, spilling muted light into the darkened room. My heart stopped. The room I remembered was no more. Once filled to the brim with neatly placed movie memorabilia and the like was now bare. Shelves empty. Desk free of perfectly aligned desk-things. Not so much as a sheet on the bed. Someone had stripped everything that Cassius had away from him and left his room barren.

I wanted to fly out the window and drag Bonnie up with me so she could see it too. Instead, I pulled my phone from my pocket and snapped a few pictures.

Most girls my age were snapping pictures of themselves in a bathroom. I was documenting evidence in a child abuse case. And I present to you, not your average American teen, ladies and gentlemen.

"Cassius?" I whispered into the hall, refusing to move from his doorway. Nothing answered back.

I made my way down the hall and to the stairs, opening every door on my way, checking every dark corner as I passed through. He wasn't upstairs. Unless there was a hidden room in the walls, which I wouldn't doubt for a second. My bones chattered with theatrical terror. The house, with or without the legends, was a worthy opponent for my adrenaline.

Making my way down the stairs, I awaited the classic sound of lightning strikes outside. Two steps in a row squeaked underfoot and I jumped. Clutching my chest, I held the banister for support. As my heart slowed to its original mile-a-minute pace, I couldn't help but picture myself as Don Knotts in the old Simmons mansion. Sneaking around, flashlight in hand, shivering like a lanky redheaded chihuahua. Except I didn't have a flashlight and the danger in this creaky old house was real. Dark and ominous, the house held more mystery than I'd ever given it credit for. All I needed was to navigate it alone, in the dark, and on the lam.

The first floor was dark, just as I remembered it. Windows covered with the same dark curtains. The sitting room near the front door was still filled with ugly knickknacks and rose-patterned everything. I assumed the old drunk bitch in the chair had decorated, so I sneered at it as I imagined it was her incarnate.

"Cass?" I whispered, and I made my way around the loop of the first floor that worked around to the door leading to the kitchen.

I knew on the other side of that door was a kitchen and through that was the living room where undoubtedly Mrs. Shooster would be passed out. The paternity of an illegitimate child was being announced in dramatic fashion on the television. It had to have been what Bonnie heard from the front porch.

Struggling with the impulse to barrel through those doors and Superman-punch the old hag in the head, I begrudgingly allowed the kitchen door to swing shut and let her be. She and I would have our day. I had an odd boy to find first.

"If I were a boy being punished, where would I be?" I asked myself under my breath, leaning against the wall behind me.

An image of Kathy Bates popped into my head. I recalled my first time in the house and the odd correlation I'd felt toward the actress. "Why Kathy Bates?" I sneered at my own shoddy thought process and pondered the relevance of the woman. A moment later, the proverbial lightbulb clicked on above my head. "You dirty-birdy." I did my best Annie Wilkes impersonation at almost zero volume and turned to find the cellar door I knew was somewhere on that wall. In *Misery*, Kathy Bates had dumped her captive in the cellar, hidden behind a secret door under the stairs. My movie-drenched subconscious had picked up on that long before I could ever think of it myself.

I pushed against the wall, allowing the nearly hidden door to release its clasp and pop open, revealing a darkened staircase. "The hole," I whispered, breath fleeting, as the sense of urgency to reach Cassius grew.

I vaguely recalled the small door from my first search of the house and couldn't believe I hadn't measured it into my equations. *Perhaps*, I thought, *I hadn't imagined anyone could be so evil except in movies.*

My heart fluttered, threatening to fly away from my chest, as I took each step downward. I touched my fingers along the wall on either side of me, brick or stone of some kind lined the narrow stairwell. No railing that I could feel, so I took it slow and easy. No sense in falling and dying down there in the hole and being no use to anyone.

"Cassius?" I whispered, feeling my way down each step. I knew the end had to be coming up soon, and I worried what I'd find.

My foot hit a dirt floor unexpectedly; it slid a half inch or so and jarred my leg. Both feet skirted around at the foot of the steps for a second before I realized the cellar hadn't been paved and likely wasn't habitable for humans.

Not a sliver of light penetrated the pit. Pitch-black, the stench of putrid church-lady perfume took over my senses.

I shuffled my feet along the floor, terrified of what I'd find down there. Worried I wouldn't find anything I was looking for, but so much more than I'd bargained for.

I reached above my head and felt around for a pull string light like the one I had in my own basement. Although, my own basement had been modernized with a finished floor and ventilation. For all I knew, the spook house still had no lighting along with the original dirt floor and stone walls. What I could only assume was a few feet in, my fingertips brushed against something smooth and solid. A bulb. Hanging from the lightbulb was the string. I tugged and it flickered to life. The aging filament in the bulb buzzed and threatened to pop overhead as it swung. Casting spooky shadows across weathered boxes and cobweb high-rises, the light hardly helped the situation, but I was grateful for what little I had.

Lying on the floor in the far corner, in a huddled pale mass, Cassius's long body was curled in a tight fetal position. His bare back gleamed with sweat and dark spots where the dirt had clung. *He doesn't like the dark.*

It took a solid second for my heart, lungs, and brain to sync up, and then I scurried toward him, kicking up dirt on the way.

"Cass," I breathed, fighting back tears.

His sad form, a lump of the human I knew was in there somewhere, didn't move. Only trembled uncontrollably from the cold and the sweat that covered him. His body had been stripped of clothes and lay naked as the day he was born. Shaking away my blush in a time of peril, I rolled him over toward me so I could see his face. He'd been worked over by Flintlock's finest, but I looked him over anyway for newer injuries.

Any fear I'd had about what Sheriff Floyd would do to me if I'd been caught were gone. All my focus was on getting Cassius out of the hole. "Hey, I need you to open your eyes and look at me." I ran my hand over his head, which was drenched with sweat.

He hadn't been down there more than a day; he would be fine physically, barring any unseen injuries. Emotionally, I prayed he would be the same boy I finally realized I'd begun to fall in love with. His lean, defined biceps flexed and gleamed in the moving light as he clung to his own body. The movement revealed thin gashes along the skin, deep and dark red from dried blood.

"That bitch," I huffed. "We're getting out of here." I wasn't going to leave him there alone to go get help. Not for one second.

I pulled my phone out again, this time calling Bonnie. A beep chimed in my ear to warn me I had no signal down that deep in the cellar. I grunted and shoved the thing back into my butt pocket. Cassius was too big for me to heft on my shoulders, so I had to try and get him up.

"Hey." I shook his face. "You have to wake up. We have to get out of here, like, now. Come. On." I shook and shoved with each word. By the last, Cassius opened his near-black eyes.

"Prudence?" Perplexed at my sudden appearance to save the day, Cassius refused to meet my eyes, focusing instead on my mouth.

Forcing eye contact, I pulled his face by his chin toward me. "Hi," I said and smiled. "You have to get up. It's time to go."

"There is no going from the hole," he said, his voice strangled and distant.

"There is today. Get up." I stood and tried to pull him with me.

"I can't, don't you get it?" he asked in a tone that would have turned my mother's face into knots. "It's where I belong," he said dramatically, curling into a ball again.

"Bullshit," I replied starkly, letting out an exacerbated huff. "Enough of this 'I can't' crap. I'm not putting up with it. I don't give a shit what your hellacious mother told you or what your father says is so damn depraved about you. You're mine to worry about now, and Prudence Penderhaus doesn't stand for this shit. Anymore." I nodded once to confirm my rationale. "Now, let's get out of here." I gave his arm one last tug.

Cassius's long legs tucked under his body and finally assisted in hoisting his big frame up off the dirt. The light had stopped its swinging and settled in a spot behind my head, my shadow casting the only cover of little—or not little, I wouldn't know—Cassius. He didn't bother to cover himself. I stood there, deer in headlights, looking anywhere but down. I swallowed hard, turned around, and awkwardly began searching for pants.

The light didn't breach the shadows that fell over corners and the far walls, leaving a good portion of the space dark. I let my long arms reach arbitrarily through the shadowy corners in search of pants that may or may not have been there. "So, any idea where your pants might be?"

His nervous throat clearing sent a wave of butterflies flittering in my stomach. I was standing in the dark with a stark naked, clearly attractive boy with nothing left to lose but my virginity. If we were in a movie—they'd label it teen and rate it R to ensure the horny masses came in droves—I'd turn around and he'd be standing there in the dim light, ready and willing. Side-boob, fade to black, and on to the next day. Then something bad would happen because we're dumb teenagers and we don't fact-check, and we would break up only to mend fences in the final scene after some comradery against a common foe. But we weren't in a movie. We weren't the cliché boy meets girl, and we sure as hell weren't about to have sex in a dirty old cellar under the feet of Broom-Hilda. Nope, instead—

"Breaking and entering?" a deep slurred voice called from the stairs. "You're working on quite the rap sheet." Mrs. Shooster stood five steps from the bottom. Her dark robe hid most of her body, but in her hand, she held something that glinted in the light, large enough to not fit in a pocket.

"I just came to get Cassius. He's coming with me." I stood my ground, leaving the idea of modesty behind.

"Like hell," she scoffed, and grunted, sounding like every other drunk middle-aged woman you see on TV. "Cass," she screeched, sending chills down my spine like nails on a chalkboard. "Get your ass back in the dark and atone." She snapped and flung her arm in the direction of the dark where I'd found him huddled.

He didn't look twice at me before turning and heading back into the shadows.

"Stop right there," I commanded. "You move one more inch, and you'll never see me again." I didn't know what made me think that was any kind of threat, but he stopped. "You're never going to the dark again. Come on." I reached my hand out to him.

"And where the *fug*," she slurred, "do you think you're going?"

Mrs. Shooster wobbled on the step, and I hoped she'd just topple right over. I'd use her limp body as a step on my way out. Cassius hadn't moved from the place where he'd stopped for me. Back to us, dirt spots looking like rotten old skin in the dim light. A zombie under the control of the witch of a woman standing feet from me.

We had to get out of that basement. Together. I didn't have a plan to speak of, but that didn't mean much. It was either going to happen or it wasn't. The time to plan and rationalize was over. He needed to get out of that house, or he'd end up dying there.

"Cassius," I said, emphasizing his whole name, unlike his mother. "Come this way. We're going to my house." I specified our destination to remove that additional anxiety from his overloaded brain. "Mrs. Shooster, I'm going to suggest politely you get the hell out of my way. I may look meek, but I won't think twice about ripping your withered old heart from between your saggy boobs if you try and stop us." That threat was real, if only in my fictional brain.

Cassius finally turned, still mostly shadowed, and watched us. I swallowed down hard the fear that I'd be leaving alone. He was taking too long. My hand had been out for what felt like an eternity. Mrs. Shooster taunted me with her stare. *Come on, Cass,* I thought. I closed my eyes and prepared to leave alone.

If he wouldn't come with me, I'd be forced to not only leave alone but ask for help from the people I worried were just as big a part of the problem as his parents. And if that didn't work, I ran the risk of never in my life seeing Cassius Shooster again. The thought was almost too much to consider.

His long, cold fingers slid over my hand. My heart began to flap again, and a self-righteous smile crept across my face.

His hand in mine, I squeezed and refused to let him go. He was mine, eccentricities, disabilities, social deficits, big feet, wild hair, all of it, mine. I put the idea that he was naked out of my mind and figured we could find him something to cover his butt somewhere upstairs once we got past the bitch. We cleared the space to the stairs in just a few quick steps and were standing below Mrs. Shooster. The glinting object she held was a bottle of alcohol, mostly empty. I wondered how long it'd taken her to down the rest of it. The last I'd seen her she was mostly through a bottle of wine at eight in the morning. Seemed things were escalating. Or maybe it was just a Friday.

"You're an idiot, girl." She pointed at me with her bottle. "The retard isn't worth your time. An abomination." She sneered at him.

"He's no such thing."

"You don't know. You don't know anything." She spun the metal lid off the bottle and took a swig. "The little shit's good for nothing. Bastard," she slurred, looking right at Cassius.

"If that's true, then let me take him off your hands. Just let him go." Cassius tensed, I looked to see every muscle on edge. Naked, he had no defense against the dark arts. No hood, no sleeves, just one snapping hand but he was too tense to even manage that.

She leaned toward us, and I hoped she'd just keep going until she tumbled right down to the floor. "I can't let him leave this house." Her breath burned my eyes. "Your *mother* forced my hand, but that's over now. He's never leaving this room again."

What a piece of shit. How in the hell was Cassius functioning at all in a house like theirs? "You're an evil human being. You didn't deserve to be a mother. And now, you won't be."

"Ha, I'm not his mother. My son died." I stopped and stared at her. Could she truly be that delusional? I couldn't understand why Mr. Shooster would leave his son home alone with a woman like that.

"You really are a nutbag, lady. Get out of my way or I'll make good on that heart-removal threat." I stepped up a step and nearly met her eyes. She didn't budge.

"Oh," she said with a laugh, "he didn't tell you? Cass,"— she dragged the S out too long—"what a bad little boy you are." His hand squeezed hard against mine, and I felt him try to pull away from me. "Murdering little bastard." The disparagement in her voice oozed, dripping over my skin.

"Move, lady, or I'll move you." I took two more steps up, dragging Cassius up with me. The narrow space didn't allow for passing, so she had only one choice: up. She didn't move an inch until I was standing on the step just below hers, looking down at her. Clumsily, she backed up one step, then another. The bottle remained clutched in her hand.

She held the wall with her free hand for support. "He can't leave this house."

I moved up another step, undeterred by her drunk nonsense. "Like hell."

"He's a killer," she proclaimed. Cassius pulled on my hand, trying to escape. I pulled right back. He'd have to take me down the stairs with him before I'd let him go.

"You're a sadist. And your husband too." I shoved an open hand in the center of her chest, just hard enough to show I meant business. I wasn't going back down, so she was going up. My heart pounding relentlessly, I did my best to ignore my nerves and fake badassery.

She slung the bottle around in front of her, wildly gesturing to prove her point. "Killed my son." I almost couldn't understand the words. "He killed my Andrew."

"Shut up," Cassius screamed from behind me and pulled frantically on my hand, nearly pulling us both backward tumbling down the steps. "Shut up!" It was the first thing I'd heard him say directly to her.

"I'll tell the world," she slurred over my shoulder at her son. I took a step up, Cassius fighting me along the way, and she followed suit. A step or two from the top she stopped. "That boy killed my son. Pushed him right down these stairs." She started to cry. "My sweet, perfect angel." She sniffed back snot and stuck out her chest. I could sense a manic moment on the fringes. "And he killed him," she growled and pointed dramatically at Cassius.

Cassius nearly yanked my arm out of socket, but I refused to let him go. His free arm flailed, slapping himself in the head, as he wailed. A sound similar to that he'd made when the thunder frightened him, whining and pitched, echoed from all sides.

"Move your loony ass out of my way, old woman," I said, and shoved at her.

"He's a killer. That bastard child killed my Andrew," she screeched over my head. "Murderer, murderer," she yelled over and over again.

Her shrill voice rang in my ears and sent chills down my spine. She was nuts, she had to be. There was no way Cassius killed anyone, ever. And who the hell was Andrew?

"No!" Cassius shouted. His breaths came fast and hard as he breathed through gritted teeth, spitting with each breath. "You're a liar. You're a liar. Shut up, you… *bitch*!" He squeezed that last word through hard and long, shooting spit from his mouth.

"It should have been you. It should have been *you*." Mrs. Shooster sobbed in a slurry of booze and spit. "Go to hell, abomination," she cried, and knocked her empty bottle against the side of my head.

The glass *thunked* when it made contact with my skull, but it didn't shatter like in the movies. Instead, it rang my bell, lighting up little twinkly lights in my vision. I swayed in my spot, and for a moment, I thought I'd fall, but I swayed forward again and righted myself. Everything went black. Blacker. In a haze, my body slammed into stone and slapped against something slick.

My eyes tried to flutter open, but in the end, refused outright. I heard a groan, but it didn't seem to be coming from me. Grains of dirt dug into my palms.

My head throbbed. The zinging pain in my arm was nearly unbearable. I winced, and a pair of arms wrapped around me.

"Look at you. Think you're some kind of Prince Charming? Retard, doesn't even know what a girl is." Mrs. Shooster's sinister voice inched closer. "What do you think you're gonna do with that, huh?" She cackled and kicked my feet.

I lifted my head, but nothing else. Cassius's arms held me close. We'd taken a tumble down the stairs together and landed in an entangled mess in the dirt. His face was contorted into something I didn't recognize. A mixture of misery and anguish.

My vision was fuzzy. All hazy edges and mostly low contrast. Cassius grip was unrelenting. I wanted to get up, move from the top of him, right myself, and prepare a defense. Maybe he knew something I didn't, because he wasn't letting me go. I didn't fight him but kept my senses focused on Mrs. Shooster's movement.

"You could've killed us," I said, eyes focused on Cassius inches away.

"Should've, my dear. *Should've.*" I expected flying monkeys to come swooping down on us from the rafter. Her upper lip snarled. "As a matter of fact, not a bad ide—" Mrs. Shooster's homicidal tirade was cut short by a *thunk* a moment before her body fell to the floor. Dust puffed up around her body, falling gently onto her fluffy pink robe.

"Hey, losers," Bonnie said from the stairs.

A heavy puff of air escaped my lungs and I dropped my forehead to rest on Cassius's chin. "Bonnie," I whispered.

"Wow, Penderhaus, didn't know you had it in you."

I thought on it only a second before I remembered Cassius was naked. I pushed against his arms and this time he let me free. In an awkward huff, I slid to my knees and rolled over to sit on my butt. My head spun, and I propped myself on my hands. Blinking away the graying edges in my vision, I realized I probably had a concussion.

Bonnie stood at Cassius's feet, holding what looked like the ugly rose-covered clock from the mantel in the rose room. I let my hand feel for a lump on my head, which it did, quickly. Thankfully my hand came back dry. The old bat hadn't cracked my head open.

Mrs. Shooster lay to my left in a heap of terrycloth and straggly hair. To my right, Cassius was absolutely still, eyes open, focused on the ceiling. For all the wailing and flailing he'd done fighting to get away from his mother he was stone now. A statue of an odd boy, naked as the day he was born, looking to the casual observer deader than a doornail. My poor boy was going to need decades of therapy.

"Damn, Templeton, you've got some serious timing," I said through panting breaths, eyes not quite open.

She shrugged, tossing the clock to the side in a clatter of metal and glass. "Yeah, it was intentional." I raised my nothing brows at her. "I waited at the top of the stairs until just the right moment. Figured we'd never in our lives have a chance to recreate this moment; wanted to make it memorable."

Though I wasn't exactly happy she'd allowed Mrs. Shooster to make her way down the stairs and kick me while I was down, her choice didn't surprise me. Bonnie had always been the type to make everything thrilling while equally being nonchalant about life in general. Also, deep down, I appreciated the theatrical intent and would remember the moment forever. However long that would be.

"Thanks," I said, my tone dry.

Cassius shifted beside me. "I didn't kill Andrew," he professed, still looking straight up at the ceiling lying flat on his back.

"I never thought you did."

Still as the dead, quiet and contemplating, Cassius took a few breaths before adding, "Mother killed Andrew. Pushed him down those stairs."

Bonnie and I looked at each other, then turned slowly to stare at him. I hadn't even believed there ever actually had been an Andrew, let alone a dead Andrew. How could it have been that not one, but *two* boys lived in that house and no one ever knew? I'd certainly never heard any stories, true or not, about a boy dying in the house. Not specifically anyway. Ghosts, vampires, ghouls, etcetera but never a real true dead boy.

An epiphany struck, bringing a rush of fear through

my body. "Cass," I cleared my throat, "Cassius... where's Andrew now?" I waited, heart thudding, anxious for the answer. Bonnie breathed loud enough to hear each breath come quicker than the last.

Cassius turned his head toward the shadowy corner where I'd found him huddled. He pointed into the darkness, creating half a dirt angel with his arm. "In the hole."

My gut sank. The moment swirled in on itself, pulling at my insides and stealing my air. "We have to go. We have to go now."

Bonnie backed up a step. "Guys, um, I'm ready to get the hell out of here if that's okay."

"Going. Going now. This is too.... Not happen.... Nope...." I rambled on as I forced my lanky body to its feet. I stood too quickly and regretted it immediately. My head swam, turning the world askew. I reached out for the wall, but it was still a foot or more away. I stumbled, vision darkening. Cassius grabbed hold of my arm. I opened my eyes and caught *sight* of his nakedness. "And you need some pants."

They say the color black is all colors and equally the lack of color, or light, depending on the context. In the context of Cassius Shooster's eyes, it was all of the above. In the right light, they were an oil slick, reflecting all colors in a prism. Standing in his basement, they were empty, absent of light, endlessly deep.

He blinked once. "Is she dead?"

I cleared the bullfrog from my throat. "I don't think so," I said under my breath, hardly paying the woman a second glance, sinking quickly in the blackness of his eyes. He needed out of that space, that dead space. I tried hard not to think of a dead body in the basement with us, just feet away. Cassius never going to school had been the tip of the murderous iceberg. Sheriff Floyd told Mom the Shoosters had a reason to keep Cassius locked away. He warned her Cassius was dangerous. Had the Shoosters convinced the sheriff Cassius had murdered someone? There was no way. Absolutely no way the sheriff of Flintlock knew about a murder and did nothing.

"Come on. We… have to call the police." The idea of a dead boy buried, or not so buried, ten feet from me turned my stomach into knots, but strangely not as much as the idea of involving Elroy Floyd in anything more to do with Cassius Shooster.

"No, no, no, no," he repeated over and over again. His hands flew to the sides of his head, whacking his face again and again.

"Stop," I said, grabbing his arms in a sad attempt to keep him from hitting himself. "Stop it." It was like a switch had been flipped and Cassius turned into a Rock-em Sock-em Robot, only his punches were aimed at himself.

"No. No. No," he wailed. "Bad boy. Bad boy."

"Cassius." I let out a frustrated grunt. "Stop it."

"Seriously, let's go," Bonnie said, this time from

inches away.

Mrs. Shooster groaned. I couldn't control the rate of my heart, and I thought I'd keel over right there. I wanted an adventure. I wanted to leave a mark. What I got was a murderer and a dead boy, both of whom I was trapped in a deep, dark place with. Cassius had to snap out of it. He could lose it later.

"We don't have time for a meltdown right now," I begged Cassius, kneading his arms.

"Bad boy, don't listen. Bad boy, not mine." His screams were unbearable. If I'd been a man, or She-Hulk, I'd have slung him over my shoulder and carried him out.

"Cass, come on, we have to go. Your mom is waking up." I pulled on him, but this time he didn't move. I may as well have been talking to myself. Mrs. Shooster started to move. Soon she'd get up. Soon she'd be a problem again. We didn't have time to wait him out. We didn't have time for anything but running up the stairs.

In the moment I'd considered hitting Mrs. Shooster over the head again, a hard slap landed across Cassius's face from a hand not his own. "Cut it out, Shooster."

He blinked once and looked at Bonnie. "It's not funny." He completed the *Fright Night* quote as though he'd been calmly watching the eighties vampire flick on a Sunday afternoon—which was the best time to watch it, by the way. Bonnie, in her mostly inappropriate abuse, had jerked Cassius from his horribly timed meltdown.

"You're welcome," Bonnie said with an impish grin.

"Now, can we blow this Popsicle stand before she wakes up?" She pointed at the woman in question, who was rousing from her knock on the head.

I didn't ask Cassius again. Instead, I wrapped my hand around his arm and pulled him along behind me. Again, he followed, but I wondered how long I had him before he broke down again. He'd been brainwashed by an abusive mother, turning him into her little zombie. I'd gladly take her place as his master until he could manage on his own. At least he'd be following someone who gave a shit.

"You...," Mrs. Shooster mumbled. "You can't... leave. They can't know...."

She talked on, but I made every attempt to ignore her. Whatever she had to say was either a lie or intentionally meant to hurt us. No, not us, Cassius. Neither of which I had any time for. Bonnie waited at the top of the stairs, moving her phone around to find a signal. I moved behind Cassius and shoved him up the stairs, doing my best not to stare at his bare butt. He followed along, but I worried he was now trapped in shock. I wasn't familiar enough with Asperger's to know the difference. I made a mental note to change that immediately. Just like any other relationship, I'd have to learn to manage his weaknesses in order to love his strengths. But first, there was the matter of murder.

"Guess who's a total nutbag?" Bonnie said to the person on the other end of the line and walked off into the house.

Cassius and I made the last few steps back into the light of day. Sort of. Though the light was still mostly gray tones, it was a far cry from the basement.

I caught sight of Bonnie, who had meandered toward the front door but hadn't opened it yet, and her expression brought to the forefront Cassius's nudity. Dust and dirt clung in random patches to his body. Blood was dried to the side of his face, likely from the busted nose he'd received the night before. The black eye his mother—or so I assumed—had given him was beginning to turn a murky shade of green. He looked more pathetic than sexy. I wanted to wash him up and take him for ice cream. From the look on Bonnie's face, she had nothing of the sort in mind.

"Where can I find your clothes?" I asked Cassius, who still hadn't really acknowledged anyone, except to complete the quote, which I thought might have been a compulsion over coherency.

"Peek-a-boo," an eerily sweet voice called from the basement door behind us.

I jumped, and Bonnie cursed, but Cassius didn't budge. I spun around to meet the hazy glare of Mrs. Shooster. She lay on her stomach in the doorway, legs laying against the stairs as if she'd crawled up from the depths of hell.

"What is this, a bad horror movie?" I groaned and clenched my hands into fists at the sides of my head. "Shouldn't you be injured or something?"

Cassius kept his back to her, eyes unfocused, face tense.

He needed something to cover his junk so we could get the hell out of that house.

"Cass, honey, you hurt Mama. My legs are hurt real bad. I need you to help me. Come on, honey, come help Mama." Her voice brought bile up my throat. Shrill, filled with ill intent. Blood oozed from her head and down the side of her face.

"Too late, *Mama*, called the cops. You're history." Bonnie stepped beside me and stood with her feet spread and her hands on her hips like some kind of superhero.

She jeered. "That murdering retard isn't going anywhere but prison. I've done him a favor, I have. Kept him from that *place*." Her words slurred together as she clung to the doorjamb trying to get up.

"No." Cassius shook his head, clenching his fists, making the knuckles white.

"No," Mrs. Shooster mocked in a baby voice. "No? No?" She laughed. "No, Mama. Don't." Her laughter cut through the room and everyone winced. "Pathetic."

"Shut up," Cassius said.

"Nobody gives a shit what you have to say," I said to Mrs. Shooster.

"Who cares about you, bitch?" she hissed at me.

"Shut up," Cassius yelled, shooting saliva from his lips.

"Or what?" she yelled back through her laughter. "Should've been you." Her head lolled side to side and her eyes rolled around. "He should've been you." She appeared to be losing steam as she slowed her cadence to a near whisper. "I pushed *you*."

Drunk mother, hidden child, dead boy, murder? Sooner rather than later, I was going to need to draw up a diagram to make sense of it all. Until then, there was still a naked guy at my back seething with anger.

"You killed him," Cassius screamed, spun on his heel, and charged his mother. He dropped to his knees, wrapped his hand around his mother's thick face and squeezed her cheeks, puckering her lips, until she turned purple. "Andrew was mine. He was all I had, and you took him from me. You killed my brother."

Mrs. Shooster struggled out inaudible words through Cassius's strong hand. A part of me wanted to let him reap vengeance for his brother and allow him to continue his viciousness. But the reasonable part of me stood its ground and realized they really would lock him away forever if he killed his mother in front of two witnesses. I thought twice about leaving the room to eliminate a witness, but in the end decided to do what I could to stop him.

"Cass," I said softly. "Hey, just let her go." He ignored me, trapped in his own head. "She'll get hers." I stepped close to him. "Don't leave me."

He loosened his grip, and Mrs. Shooster's face instantly began to return to normal. He hadn't been choking her so much as squeezing her face between his hands like a massive pimple.

"She lied."

"I know."

"You don't," he screamed. "You don't know. She killed him and locked me away for it. I lost my entire life because of her. Because I wasn't perfect. Because I wasn't Andrew, he died and I didn't."

"I know," I agreed. "But now you have me," I said, and instantly regretted it. It sounded so stupid once it came out. So cliché. "It's like a movie, right?" I let out a nervous laugh. "All of this." But it wasn't. It was his life. "You and… me…." I really didn't know what to say or do in that moment. Cassius ignored me, glaring at his mother with unadulterated loathing.

Panic-induced sweat fell down the center of my back. Cassius had loosened his grip but hadn't released her face. She was conscious, but barely. Unable to form words, I wondered how much was due to her level of intoxication, the conk on the head, or the pressure of her surviving son's grip on her jaw.

He had to let her loose. We had to get help. Murderer or not, she was injured, drunk, and now she couldn't breathe. She could easily die too and then where would we be? There was no way in hell Elroy Floyd was going to do anything in favor of Cassius. There would be no self-defense. No reasons. No excuses. And without Mrs. Shooster there to say otherwise, as far as anyone but Cassius knew, he had also killed his brother.

"Cass," I laid my hand flat against his back. "You have

to let her go."

"No," he growled through his teeth. His jaw tight, the muscles at his temple bulged.

"You're going to kill her," I pleaded and pulled on his shoulder. "Cassius, stop," I cried, yanking him with all my body weight. He flung his arm, shoving me off of him and almost off my feet.

My hands flexed at my sides, stomach turning in my gut, and I knew I had no time and no choice. My strength was no match for Bonnie's, though she was almost a foot shorter than me, but I was out of options and desperate to stop the situation.

Mrs. Shooster wasn't talking anymore. Her eyes were closed, and she was mostly limp, her head propped in Cassius's grip. "I'm really, really sorry."

The thwack of my open hand against his skull echoed together in harmony with the bang of the door creating a theatrical effect worthy of any slapstick comedy. Bonnie's hands flew to her mouth. She'd heard more than she saw and assumed the sound was my wimpy slap colliding with his head. Cassius released his mother, whose head dropped to the floor with a thud. Less than a second later, men began shouting as they filed into the house. Cassius had rocked on his heels but hadn't gone down under the weight of my smack.

"Look out," I screamed and tackled Cassius to the floor. *And the Oscar goes to…*

His naked body fell with a slap against the hardwood,

and I landed on top of him. Again. Mrs. Shooster came to life and grumbled something from the basement doorway. Bonnie took to action, shoving her back in and slamming the door dramatically. *Best supporting actress goes to...*

She ran toward the front of the house to meet the men. "She's in there. She's in there. She tried to kill us." Bonnie's voice cracked, and crocodile tears fell down her round cheeks.

Sheriff's officers rushed in, some with guns, some without, but no Sheriff Floyd. Bonnie continued to play the damsel in distress as the officers moved past her and to me. They stopped, one by one, nearly piling on top of each other. My cheeks flushed red at the expression on their faces when they realized the boy I was laying on top of was naked.

Bonnie followed behind them. "She's an awful woman," she said in explanation. "She kept this boy chained up, naked in the basement." When the officers ignored Bonnie to focus on the baby giraffes tangled up on the floor, she grabbed one by the arm. "No, in the basement. His mother. She's a monster."

I stammered, mouth refusing to form words I didn't really have anyway. "I-I-I had to protect him from her." It was a poor excuse to be on top of a naked boy and their expressions proved it.

I scrambled to my feet, leaving Cassius exposed, lying flat on his back. He had completely shut down, lost, again, somewhere in his own head.

Cassius refused to look at me, at anyone, just stared at the ceiling, whispering something under his breath. The partner of Officer "bun head" Phillips took off his jacket and used it to cover Cassius while another pulled him up by his arm like he weighed nothing.

Someone had found the hidden basement door and popped it open. Mrs. Shooster grumbled, sprawled across the few steps from the top. An officer pulled me by my good arm—by sheer luck—away from the basement door, depositing me at the foot of the stairs with Cassius and Bonnie.

Cassius huddled against the banister, hands over his ears. I held the police jacket sleeves around his waist with one hand and felt the knot on my head with the other. Mrs. Shooster *oofed* and *guffawed* as officers attempted to drag her from the stairwell.

Officer Phillips's partner, a handsome young blond with a butch cut, rushed us, and wrapped his meaty hand around Bonnie's arm. "Are you okay?" he asked Bonnie. And only Bonnie.

She nodded, her blonde curls bouncing around her face. "I'm fine." Her eyebrows raised. "What a nut," Bonnie said and stuck her thumb in the direction of the basement.

He chuckled. Nervously. "Yeah, right." He ran a thick paw over the back of his neck. "I'm glad you called—"

"Mm," Bonnie cleared her throat. "Not right now," she hissed through a gritted smile.

Wrinkles formed at the center of my brows. Something was afoot in Flintlock. Something *else*.

"Um, hi, best friend here. Who the hell is this?" I jammed my open hand in his direction, clutching the sleeves of the jacket with the other, and completely ignoring the dire situation that surrounded us.

"*He* is Heego," Bonnie answered, and the man cleared his throat. "*Officer* Heego," she added, her tone in the realm of condescending.

"Thanks," he retorted sarcastically.

I stared at them. Two hazel eyes, burrowing into their sneaky little souls. Nearby, officers wrangled Mrs. Shooster. She hollered and wailed and made a scene, but it was mostly incoherent drivel. They had her out of the basement now and were making their way to the front of the house. Against everything I'd fought a whole week for, I ignored the manhandling of Mother Shooster.

Bonnie succumbed to my glare. "We have a thing." She looked at him, and he smiled. "It's a thing," she said again and brushed it off, but I knew there was more. She'd hidden an entire man from me. Six years of bestfriendship and she was lying to me. In her defense, I'd been hiding my entire lifespan from her.

"Bon?" The one word said everything I'd been thinking. It may have also been the tied-up expression on my face.

"What? I'm an adult. I can date who I choose"

"He's a cop," I said as though he wasn't standing six

inches from me.

A devilish grin tugged at one side of her mouth. "Yeah, he is."

"Gross. Where's the sheriff?" I asked *Officer Heego*, intentionally changing the subject.

"He's—"

"Right here," said the jerk in question, rolling onto the scene like he was John Wayne. Elroy Floyd ruffled his mustache between his lip and nose. "What'd you go and do now, girl?" He pointed at Cassius, purposefully calling me girl just to piss me off. "And why's that boy in his birthday suit?" He gripped the butt of his pistol in its holster. Likely a substitute for something he wished was similar in size. "Will someone please tell me what's going on here?" he demanded.

Officer Heego stepped forward, mimicking the sheriff's position. "Sir—" His radio crackled, interrupting him before he could finish.

"He killed my boy," Mother Shooster, loose from the grip of the officers, charged us. Cassius flinched, pulling against my grip on the sleeves of his only clothing in an attempt to escape his mother. "That retard killed my boy." In less than three steps she was under their control again. Sort of. The wibbly-wobbly, drunk-and-sloppy, flippy-floppy scene looked more like two grown men trying to put a shoe on a fish. "My Andy," she screamed over and over again. "He killed my boy."

"She's a damn liar," I screamed back, pointer finger

aimed at her. "She tried to kill us." Mrs. Shooster struggled against the officers; rage lit her eyes. "*She* admitted to killing Andrew." Everyone stopped. Silence spread through the chaos frozen in motion as all eyes fell on me. "He's buried in the basement," I exclaimed, accentuating every word for effect.

No one said anything for a full minute. I know that seems like a long time, and it was, but it's no exaggeration. Even wildly drunk, Mrs. Shooster was silent. She'd been outed. She couldn't hide behind her living son anymore. Her lie was over. There was no way Sheriff Floyd could sweep murder under the rug. Not when there were witnesses.

"Now, you listen here, girl," Sherriff Floyd broke the silence. "We won't have any of that trash talking, you hear me? This fine lady has been through the wringer with this boy, and she's just about lost it." He called Cassius boy in the same tone he called me girl. "We all know there is no boy buried in that basement." He scoffed. "Cassius had no brother."

"Damn it, Elroy, you didn't even know *he* existed until last week. How the hell do you know there was no brother?" We all talked about Cassius as though he wasn't huddled behind me, naked, wrapped in a rayon loincloth. It was rude, but he made zero attempt to take part in the conversation. I was fine acting as his mouthpiece. Someone needed to.

The sheriff rocked back on his heels and sucked his teeth.

"I never did see two boys over here."

"You never did see *one* either." He was clearly up to something. No officer of the law refutes allegations of murder that flippantly. Sheriff Elroy Floyd knew way more than he was letting on. "What's the game here, Sheriff?" Flintlock was too small of a shithole to be harboring such dark secrets. Or maybe I'd been stuffed in my own head too far too long to have noticed.

"What exactly are you accusing me of here, girl?"

Bonnie, Heego, Mrs. Shooster, and five of Flintlock's finest watched our interaction in silence. Cassius hummed, a constant single-pitch tone that almost melded into the noise of ten people breathing at once.

"First of all," I started, folding my arms loosely across my chest. "Stop calling me girl. You know my name and you're intentionally trying to put me beneath you. It won't work. I've got bigger things to worry about than you and that mustache. Second, that woman had two sons." I held up fingers to match. "One died. She killed him. Blamed Cassius his whole life. Kept him locked in this house and threatened him with imprisonment should he ever leave. She became a drunk, obviously, because hello, murderer. And now we're here. The boy's name is Andrew, and he's buried in that basement. The basement this boy, Cassius, had been locked in naked as punishment for defending himself against that meathead Morgan. As I stand here and say this, I know you already know every word I'm about to say before I say it, because you've known all along."

The words just spilled out. It wasn't even something I'd thought on more than to form the letters with my mouth. Detective work by the seat of my pants. "You knew about Cassius, his mother, and the dead boy in the basement." Mic drop.

He didn't breathe. My own heart beat four or five times before he finally came to life again. "You just stop right there. No need for hysterics. There is nothing tying me to this house or this family. Your allegations will get you into trouble, missy."

"Not yet, but there will be," I promised, as though I could come through on it. His incarceration would be based solely on what his fellow officers chose to do about it. "Check the basement, Sheriff. If you're so sure. Go take a peek."

"I will do no such thing." He ruffled his shaggy mustache.

"Okay," Bonnie said, grinning until her cheeks peaked beneath her eyes. "Channel Four News is always interested in cases involving corrupt government officials. I'm sure we can get them to front an excavation of the basement. Until then, surely Mrs. Shooster will be brought up on some kind of charges for that child abuse and, what, going on eighteen years of neglect?" She looked at Cassius; it was the first time anyone had addressed him directly. "Hey, Cass, you've *never* left this house, right?" He didn't respond, stopped humming and looked at her. "Say, how old was Andrew when you killed him, Mrs. Shooster?"

"I was four years old. Andrew was four years old," Cassius spoke before his mother could respond. He hadn't moved, not even his hands from his ears.

Mrs. Shooster sneered at her son. "Shut up. You're an abomination. A mistake. They should have thrown you in the garbage," she hissed.

If someone had been filming me, a lightbulb literally would have popped on above my head. "Twins," I exclaimed to mostly myself, letting my epiphany take over. "No wonder you…." I stopped and stared at Cassius in awe. "She thought he was you." Tears stung the edges of my eyes. I couldn't hold them in. The drunken ramblings of a lunatic had been 100 percent true. His own mother tried to kill him.

Mrs. Shooster's wranglers looked at her, disgust passing over their faces. She didn't say a word, just stared a hole into Cassius. I stepped in front of him, blocking him with my body.

I looked Officer Heego in the eyes. "Check the basement."

He swallowed, glanced at Bonnie, and nodded once before moving away from the staircase. Floyd put his hand up to stop him.

"Now, hold on, we're not going to go snooping around this woman's house looking for ghosts. We have no warrant."

"Reasonable grounds," Heego said, and the sheriff grumbled. "Sir, I think we should listen to these girls.

They've been in the basement. If there's nothing there—"

"If there's nothing there, then we've torn up a family's home for nothing. For a bunch of lying kids who can't handle a little punishment."

Hackles up, I stepped toward him, fully prepared to go to prison.

"That's a black eye; that's not punishment," Heego argued, stopping me from doing something stupid. "I became a cop for a reason, and that reason was this." He waved his hand toward the sheriff. "Someone help me," he said, still looking at Elroy. "We won't dig. Just look." It seemed Officer Heego was the most rational of the bunch. Perhaps Bonnie had chosen wisely after all.

Sheriff Floyd held firm, refusing to move and let him pass, but Heego took the initiative, stepped around the stout sheriff, and made his way to the basement. A moment later, a few more men, those who I was sure had grown sick of the sheriff's shit, and Officer Phillips left the side of their imperial leader to join the rebels in the basement.

Mother Shooster's eyes were saucers, mouth hanging to her knees. Drunk or not, she knew the jig was up and there was little to be done about it. For the first time since I'd seen her snoring in front of *The Maury Show* she was stone silent.

Down in the cellar, the officers made little noise as they went to work searching the dark space. Muffled voices and flickers of flashlight beams flittered out the doorway and danced on the walls. We, the three of us, waited at the foot of the stairs on the first floor. Sheriff Floyd stood watch over the basement door. His face remained stoic as he stood there awaiting his fate. He didn't so much as glance in the direction of Mrs. Shooster.

I had zero proof aside from the excited utterance of the naked dirty guy covering his ears in fear behind me there was, in fact, a body in the basement. And, should there be a boy in the basement, it would only prove there really was an Andrew. It would then depend on the detective work applied to prove who the killer really was. But I didn't need all that. I knew, knew it in my gut, the crazy drunk lady had killed her son in cold blood. Proving that was going to be the difficult part.

Scuffling brought all eyes to the basement door. "We got it," someone called up. "We got a body."

My stomach plummeted. Andrew. The dead boy in the basement was real. All the stories about the spook house were real. My mind spun with the thought there had been a coffin down in that basement all along.

A dozen chest-heaving breaths later, Heego emerged from the cellar, a small bundle of fabric and bones laid over his beefy arms. He'd found him. Down there in the dark. In the hole.

The legal ramifications of what Heego had done wouldn't sink in until later. In that cluster of breaths, I, Prudence Penderhaus, had officially uncovered a deep, dark secret that someone had gone through a lot of trouble to keep hidden. My life, the lives of the people of Flintlock, would never again be the same.

The scene was right out of a horror movie. The noises around me dimmed until it was hardly focused on Officer Heego. A dark gray tunnel surrounded my vision, focusing only on the child he held. His small body, mostly murky brown tones, was wrapped in an equally colored blanket. A dried rose clung to the blanket, daring to come free and fall to the floor.

"It's a little boy," Heego said, voice high and shaking, sheer adrenaline guiding him. His words came to me in slow motion. "Someone call the state police," he shouted, but it hardly made a sound in my ears.

The thrumming of my own heartbeat took precedence over all else. Sheriff Floyd backed away from the crowd. He refused to look at the body, or Cassius, or me. Feigning disinterest, he leaned against the wall near the front door. Mrs. Shooster looked on in drunken awe. I was unsure if she was grasping the situation fully or not. Someone had just brought the remains of her dead son up from her basement; there was bound to be some sort of reaction. Eventually.

"My baby boy!" *And there it is.* "It's my Andrew. Don't touch my boy." Her theatrics were enough to draw attention away from the dead boy and toward her.

He'd been wrapped in a blanket and intentionally placed in the basement. Someone, an adult, had done that. Cassius Shooster had been her scapegoat, but why not just call it an accident? Why not have a proper funeral? Because there was a witness.

Hide the body, hide the boy. The living boy. The only witness to your crime. Why not kill him too? Clean and easy—that felt gross even thinking about—no one would ever know. Mr. Shooster may have had a hand in keeping his living son alive. Teaching him, helping to keep him somewhat human. And safe from his wicked mother.

Oh, Mrs. Shooster, you sinister bitch. Judging by his expression, Heego realized this too. Even Sheriff Floyd couldn't hide the obvious from his face as Heego laid the remains on the floor.

Sheriff Floyd shook his head, but he didn't let on why. It could very well have been Heego's obvious evidence tampering. Or, it could have been his own conscience coming to bite him in the ass.

Mrs. Shooster wailed about her son, throwing herself to the floor, putting on a performance as if she were only just finding out about the dead boy in her basement. The small heap of decaying human lay there as blinding proof Sheriff Floyd had been full of shit. Cassius hadn't been the trouble; he hadn't been the dangerous one. Something was rotten in the town of Flintlock.

Too lost to snap and too naked for a hood, Cassius pressed his face against my shoulder away from the scene; humming his constant tune. His body shook, breaths came in sharp, ragged bursts. Shock. Panic was setting in. I needed to get him out of there.

I wrapped my arm around him, careful to hold his jacket-pants in place. I couldn't fathom for an instant what state his mind was in. There were too many variables surrounding him to make assumptions. That bitch had taken away his childhood to cover up her selfish homicide.

Cassius trembled, knees knocking, hardly able to stand. Mother Shooster sobbed, screeching her lies, still on the floor where the officers let her stay—she clearly wasn't getting up again. A few officers, the ones that didn't follow Heego into the basement, seemed affected by her screams. As though a toddler could have truly murdered and hidden his own brother.

"You'll see," she slurred, "you'll all see. He's the deviant. He's the killer. It's in his brain."

His knees buckled. I couldn't hold him. We turned, more me than him, and I did my best to aim his butt at the third step from the bottom. Mother Shooster's screeching unraveled my last nerve. I kissed Cassius on the cheek. "Be right back."

Bonnie took over sleeve holding, and I stomped toward Mrs. Shooster, clearing the distance in a few long strides. The two cops had given her some space to flail, which granted me enough room to get close to her.

"You're a cold, heartless bitch, and I hope you rot." She looked up at me and smiled. Through all those tears and screams, she smiled at me. A sickening twist of her lip proved her apathy.

A sociopath if I'd ever seen one. I hadn't really

seen one, to my knowledge, but movies depicted them beautifully, and I was going with that.

She glared, the corners of her mouth curled. A rage, fiery and unyielding, filled my soul. I wished I'd killed her. I wished she had died at the foot of the stairs, an ironic end to the hell beast.

Mrs. Shooster leaned on her heels, swaying. "He's going away forever, little girl," she whispered, still pretending to cry for anyone still listening to her. "Retard's going where he belongs."

Tweedle Dee and Tweedle Dum moved in on us, I only had a second. I let a hard slap loose, stinging my palm on her face. The other officers who had been milling around stopped and watched me. My violence was unexpected, and the wranglers stopped in shock. One slap wasn't enough to quench my vengeance, and another rang through my hand with a bite and sent Mrs. Shooster to her hands and knees before the officers could react. My knuckles stung, and I realized I hadn't slapped the woman; I'd decked her. She looked up at me, unreserved disgust scratched across her face. I felt then that we were on the same page of hatred and if allowed we'd fight it out to the death.

An officer wrapped his arm around my waist, dragging me back to the stairs. Four spindly limbs flailed through the air, finding no purchase.

"Get up," I yelled at her. "Get up so I can hit you again. Don't act like you don't deserve it. You murdered your son. You locked your living son away in this prison you call home to cover it up." The sheriff cleared his throat as if to interject. "And you"—I pointed an accusatory finger at him—"you shut the hell up. This woman should be in handcuffs, not flailing around on the ground crying about her long-dead son." No one else attempted to stop me or made a move in any way. Sheriff Floyd was quickly losing cohorts as he stood there defending his actions.

"Now, hold on there, girl. You're no officer of the law, and you will not be telling me how to do my job."

The officer who'd pulled me away from Mrs. Shooster had me seat-belted against his body.

"What were you, a deputy at the time? How long have you been sheriff? Ten, fifteen years?" He'd gone to high school with my parents; he couldn't have been more than midforties. I'd been too young to remember who held the job before him, but I'd bet my life he wasn't sheriff in his first few years on the job.

"I don't see how this is—"

"Establishing a timeline." Thank you, *Law and Order*. "Will you please?" I grumbled at Officer Seatbelt, pushing his arm off me. He relented quickly, freeing me to pace in true ADA Cabot fashion. "How long did you think you could cover it up? How long before someone noticed there was a *teenage* boy living in this house who no one had previously known existed? Did you really think you could keep him enslaved here forever?" I asked Mrs. Shooster. Before she could answer, I redirected my questions to the sheriff. "You knew he was here," I accused. "You made sure no one else suspected a thing. Damn, Sheriff, you really are dumber than you look."

Officer Heego stifled a laugh along with a few other officers. The body of a dead boy on the ground proved they had no room to chortle over stupid decisions, but I ignored that fact and focused on the life and death issue.

"The only thing I don't know yet is why. What role did you play in this child's murder, Sheriff Floyd?"

No one spoke. All eyes darted between me and the sheriff. Any other crime scene would have been covered in police and forensic people, but not in Flintlock. Where the sheriff's office covered two counties and consisted of a little over a dozen officers, there wasn't much room for anything other than hypocrisy and nonchalance. Nor was there room for advancement. Elroy Floyd had been sheriff for the better part of my memory, but I knew the sheriff before him had been in office when my parents were my age before he finally croaked and made room for Elroy. Surely one of the eager officers standing around gawking had the sense in him to step up and take control of the situation. I waited for someone, anyone with a badge, to back me up.

"State police," a voice bellowed from the front door.

"In here," Heego called back, standing guard over the mostly decomposed little boy.

A gaggle of officers filed in one at a time, each mouth

gaping at the situation. Drunk woman on the floor. Naked guy crying. Dead boy rotting. And me, standing there asking questions like I knew what the hell I was doing.

"I'm going to need everyone to clear out of here," said a guy who seemed to be in charge. "What are all you people doing in here?" Small town law. "Did you move this body?" he asked. Disappointed suspicion danced over his face as his shoulders slumped at the sight of tampered evidence.

"Officer," I said, my stomach flipping over into knots. "This woman killed that little boy." I pointed to the bundle. "Then locked this boy, Cassius, up in this house his entire life, forcing him to believe he'd killed his twin brother." The officer looked at me, blinking thick black lashes twice in a row, and I suddenly felt like I was retelling the events of primetime television. "And our lovely sheriff helped her cover it all up. I think." I smiled and folded my arms across my chest. I couldn't prove the sheriff had any involvement in it all, but any movie buff worth her salt knew when law enforcement refused to act, they were not the good guys. "Oh, and there's a dad too, but he won't be home from work until 5:00 p.m."

His officers went to work around him, shuffling Flintlock badges out of the house. "Who are you?" he asked me.

"I'm Prudence Penderhaus. I live down the street." His dark brow raised, questioning. "I'm the one who found the boy." I stopped myself. I'd been calling him a boy when in reality he was more of a man. "I found Cassius here in this house," I rephrased, "and set into motion all of this."

He took a moment to consider what I'd said. Nodding, he said, "Ma'am, Sergeant San Dimas." He shook my hand. "I'm going to need a statement from you." He pointed at me. "No one leave the property," his voice called out over the top of murmured discussions.

Cassius sat in silence, still focusing on nothing. He'd stopped humming. "Sir," I said sweetly. "Can we wait at my house?" I wanted nothing more than to physically witness Mother Shooster in handcuffs, but Cassius outweighed my need for smug victory. "It's only a few doors down. He really needs a break from this. And pants." Sergeant San Dimas sized me up, skeptical of my intentions. "We'll take Officer Heego with us."

Eyeing our motley crew, he thought on the idea. "Fine. But don't leave the house. I'll be down shortly to talk with you. And get him some pants."

The four of us wasted no time skirting out of the house. I wanted to stay behind and make sure Mrs. Shooster ended up in the back of a squad car. Someone had to. The standing clock that stood near the door read half past three. It felt like only minutes before I had been scaling the Shooster's porch. Mr. Shooster would be home soon. Mr. Shooster. There was no way he didn't know a thing about his dead son in the basement. I found it hard to believe the man spent nearly fourteen years of his life never asking,

"Dear, where is that little scamp, Andrew?" No, he knew. But how much of his participation was to save his son? Not from his mother, but from incarceration.

"Hey," I said to the sergeant. "Just a warning. That woman has everyone fooled. She's a sociopath and murderer," I said dramatically.

"Miss, go home and get that boy calmed down. We've got a lot of ground to cover to make sense of all of this. I promise you, whatever has been going on here"—he used his hands for emphasis—"stops now."

I stepped in closer, our eyes nearly meeting in height. "Sir, please don't take this the wrong way, but this boy means a lot to me, and if that woman spends another day in this house, I promise you I won't stop until every single one of them is dead or in jail." I had no clue what the hell I was talking about, of course, and I was sure to end up in handcuffs again, but really did mean it. Definitely watched way too many movies, but it was looking to pay off.

The sergeant laughed, crinkling his eyes at the corners, and patted my shoulder, bypassing my threat to kill things. "I don't doubt that for a second. Now go home," he said, his tone somber.

Mrs. Shooster whined and grunted against the state officers as they tried to put her in cuffs. The fish was getting her sock. I stood for a moment and soaked in the victory. Sheriff Floyd had attempted to slink to the kitchen and out of sight, but the valiant sergeant caught him at the last minute. Mommy Dearest in cuffs, the sheriff under scrutiny, I was beginning to like Sergeant San Dimas. Even if he brought out in me a rash of movie quotes, I didn't think I could stifle.

Bonnie had Cassius out the gate and on the sidewalk by the time I finally stepped out the front door. Someone had begun winding yellow police tape around the property, and police cars lined the street. Every neighbor home at the time was out on their lawn watching the show. Flintlock didn't have a local news media, but soon they would come from cities and towns all around the state for a glimpse of what would surely be called the Flintlock Bloodbath or something equally tantalizing and absurd.

I caught up with my people, who'd made it to the corner of Mr. Horowitz's picket fence, and I took Cassius's left hand. Heego followed, blocking his bare tush, and Bonnie held Cassius's right arm, standing half his height, still hanging on to his jacket-pants. Together we did the best we could to block the naked spectacle from the prying eyes of our nosy neighbors.

All those eyes that had never once glanced up long enough to notice a boy in a window looked on with ignorant judgment. I fought the urge to scream at them all. Their stares were shallow, and in the end, most of them would either take pity on the retarded boy whose mother went nuts or deep down believe he really did murder his brother. In my heart, I knew Cassius Shooster would never really be accepted in Flintlock. But anything had to be better than living in a house with your dead brother under your feet.

11

MOM WASN'T HOME, AND FOR THAT I WAS GRATEFUL. SHE would have made everything worse with her recent blossoming of moxie and abrupt desire to keep me from Cassius. We needed time to gather the facts and get our heads together. Not that one of us had done anything punitively illegal, but the last thing I wanted was Cassius in the slammer, or worse, institutionalized, and the Shoosters out free because we couldn't get our shit together. That just wouldn't work for me. Not one bit.

We stood in the entryway for a moment, breathing in unison, processing what had just happened. Cassius wasn't the only one who would be needing therapy. In the matter of a week, I'd learned I was dying—possibly—uncovered a secret boy, discovered my delinquent best friend was dating a cop, and opened a can of murder worms onto the town of Flintlock. And I punched someone. Twice. Two people. I was becoming some kind of badass.

I looked at my friends. A new group of rabble-rousers. The Scooby gang. Unmasking the villains in the final scene. Cassius, face slack, emotions trapped in the steel vault of his mind. Bonnie, least affected outwardly, but I knew my girl, she felt it. Where it counted, she felt it. Heego, his face was new to me, but it was still clear the cogs and wheels churning in his head as he put the pieces together. Whatever we were, whatever we'd evolve into, for one day, we were heroes. My only worry, how much of the story had yet to be told? Instinct promised there was more to come. Lots more.

"Get him to the bathroom and in a warm shower," I instructed Bonnie, snapping everyone out of their thoughts. "I'll see if I can find some of my dad's old clothes around here." Officer Heego stood in the entryway, waiting for instructions. "You... just wait." He nodded, resting his hands on his utility belt.

"You might want to photograph his wounds before he cleans up." This from the man who moved a corpse. "Just in case." He was clearly trying to cover his ass after his major blunder.

"Is that something you should be doing as the cop here?" The last thing I wanted was to take photos of a naked Cassius.

He looked back over his shoulder toward the bathroom. "I'm not sure I'm the right man for the job."

Yeah, tell me about it. "Look, you're the only law enforcement here. He is naked, cold, scared, and filthy. He needs a shower and some clothes. We can't wait around for someone to come down here." I placed a hand on each shoulder. "It's just pictures. Besides, the most important evidence was the body…" I pressed my lips together and raised my brows.

Thankfully, he got the message without me having to go any further. "Fine."

"Thank you. I'm going to get him something to wear."

In the back of my parents' walk-in closet, I found a stash of Dad's stuff, still hanging where he'd left it. It'd been five years since his death, and Mom hadn't gotten rid of any of it. I was glad she hadn't but worried she was hanging on to it for all the wrong reasons.

The shower was running when I came back downstairs, and steam billowed from the open door. Bonnie and Heego stood in the hallway between the bathroom and living room, leaving Cassius alone in the bathroom. The innocent loser inside me screamed to stop before I walked right into the room. I'd already seen everything he had to offer, what was another glimpse?

"Hey, I brought you some clothes," I said in the seconds before I breached the open door.

Cassius stood facing the shower, his backside out for the world to see. The pale skin covering his lean body was marred by patches of dirt and raw, bloody scrapes. I'd only known Cassius for inside of a week, but in that week,

I'd uncovered a soul deeper and more stunning than any I'd met in my albeit short life. My heart hurt for him. I wanted nothing more than to reach out and hold him. Cuddle him until he'd forgotten all about the witch he called mother. I didn't honestly know what love was like or how long something like that should take to develop, but I knew if it were any other naked boy standing there in my bathroom, I'd have blushed red and thrown pants in his direction while I raced past the open door.

"I…," He started, but trailed off for a moment, chewing on his words again. "I'm having a really hard time right now." His voice was fast and warbled.

I pushed air through pursed lips, hiding tears from my voice. "You've been through a lot. But it's almost over. You can let go now." I didn't know why I'd said that, but it sounded good. "You never have to go back to that house again."

"But that's my house."

I thought, just a second, I heard the sound of my heart breaking. "Not anymore, honey." I didn't know that to be true but couldn't see how he'd ever want it in the first place. Taking a step forward, I put my hand on his back. He jumped but didn't shy away from it. "This isn't going to be easy, and I won't lie to you and tell you otherwise. But I will tell you I'll be here with you through it all. I started it, and I'll see it through. I promise." Secretly, I told the mass in my arm to chill the hell out long enough for me to make good on that.

"Prudence," he said quietly.

"Yeah?"

"Do you own *The Breakfast Club*?" He didn't turn to look at me. "The wicked woman I called mother destroyed it before my very eyes when she threw my things away last night."

I laughed and pushed back the rage that billowed up from the depths of me. The question seemed out of place for the situation but absolutely perfect for Cassius Shooster. "Yes, I do, and we can watch it. But first I want you to wash those scrapes off before they get infected."

I felt like a mother and realized that regardless of the role I took on in his life, I would need to take on some responsibility for him. At least at first. His heart was pure, and his head was smart; I had no doubt he would be just fine eventually. He'd need years of therapy, but then again, so would I. Dead things will do that to you.

Stepping into the shower, the water hit his raw skin. He yelped in pain, and I winced right along with him. I moved quickly to the shower to turn down the heat for him. Before I got there, he gripped the dial and turned the water to cool. It was a simple thing, but for whatever reason, in my head, I hadn't assumed he could manage common sense things like that. It was stupid to think that way. His parents, well, his father, hadn't locked him in a dungeon his whole life. He'd taught him how to speak, how to add, how to use the bathroom and his DVD player. It was becoming apparent he was capable of more than

I'd given him credit for, and I should've listened to my pretty doctor.

"You got this?" He didn't respond. "Cass," I said, grabbing his attention, "do you need anything else?"

He shook his head but didn't say anything. I turned to leave the room.

"Prudence," he called to me before I passed through the doorway.

"Yeah?" I said over my shoulder.

He was quiet until I thought he'd changed his mind. "Thank you."

I smiled. "You're welcome."

"Prudence," he said again, just as I was outside the door.

"Yes?"

"I'm not a retard."

"I know that."

"I know what to do with you... also."

I blushed. He was referring to the statement Mommy Dearest had made about his inability to be a man or understand women. Luckily for him, I wasn't anything like most women. Glad the curtain was closed, I smiled and my cheeks flushed red to my ears, surely visible even from behind.

"We have all the time in the world to figure that out," I lied. "Wash up. I'll get the movie going. Popcorn?" It wasn't really a popcorn and movie sort of day, but if it made him happy, I saw no reason it couldn't be.

"Yes, please."

"You got it." I left the room feeling as though I were walking across a bank of billowy clouds. When I'd met Cassius, I never imagined our lives would become so intertwined. Never did I think for a second, I'd be blushing over him. Even the image of his brother's corpse was shaded in rose tint in my mind. There was also a good chance my head wound played a role in the ethereal sensation.

The popcorn popped in the microwave as Bonnie, Heego, and I discussed the events of the day.

"How are you holding up?" Heego asked in his cop-type way.

"I'm sure I'll need therapy, but for now, I'm okay. Cassius is going to need a lot of support."

"Certainly. I could only imagine," Heego said.

"I don't think any of us could."

"The entire thing is just too weird for Flintlock. Too weird. How did no one know there was a set of twins in that house?" Bonnie's statement held truth that only Flintlockians—Flintlockans,   whatever—we   could understand.

"I've lived in this house my entire life and never once suspected a thing. I've never even seen Mrs. Shooster in all my seventeen years." My four-year-old self may have, but certainly it wasn't in my memory bank.

"How could a mother kill her own son?" Bonnie asked.

"She thought it was Cassius."

Heego didn't seem satisfied with my theory. "Why just the one?"

"He was the abomination. Couldn't handle having a kid on the spectrum, I guess. And she's also a flipping nutbag. I want to know why, too, but I don't think I ever will. She can't even admit to herself what she did. Instead, she just became a raging alcoholic."

"Spectrum? Like Autism?" I nodded at the officer. "Wow, and she locked him up in that basement with the remains of his brother? What a sick bitch."

"Yeah, real newsworthy. How did no one smell a dead body in the basement for over a decade?" Bonnie asked, and reminded me of the sickeningly sweet putrid smell I'd caught when I first entered the basement.

"The body was covered in roses," Heego chimed in. "Piles of them. I was right on top of it and had no idea that there was a dead body underneath. There were bushels of them dead all around the area. She had to have been using them to mask the smell for years."

I hadn't been smelling a body. I'd been smelling years of decaying matter engrained into the porous stone—flesh and flower alike. Then it clicked. Roses. Just like the living room. "That. Sadistic. Bitch." They looked at me. "I couldn't figure out why, but now I've got it. She created a hatred of roses in Cassius by forcing him into the basement with the rose-covered body of his dead brother."

"And?"

"Did you notice all the roses in the sitting room by the door? Cassius hated them; he would've avoided them completely. ASD 101. She used them to keep him away from the front door and in the house." That random Tuesday morning popped into my memory. "He opened it for me…."

"Must've really wanted to talk to you." Heego chuckled, but it wasn't funny. Ironic, but not comical.

If he hadn't opened the door for me, he'd still be in that house with that woman. I hadn't thought it was that bad, but it really was *that* bad. She didn't have to tie him up in the basement, or lock him up in his room, she just had to use his own faults to keep him in line.

The movie was on and the popcorn was ready when Cassius came out of the bathroom. His wet hair hung in pieces like icicles around his face. Dad's pants fit him well, but the ancient Bon Jovi shirt I'd picked out for him was a bit snug and clung to his body. Anthony Michael Hall began his monologue intro on the television, and Cassius followed right along with him. Bonnie and Heego looked on, all raised eyebrows and crinkled faces.

I grinned at his eccentricity and followed along. I got it because I did it too. Sometimes the universe only gave us one person, but when that person came along, we had to hang on to them for dear life because never in our existence would we ever be so accepted.

The clock on the mantel tolled five. "Dad's home. He's going to come get me." The fear in his voice was apparent, and each one of us grimaced flinched at the sound.

"Probably not," Heego assured him. "I think the police will want to talk to him too."

Cassius's whole body tensed. Humming rumbled in his chest. *Snap, snap.* I wanted to get up and hug him. Take him by the hands, drag him outside, and dance in the rain. I wanted to grab him by his floppy hair and plant cheesy, Harlequin kisses all over his face. I didn't. I didn't do anything. Because I was an idiot.

"Cass—er—Cassius, that is something you never have to worry about again. You're here and you're safe, and those people can never, ever control you again. Okay?" He nodded, clenching his jaw until the muscles flexed and moved. "Let's sit down and watch the movie while we wait." I kept my tone even, not condescending or demanding, friendly and helpful. I longed for the day Cassius Shooster was just another dude. Well, odd, and strange, and quirky, but not scared of the wicked witch of the Pacific Northwest.

We sat together on the couch and watched in silence, other than random outbursts of quotes from Cassius and me. Soon enough, Bonnie and Heego were doing it with us. And by the time John Bender was pulling the pins from the door, we were all acting out the movie as though we were on stage. For an instant, we forgot why we were all sitting in my living room. That instant was perfect.

The knock on the door stopped us all in our tracks. Time was up. Perfect moment over. Reality came rushing back, and in the form of a state police officer. Heego answered the door while I paused the movie.

Sergeant San Dimas moved into the living room, stopping first at the rug to stamp the rain from his boots. Mom would appreciate that. I stood to meet him. Cassius stayed on the couch, tucked his head, if he'd been wearing his typical uniform, he'd have flipped the hood over his still damp hair.

"Glad to see you're feeling better," the sergeant said to Cassius. "And wearing pants." Cassius looked at his feet. "Can we talk, son?"

"I'm not your son."

"Mm-hmm," the sergeant said, softly nodding. "Okay."

"Sir," I said, stepping closer to him. "It might be easier for him to talk if I were there too. He's been through a lot, and I don't think he has the wherewithal to do this alone."

Sergeant San Dimas closed the space between us. He lowered his voice. "I understand Cassius's difficulties, and I think I got this one. 'Kay?"

"I don't think you do—"

"I spoke with his father just before coming down this way. He explained everything."

"Explained?" *Oh, really?* Defenses, engage. "Explained what? How he and his wife hid a body in their basement for fourteen years?" I slapped my hands against my thighs.

"Fifteen."

"What?"

"Fifteen years. In just a few weeks, actually," the sergeant clarified. My head spun. Mr. Shooster just gave up all the information they needed right out of the gate? "Mr. Shooster knew the boy was in the basement but hid him away under the roses to protect his son. His living son."

I knew it!

"Cassius? He was four years old. How did he kill anyone?" Heego said. He was quickly becoming our only ally.

The sergeant smiled. A grin that pushed parenthesis around his cheeks and wrinkled the corners of his eyes. "I promise your boyfriend isn't a suspect and likely will never be. For now, I really need you to wait here and finish your movie. Looks like you're about to find out what happens when you spill paint in the garage." The sergeant, who I'd at first assumed was a douche with a badge like the others, hit my soft spot, and I backed down. I hoped that meant he wasn't an idiot like the Flintlock sheriff's department.

"He's not my boyfriend," I argued.

He leaned in closer and whispered, "You should tell him that."

The sergeant walked past me toward Cassius, who

now stood behind me. I turned and caught the hurt on Cassius's face before San Dimas guided him into the kitchen. The two disappeared into the dining room and out of sight.

Bonnie, Heego, and I sat and waited for what felt like a million years. Brian was a cherry, 80s slang for virgin, when the front door flew open and a blonde mess burst into the house.

"What in the shit is going on here? Prudence?" Mom screamed, and slipped on the tile at the entrance, catching herself on the coatrack, but spilling the bag of groceries she held in her arms.

Heego instinctively reached out to catch her, though he was feet away and would've never made it in time had she actually fallen.

"Mom, slow down, we're fine." Mostly.

"What? How? Who?" She pointed at Heego. Her hair was a mess, scarf half on, half off, jacket one button off kilter.

"It's a very, very long story. But the long and short of it is Mrs. Shooster is a murdering psychopath, Cassius had a brother, and he's in our kitchen with an officer right now. Cassius, not his brother. His brother is dead."

Mom blinked slowly. It was a lot to handle, but she'd get it sooner or later.

"Mrs. Penderhaus?" the sergeant asked from the other side of the room.

I dropped my head into my hand, regrettably unable to

soften the blow with Mom before she discovered a state trooper in our kitchen.

"Yes," she said in a daze, half-empty paper bag clutched in one hand, house keys in the other.

"Can we have a word, please?"

Sergeant San Dimas, middle-aged, dark and handsome, grinned with the side of his mouth. His eyes twinkled and Mom blushed, making it clear she noticed the officer like I had.

"Take your time to…" He let his gesture finish the sentence.

She quickly snapped out of her bewilderment. "Oh, oh, my." She giggled. "Oh, what a mess." It'd been five years since she'd spoken to a man that she hadn't known when my dad was alive. An attractive one in a uniform to boot.

Heego took the bag from her and started picking up the stuff that had spilled. Thankfully, it wasn't anything glass. Just a quart of ice cream, bunch of bananas, an *Esquire*, and a box of Kotex—which Heego didn't stop to cringe over.

"Thank you, Officer."

"Heego, ma'am."

"Yes, whatever that is. Thank you." She took the bag from him and the sergeant promptly relieved her of the bag.

When he turned his back to her, she shot me with a glare. I held my hands up in surrender. I hadn't done it.

I wasn't in trouble. She fixed her hair and followed him into the kitchen.

Minutes passed. Ten. Fifteen. I couldn't take it anymore. Bonnie and I looked at each other before silently slinking toward the dining room. We pressed ourselves against the wall so as not to be seen.

"You can see my predicament."

We inched closer.

"Oh, yes. Well...." Mom sighed. "He has a home here if there's no one else."

My eyes went wide. Were they really discussing Cassius *living* with us? I hadn't even considered where he'd stay if his parents were locked up. Apparently, he would be living with us for the time being. Though I felt stupid and selfish for overlooking the big fat homeless elephant in the room, there was no way I could go through everything I needed to go through with him in the house all day every day.

"Might as well come on in here, guys," the intuitive sergeant called to us.

The three of them sat at the kitchen table. Cassius stared at his hands. "You okay?" I asked him, and he nodded. Tears ran down his face, but he hid them behind his hair.

To keep them from running through his mop, I shoved my hands in my back pockets. "So... what's the plan, then?"

Mom looked at San Dimas, then me, her blonde

brows raised in the middle. Bonnie bit her thumbnail, mostly disconnected with the conversation. After a quick moment of awkward silence, Heego piped in. "Wanna live with me, kid?" Officer Heego offered out of nowhere. We all looked at him. No one really knew him, other than Bonnie, and it seemed odd for him to even offer. "We hung out at the jail for a bit. We're buddies now." Heego's grin spread wide. "Right?"

"Buddies." Cassius nodded and agreed. "Heego saved my life from the meatheads." He spoke of the boorish officers who'd taken it upon themselves to teach Cassius a lesson.

"It's nothing fancy, but I've got a pullout and a sweet big screen." Cassius looked up at him. "I also have cable." Cass blinked. "Netflix." Heego dragged out the end of the word.

"Sorry, Prudence's mom, but I want to stay with Officer Heego. Because he's a man and can teach me how to be a man. Unfortunately you can't. Or you." He looked at me. "You're a woman."

"I'm going to take that as a compliment."

As a group, we chuckled, but his words meant more to me than anyone else in the room and it really wasn't funny at all. For the first time in his entire life, he was free. Free to go and do and be whatever he wanted to be. Free to be human but not free from the physical and psychological damage he'd be stuck with for the foreseeable future.

"Just don't teach him to be a dick, eh?" Bonnie added,

and I couldn't have agreed more.

"Deal. What do you say, dude? Hang at the bachelor pad tonight?"

Cassius's dark eyes darted in my direction, then back to Officer Heego. "Yes," he said and looked back down at the table.

"Officer…," the sergeant started, and waited for his response.

"Heego, sir."

San Dimas turned his body away from Cassius but didn't leave the table. "You are aware Cassius is an adult and won't qualify for many services he should have received years ago."

"Yup," Heego said.

"Wait, what?" I asked, not trusting the ability of my brain to comprehend basic math.

"Cassius will be nineteen in a few weeks, end of November, according to his father." Sargent San Dimas directed his attention at Heego. "From what we know so far, he's never been to school. We have no medical records for him yet, so he's not considered disabled in any way. He's really just sitting in limbo for the time being. Basically, you'd be taking on a big responsibility."

"I'm sitting right here," Cassius grumbled from beneath his hair veil, exasperated.

"Gotcha." Heego nodded and pointed a friendly finger gun at the sergeant. "We got this, sir. I have a huge movie collection." He shrugged.

Whatever the motive behind Heego's offer, he appeared genuine and Cassius seemed happy enough to go with him. Although it did hurt a bit that he didn't want to live with me, I could get behind his reasoning. I wasn't, after all, a man. What could I teach him? And there was the whole dead-girl-walking thing.

"Since you're an adult, Cassius, the choice is yours," the sergeant said. "I'll do what I can to make sure you've got access to the house as soon as possible so you can get your stuff or move back in. Forensics will probably come across your birth records, and I'll make sure you get those things as soon as I can. You'll need them."

"He's registered at Flintlock," I said, pointing out someone outside of that house had to have some kind of documentation. "The school has to have his records for enrollment. Right? I mean he only went the one day, but I think he was on the schedule." The more we peeled back the layers of Cassius Shooster and the whole of Flintlock, the more I came to terms with the fact nothing here was right.

"Hmm." The sergeant jotted down the information into his tiny notebook. "Thanks. I'll look into that." He played it cool, but his wise eyes told me he saw a bigger picture. A picture I hoped I lived long enough to see unveiled. "Until then, do the best you can, and we'll make sure you come out on the winning end of this. Okay?" Cassius nodded but didn't look at the sergeant.

"And the sheriff? Who's handling that?" Heego asked

what I'd been thinking.

The sergeant looked at Heego for a long time, gauging his trust in the officer. After a deep, grumbling breath, he said, "Sheriff Floyd is currently under investigation," and left it at that.

Heego nodded once, jaw clenched. We weren't satisfied, not one of us, but we weren't stupid and knew that was all we were going to get for a while. Having Heego as an inside man would hopefully prove itself an asset in the future. The sergeant hadn't yet proven himself an ally completely, but he was the best option at the time. And oddly, through his gruff demeanor, his soft spot for Cassius showed, for that I was grateful.

Bonnie and Heego left the kitchen first, choosing to stand far too close together in the dining room, whispering something between them. Mom left the table and began unloading her bag of groceries.

"Prudence," Sergeant San Dimas said, motioning for me to sit in Mom's chair. "We need to talk."

"Figured that was coming."

"Cassius, can you hang out in the living room until we're done? Mrs. Penderhaus? If you wouldn't mind, please."

"Hm." She looked at him, eyes on the verge of dreamy. "Oh, yes. I'm sorry."

Mom shoved a half gallon of milk in the fridge and shuffled out of the kitchen. Cassius followed behind her. I shot a glance at Cassius as he passed. The corners of his mouth were turned down, lips pulled tight together. Anxiety played over his face, pulling his brows up in the center and dragging his dark eyes down at the edges. I ran a hand over his shoulder before he was too far out of reach. His whole life had been upheaved, churned up, and thrown in the wood chipper. It would be a miracle if he came out unscathed.

I sat alone with the sergeant at the kitchen table. He flipped his notebook open, and without prompting, I started talking. He didn't ask many questions, but really he didn't need to. Every question he had I had too and neither of us had the answers. We discussed my thoughts about Mrs. Shooster and her role in the events that led up to the day I coldcocked a drunk woman and uncovered a long-dead four-year-old. We agreed that it seemed likely Mr. Shooster had done just as he said he'd done. I wouldn't be surprised in the slightest to learn that Mother Shooster had lied to her husband, just home from work at 5:00 p.m., that their *retarded* son had killed his brother and they'd surely lock him up if he were caught.

"I just can't figure out where the sheriff comes into play," I pondered before we wrapped up our conversation.

"So far, neither can I." He tapped his pen against the table to click it shut. "Rest assured, I'm looking into it."

"But you're with me on thinking he's not innocent in this, right? I mean, I know you must think I'm just some dumb kid, but—not to toot any horns—my dad was a pretty prolific journalist before he died. The apple can't fall too far, right? I've got to have some sort of intuitive investigative chops running through my veins. Right?"

Sergeant San Dimas let out a long sigh. "I think you're a very smart girl." He held his hand up. "Sorry, woman, and I think you care a lot for Cassius." Mulling over what he'd say next, the sergeant pretended to flip through his notebook. "What I'd like to know is what really brought you to their door in the first place?"

"I told you, Morgan—"

"You could have gone home," he retorted. "It is just three houses away." His honey-brown eyes focused dead center on mine, forcing my confession with willpower alone. He was a better detective than I'd given him credit for.

"Because I'm dying," I admitted, indignity subconsciously pulling my hands to cover my face.

His eyes fell away from me. "I see."

"I haven't told anyone yet, so please…."

He cleared his throat and tucked his notebook into his breast pocket. "Yeah. Sure. Well, I'm glad you had the guts to ring the bell."

"Seems I have the guts for a lot of things now." Except telling the people I loved I'm dying.

Sargent San Dimas stood and leaned on his hands across the table. "Let's hope that's true."

A couple of paramedics eventually came down to the house to check me and Cassius for anything more serious than cuts and bruises and post-traumatic stress. San Dimas questioned Bonnie, then Heego, not taking more than a half an hour each. I had a feeling he'd be calling everyone in for more in the coming weeks. Before leaving for the night, he shook our hands and talked to Mom for a long time on the porch. Me, Cassius, Heego, and Bonnie watched them from the window. Like children with their noses pressed to the glass at a candy store, we grinned and blushed and hoped for the best. Except Cassius. I was pretty certain Cassius was just trying to be normal. Even if only for a moment, squeezed on my couch with the only people he knew in the world who weren't behind bars.

They'd arrested the Shoosters officially, and eventually there would be a trial. Cassius would have to testify. My heart ceased beating at the thought. Cassius had a life ahead of him that I couldn't know for sure he was ready for. Then again, for all I knew, he was totally capable of everything coming his way.

The dying part of me smiled with pride that maybe I would get to see him succeed. The other part, the part that fell in love with the peculiar boy at 17 Marigold Lane, cried at the notion I wouldn't be there for any of it. Maybe. Sixty percent seemed like good odds until it came to life and death.

12

SATURDAY. THE DAY HAD NEVER HELD MUCH BY WAY OF anticipation for me. Other than my monthly date with Angus Libbit and, of course, no school. But with my impending graduation from institutional learning, that wasn't so much an issue anymore.

Too exhausted to sleep, I'd stayed up long after Heego had taken Cassius to his temporary home, categorizing my DVDs, organizing my books. Through the night, as the storm raged on, I'd fretted over his well-being. The guilt I'd been working on had settled in nicely and was plotting to destroy me, one overprotective worry at a time.

I didn't want to open my eyes, but the slice of sunlight that broke through my curtains had other plans. It fell over my face, warming my cheeks, penetrating my eyelids. I pulled the covers over my head and rolled away from it.

That morning, the sun shone for the first time in weeks.

Bright and warm, it made quick work of drying up wet lawns and soggy pumpkins. Remnants of wind-whipped Halloween decorations fluttered from eaves, holding on for one more day.

The storm that had come through had whipped around the tree out front and flooded the garden out back. Lacking in theatrics, I was thankful it hadn't pelted us with lightning and thunder, for the sake of an odd boy I knew.

The week had been, to say the least, trying. It wasn't Cassius, or even his mother. In fact, without him, I'd have been forced to face what lay ahead. I'd skillfully ignored my body and it's screaming attempts to slow me down. It wasn't that I was sick, not yet anyway; it was the constant pain. Always there, lurking in the background, threatening to take my very existence.

"Pru," Mom's voice sang quietly from the other side of my door as she knocked softly, pulling me out of sleep completely.

"What?" I said rudely, face smashed against the pillow.

"Cassius is here," she said mockingly.

It was a milestone moment for a mom and teenage daughter, announcing the arrival of a boy, but it wasn't. She enjoyed the moment, her tone proved that, but under it, in the way her voice lilted at the end, was contention over the situation. If not for the boy entirely.

"Okay." *Shit.* I jumped from my bed and scrambled for a pair of pants with my eyes still half shut. "Gimme a minute."

My left leg slid in without a hitch. Plunging my right foot into the hole, my big toe caught the crotch seam, sending me hobbling on one foot trying to maneuver the space blind.

"Prudence," Cassius's voice sent my stomach careening to my butt. "Why are you in your underwear?"

With my back to him, he couldn't see me blush. It was an unattractive mess of pink-tinged freckles anyway, so the better for it. I was, however, standing there in my underwear. Blue, if I remembered without looking.

"Uh…." I chuckled. "I was asleep."

"It's three in the afternoon, Prudence."

"No it's not." I looked at the clock. Yes, it was. "Fine, I was really tired, okay? I stayed up all night… worrying about you." I turned, pants on and in desperate need of a toothbrush. "How'd it go with Heego?"

"I slept on an inflatable mattress," he said, matter-of-factly.

Laughter was my first instinct. I ignored it and settled for a grin. His new life, no matter how much better than where he'd been, would never be home. His existence would forever be changed. Monolithically.

"Cool, like camping." Casually, I crossed my arms over my chest, covertly covering my braless boobs. "Have you heard from Sergeant San Dimas?"

He steepled his hands, twisting his fingers together nervously. "How are you not doing it?" he asked, astonished over whatever his cryptic question was about.

"Doing what?"

He let out a long, annoyed sigh. "Prudence, I thought you liked movies, too." I stumbled over my words, but he didn't give me a chance to answer. "How are you not saying San Dimas High School football rules? A quote from the 1989 cult classic, *Bill and Ted's Excellent Adventure*."

I stared at him for an uncomfortable span of seconds. "You're ridiculous, you know that?" I joked and his face fell.

"Yes, I do."

Clever, Pru, real clever. I reached out to grip his arm, and he didn't shy away. "I spent an hour saying his name last night. It *pained* me not to say it, but more importantly, I believe that was the first logical, socially appropriate sentence you've ever said to me. Where were you hiding?" My eyes locked on to his.

He fell silent, held eye contact only a few seconds before looking at his feet; he grumbled, "I should tell you I have no idea what I'm doing."

I stepped closer to him. "You should be forewarned, neither do I."

His eyes lifted, finding mine again from beneath his lashes. "Prudence, I have to tell you something."

My gymnast heart summersaulted in my chest. "Yes?"

His eyebrows came together in such a way that I worried what would come out of his mouth next. "Your breath smells bad."

I clamped my hand over my mouth. My cheeks flushed red instantly, and all reservations I'd had about pink freckles were out the window. "I'm gonna brush them," I said through my hand, shuffling out the door. "Meet me on the couch," I shouted over my shoulder before shutting the bathroom door.

Minty fresh and de-caveman-ed, I joined Cassius in the living room, where he sat on the couch watching classic cartoons. I'd wondered why he suddenly used the front door and not the window before I realized he hadn't come alone. Bonnie sat on the couch next to him, and Heego leaned against the wall next to her. They were an odd couple, those two. A hooligan and a man of the law. Bonnie, having screwed the pooch the first time, was a senior for the second year but an adult by the letter of the law, therefore fair game for whatever man caught her fancy. Heego was the strangest fancy she could've had.

"I'm having a hard time drumming up a good insult for that…." She pointed at me as a whole. "Just know you've looked better."

"Thanks, Bon. Not that I don't adore every last second of the time I spent with you yesterday, but why are you all here?" I didn't typically berate my friends for visiting me. I'd slept until three in the afternoon for a reason. I was exhausted.

"Because, my dear, it's Halloween. Where else would

we be?" I'd spent every Halloween for six years with Bonnie.

"Bonnie wants me to go to the Halloween party at the high school," Cassius added, not taking his eyes off the television.

That was the dumbest idea she'd had to date. "That is the dumbest idea you've had to date." No reason to be dishonest among friends. Right? "Do you know— Cassius?" He looked away from the TV finally. "Do you know who's going to be there, without question? Give you two guesses, but you'll only need one," I said to him. "Morgan," I added when he took too long to reply.

His jaw flexed. "That guy's just… like, just a bunch of… poop or something." Cassius's bag of insults was about as diverse as mine. Although, I had a feeling he had a few good ones brewing in there. And if all else failed, always fall back on the classics.

"Poop indeed," Bonnie agreed. "He's a tool. Who cares? Heego will be there, nothing is going to happen."

I lowered my head to meat Cass's eyes. "Is this something you actually want to do?"

He shrugged. "I've got nothing else to do tonight."

"Is this your first one?" Heego asked. "Halloween, I mean."

Cassius took his typical dozen or so seconds to answer. "Dad brings me a pumpkin on October 25th. I carve it in the upstairs bathroom on the 26th. Then I watch the Halloween franchise films. Even *Season of the Witch*, even though most people don't count that one into the series." He stopped to look at Heego, then Bonnie, and finally me. "My house scares children on Halloween. I watch them run from the gates wearing costumes and carrying flashlights." He sat back against the couch, no hoodie to hide behind. "Halloween seems like something I could get into," he mumbled.

"A man after my own heart," I said with a weak smile.

"Every day this week," he said, and they both looked at him.

I, on the other hand, looked away. Because that's what I do. When the moment became too awkward to stand, Bonnie broke the silence.

"It's a dress-up kinda thing, so we'll have to get you ready."

I nodded at Cassius before realizing it was me she was talking to. "*Me?* Dress-up? Like a costume? I don't want to wear a costume," I whined.

I was honestly tired, and despite my all-around adoration for Cassius, I could have done with a day off from it all. My emotions were all over the board. Attributing that to lack of sleep, it made sense that I was cranky.

It took Bonnie exactly seven minutes to convince me I would be wearing a costume whether I liked it or not. She'd decided what I would wear based on the availability in my closet and insisted on helping me get ready. Fearful she'd easily spot the lime-size protrusion in my underwing, I awkwardly stripped my T-shirt and replaced it with a fuzzy pink sweater I hadn't worn since 8th grade.

"The sleeves are too short," I complained, holding my arms out like a mummy in the mirror. "I actually look like Lurch now."

"No," she grinned and leapt from the bed. "It's perfect." Bonnie stood behind me, watching around my arm in the mirror. She pulled the sleeves into a slouchy bunch at my elbow. "Perfect." She grinned, crackling the peeling skin she had glued around her mouth.

Cassius opted for a simple getup that I was able to provide by way of Dad's closet. Mom pretended like it was okay, but I knew deep down she wasn't happy we were in there taking things.

By five o'clock, we had one dead hippy, one marine, one member of the Brat Pack, and one finely dressed Doctor.

"Suit fits you perfectly," Mom said, fingering the cuffs of Dad's blue blazer.

"You need a trench coat," I added, from the third step from the bottom.

"The prom queen," Cassius said in return, his black eyes shimmering in the dim light.

A blush heated my cheeks. "I still think it would've made more sense if we *all* dressed up like *The Breakfast Club* and not just me. As it stands, I'm just a redhead in a pink sweater. Whoop-dity-doo." I spun my finger around above my head.

"Oh, but you're a lovely redhead in a pink sweater." Cassius took on the persona of the tenth Doctor with ease.

My head fuzzy, everything felt like a dream. "Thank you." How could we be preparing to go to a party hardly twenty-four hours after Heego himself had pulled a dead child from Cassius's basement? How could any of us be functioning?

"Pru, you okay?" Bonnie asked.

I softly shook my head. "I don't know. No? Doesn't this seem weird to you? Shouldn't we be mourning or in shock or something? Is it normal to get dressed up and go out the day after… something like that?"

For a moment, maybe even two, no one breathed. Eyes focused on feet, no one spoke. They'd all been thinking it; I'd just said it out loud.

"What is normal?" Cassius pointed out.

I pinched my lips between my teeth. "Nothing about the last week of life."

"Then I guess we've not deviated from the plan," said Heego in his military garb.

"Pru," Bonnie laid her hand on my arm. "I get it. I'm totally fu—" She stopped on account of Mom. "—screwed up in the brain right now. I can't get that… I just want to think about something else, okay? And I think if you let yourself, you do too."

That was all I'd been doing. "Yeah."

"Prudence, honey, you've all been through something... more than most people. You do whatever you need to do to process that. And it's totally normal to want to feel normal. Even if just for one night." Mom's neutral grin validated my thoughts. I wanted to be with my friends and ignore everything I should have been worrying about, but everything about the idea felt wrong.

"Cassius?" I questioned. "How are you feeling?"

He fingered the cuff of Dad's jacket. "This is good. I want to pretend to be normal."

That I knew for certain. I sighed. "Then we party." I'd keep pretending too. Just one more night. I wanted to give him, and myself, just Halloween, before I threw a cancer wrench into things.

"All right, let me get a picture." Mom shoved us all in together side by side. "Smile." The light flashed, and for a moment, I was blind.

"I like your hair," I whispered to Cassius before Mom snapped a second shot. I was certain the end result was a lovely photo of my friends standing beside a tomato in a pink sweater.

"Okay, go have fun. But not too much. Be careful," she said directly to Cassius, who promptly saluted her. I liked Cassius pretending to be normal. I didn't worry so much about that Cassius. But I knew it was all superficial. Under the surface, he was just as terrified as I was. More so, surely.

My lungs pulled in the crisp autumn air. The sun had

disappeared behind another ominous bank of clouds. Shades of deep blue and gray filled the sky. The sun was setting, and soon the colors would disappear altogether, leaving behind an inky black mess.

We passed the white house next door, Mrs. Holloway, porch light on ready for trick-or-treaters. An orange pumpkin smiled at us from the top step. A black cat ceremoniously wound its body about the gourde. One of the dozens the old woman fed.

The vacant house before the end sat empty as it had since its owner passed away over spring. Dark, it held an eerie silence made more apparent by the time of year. In the light of day, it was blue, mostly well-tended. The century-old gingerbread cottage, surrounded by a white picket fence, beginning to show wear—a loose board or two and aging paint—was almost covered in leaves. Leaves on top of leaves. I didn't envy the person who had to clean up that slop hidden beneath the top few layers.

At the end, the old brown house that held so much mystery within its walls sat empty as well. Darkness filled each window, and as we stood there, momentarily locked on the building, it became increasingly difficult to look at.

Series of images—Mother Shooster, Andrew, naked Cassius—flashed the longer I stood there. Bonnie was the first to break away, Heego towing along behind her. Police tape flittered in the breeze. Cassius stood steadfast in front of his house although we'd begun to move along. A sad shell of the worst years of his life.

"Hey, let's go. It's party time, Cinderella," I said, pulling on his arm. Though I didn't want to party, taking the wind from his Halloween sails wasn't going to happen on my account. Pretend to be normal.

Letting out a long sigh, he finally looked away from the house. "This is never going to work," he confessed. "A party? After all that happened? How stupid. How completely and totally preposterous."

He'd stolen the words from my head. "I couldn't agree with you more. But we're already dressed, and really, we don't have anything else to do tonight. Right?" I shrugged.

"What if—"

"Nope." I waved off his words. "There isn't room for what-if. Not anymore." I stuck my hand out for him to take. "I'm living my life. Normal or otherwise. You coming with me?"

After a long, reluctant moment, he placed his hand in mine. I realized my tone had been anything but friendly and was thankful he hadn't picked up on it. Or if he had, he didn't say anything. My head wasn't with it, and my grogginess was making for a bitchy Penderhaus.

Flintlock High School gymnasium, a mecca for the Brady Miles crew and the home of many years of my torment. Black and orange streamers stretched the space of the room overhead. Paper skeletons and rubber bats dangled from the ceiling. A textbook Halloween party, as some would call it, the Basic Bitch of October 31st.

"Look at all the imagination put into this place," Bonnie said sarcastically. "I am in awe."

Cassius leaned closer to me. "This is like from a movie," he whispered.

"You don't have to whisper. And yes, it is." From Cassius, that was a compliment. At least someone was enjoying the lack of creativity.

People of all ages mingled and danced and drank watered-down punch. Flintlock High School put on two parties a year open to the public, Halloween and New Year's Eve. The public reasoning behind it was to raise money for the school in ticket and photo sales. But we all knew it was the town's way of keeping everyone in check on the rowdiest party nights of the year. According to my dad, it all went back to his high school years and some tragedy no one would ever talk about. I was learning my town had more secrets stuffed in its closet than a dirty politician.

Bonnie snatched Heego by the hand and dragged him to the designated dancing area. She'd forced me to attend the shindig only to subsequently ditch me for a guy. *Joy.*

I leaned against the far wall behind the basketball hoop and loosely folded my arms over my chest, Cassius followed, exactly.

"Psst, hey, if you're looking to pretend normalcy, don't copy *me.*"

"Hey, Pru," Marlin called to me with a smile plastered across his face. "Lemme guess," he said, looking my costume up and down. "I don't get it."

I grunted and smiled smugly over being proven right even though Bonnie was nowhere around. No one would get my costume. "Claire," I said and held my arms out. Marlin shook his head, indicating he was clueless. "It's a family name," I added begrudgingly.

"It's a fat girl name," Cassius said from behind me.

Marlin's face went wide with shock. He held his hand over his mouth dramatically. I closed my eyes and stood stoically for a full second before laughter took purchase and doubled me over. Of all the things he could have said, he said that. My cranky mood hadn't left me; Cassius had just found a way to gloss over it and make it livable.

"Oh, boy, this is going to be fun," I grumbled under my breath. "Marlin Sheave, Cassius Shooster," I introduced them.

Marlin stuck a hand out to shake but became hesitant when he realized who he was being introduced to. I hadn't watched it, but I would lay money the local news had covered the story. I'd only seen one van on the street, Channel 10. How many others would find the story of the hidden boys and run with it?

"Is this him?" he asked me. "Are you him?" Cassius shook his hand just like I'd showed him but otherwise looked confused. "You're the boy they found in the spook house." Marlin smiled and looked Cassius up and down. "I was honestly expecting someone more… boyish."

"He's big for his age." I sniggered and moved right along. "Cassius," I said, "Marlin here is going to be a big-time science guy over at MileStone GenTech."

"Oh, please," Marlin said, feigning modesty.

"My dad is a geneticist at MileStone GenTech Incorporated."

"Oh, well, put in a good word." Marlin laughed and looked at my stern expression. "Oh, no? Oh… just a joke." He looked away, embarrassed at his oversight. "Well, you look amazing,"—he pointed to me—"and you, loving the suit." He patted me on the head as though I wasn't standing six inches taller than him. "Well, have a blast." He waved over his shoulder as he sauntered back toward the thick of the party.

"That's gay, right?" Cassius asked, and I laughed. "He's a gay guy?"

"Shh," I hushed him. "Not today," I said, chuckling. "Want something to drink or something?"

"No."

"Want to get our picture taken?"

"No."

I blew air through my lips, making a farty sound. "You let me know when you figure out what you'd like to do with your time here."

I leaned against the wall again and surveyed the room for dangers. Brady hadn't arrived yet. All girls fourteen and over would not have been caught dead slouching, or God forbid, eating in the presence of field god Brady Miles. He seemed to bring out the robot in half the female student body. No Brady meant no Morgan, and no Morgan meant no worries. Yet.

Elvis Costello began over the sound system. Cassius bobbed his head to the tune and sang the first few lines before I joined in. The song was a classic, and I knew every word. By the first chorus, we were singing along together leaning against the back wall in the dark. As the song slowed, I took Cassius by the hand and spun under his arm like a ballerina. He laughed and made me do it again. We held our hands together and continued to sing flawlessly to every word, dancing as best as two baby giraffes could manage.

"I love this song," I yelled to him over the music as we danced alone on the fringes of the party. "I didn't know you were into music."

"That is a silly assumption, Prudence."

"Sorry. I'll try not to assume things about you anymore. I'll just let you surprise me." I laughed, he didn't. I cleared my throat and looked out at the crowd, avoiding Cassius.

The song ended and Cassius let go of my hands. Cyndi Lauper bellowed her iconic ballad next and everyone else moved in close to each other. I wasn't sure who was running the tunes, but I had to congratulate them on excellent taste in music.

Cassius eyed the crowd of close dancers, before looking back to me. His stare at the side of my face was palpable. If I looked back at him, would he look away?

I swallowed hard and found something to talk about. "Well, Doctor," I said, "how are you finding this planet?" I looked.

He smiled, no teeth, but all dimples, turning his dark eyes into handsome half-moons. "Unexpected." *Snap, snap.*

Before I had a chance to curl my lip and say "What," his large hands found either side of my face. Not a moment to breathe, he pressed his lips to mine. Abyss surrounded us. Nothing and everything in one ethereal cloud. His hands on my cheeks, lips on mine, the only things in existence.

Life was full of firsts. First kisses topped that list. In the dark, on the fringes, two peculiar giants kissed like they were the only two people on earth.

The moment played on for an eternity. I found myself wishing it would never end. Seventeen was a bit old for first kisses, but I didn't care. I'd have waited another twenty years for that particular kiss. That particular boy. Love didn't happen overnight. It took time and effort. But sometimes, love took a back seat to something so much bigger. Fate.

"Someone stop them before I puke," Morgan yelled over the music. "Think they'll make baby Lurches?" He laughed, and his buddies gave him congratulatory slaps on the back.

The moment ruined, I felt my face turn fiery red. I wished I had the opportunity to turn green and muscular instead. Pru, smash. "Get bent, Pennington," I said.

"Already did with your mom."

"Did she provide the magnifying glass or did you?" I asked, and secretly congratulated myself.

Morgan smiled for a moment before he figured out what I'd said. His goons laughed and slapped his back again. I wondered if that was all they were programmed to do.

"You know what—"

"Do you want your ass kicked again?" Cassius stepped up beside me, sounding more badass than I'd ever given him credit for.

"Hey," Brady called to Morgan from a dozen feet away, "let's blow. This sucks." He held up his hand in a beer-drinking motion.

Morgan stepped up to Cassius, who stood a solid five inches taller. "Hey, freak, tell me, how'd it feel when you killed your baby brother?" He snarled and glared at Cassius from under his brows. "Huh?" Morgan macho-sniffed. "Freak."

My vision flashed red, and I was on him like a spider monkey. My long arms and legs flailed, trying to reach for him but were hindered by thick hands and arms. Heego had arrived just in time to save Morgan's pimpled face from attack.

"You need to leave," Heego demanded.

"Already on it." He waved off Heego. "See ya," he said to Cassius with a snarl.

"Let me go," I said and pulled free of his grip. "I can't

believe his shit. Ugh!" I grunted, and my face flushed with angry heat. "How can anyone want to be around that ass?" I clenched my fists over and over again, my rage settling viscerally deep.

"Hey, you need some air." Heego examined my face and pulled me by my arm to the doors that led outside.

Bonnie and Cassius followed. "Hey, were you kissing over there?" Bonnie asked from behind me. "Were you?" Everyone ignored her question, but she'd ask again later, surely.

I pushed out the doors with gumption and stumbled out into the cool night. Wiping anger-induced sweat from my brow, I closed my eyes and tried to slow my breathing.

"You all right?" Heego asked, his hand on my shoulder.

"I'm fine." I shrugged out of his grip and walked away.

My first kiss, the moment I wanted to remember forever, had been ruined by Morgan *fucking* Pennington. He was a life ruiner. Plain and simple. Douche McGee, the life ruiner.

My head wouldn't stop spinning even in the cool night air. I could hear my friends talking behind me but couldn't make out what they were saying. Rage had completely taken over my body. I stood on the sidewalk in front of the school and looked down Marigold Lane. The street was brimming with herds of kids in costumes begging for candy. I watched as they hit one house, then the next until the last left was 17 Marigold Lane. The spook house. They stopped long enough to dare each other to go up to the door and run away when the idea became too scary.

I shook my head at the scene. It had been the norm for so many years, fearing the spook house. Even now that the truth had come out, even five years from now, it would still be the spook house. It could never be anything else. They'd do well to tear the damn thing down.

In a window on the second floor, light flickered between the curtains. I stopped moving. Stopped breathing. Yellow police tape still clung to a few spots on the wrought-iron gate and a crime scene notice was plastered on the front door. Cassius hadn't even gotten clearance to enter the house again. There was no logical reason for anyone to be inside.

Bonnie said behind me, "Hey, Pru, let's just get out of here. We can go to your house and watch a mov—"

"Shh, look." I pointed to the darkened window.

"Yeah, it's scary. Let's order a pizza." She pulled on my arm.

The light flashed over the window again. "No, look."

Bonnie gasped. "Heego." She pointed to the house. "Someone's in the house."

Heego planted his hands on his hips and stared up at the house across the street. A moment later, the light glinted again. "Shit. Stay here," he said.

Bonnie and I looked at each other. "Ha," we said together. "Not on your life."

Heego crossed the street ahead of us. Clad in fatigues and without his badge and gun, I wasn't sure what he planned to do once he got there. We followed, Cassius taking up the rear. Children scattered from one house to the next, skillfully avoiding the spook house on Halloween night.

The light flittered passed the window one last time before stopping just as we approached the gate.

"Seriously, stay right here," Heego said, gesturing to get his point across, and made his way around the building, shining his trusty flashlight in the windows, skillfully alerting whatever prowler was inside of his presence.

Emerging minutes later, shaking his head, Heego seemed disappointed with his lack of criminal. He stood near the front porch, where we'd congregated, with his hands on his hips, shaking his head.

"There's someone in there," he whispered. "I just don't know where or how. That door tag hasn't been tampered with and the back door is boarded up."

"Mom nailed the boards from the dog house over the back door when I was ten years old," Cassius added.

"You don't have a dog."

"Anymore," Cassius said, surveying the land. His tone sent chills down to my toes.

Without another word, Cassius bounded off toward the driveway. Like a gazelle, he leapt onto the porch railing and pulled himself onto the awning roof.

"Hey, I don't think so," Heego shouted up to him. "Come on down now. I'll call down to the station and get—"

"Who?" Bonnie asked defiantly. "Who can you trust down there right now?" She had a point.

"Phillips. I can trust my partner."

I nodded to agree with him and looked up at Cassius. It was too late. During their few-second skirmish, Cassius had slipped into his window and disappeared in the darkness of the house.

"Shit," I said. "He's in. We can't leave him in there alone."

"Damn it," Heego huffed, before stomping off to the edge of the porch. Calculating the distance, he shook his head. "I'm killing my manhood saying this, but I'm too short to reach, I think." His stature, though stocky and strong, was nearly a foot shorter than Cassius, who stood inches taller than me.

"I'm not."

"You're not going in there alone." Heego began checking the few windows downstairs to see if they were locked. "Shit." He slammed his palm into the frame of the window.

"Bonnie, how did you get in when you bonked Mother Shooster on the noggin?"

She moved to the side of the porch. "I used this piece of wood—" She stopped when she discovered the piece of wood was gone. "—as a ramp. Crap."

Heego searched the area with his flashlight, finding nothing. "We're wasting time." As the seconds ticked on, my fear for Cassius began to rumble my gut.

"Why don't you just bust in the front door?" Bonnie asked.

"Because, Bonnie," he said with snark, "like you said, I can't trust anyone and therefore can't call this in. If I break in there, we might as well throw the Shooster case out the window. Without cause, a good lawyer could call that evidence tampering. I just need to get him out of there. Then we'll deal with whoever broke in."

After screwing the pooch by moving the body, Heego couldn't risk another rookie move. The spook house on Halloween night, an impossible temptation for the teenage population of Flintlock. *Cassius should be fine*, I lied to myself. I must've been a couple of kids just looking to scare themselves. Just teenagers looking for a thrill. I looked up at the window I'd climbed in once before. My head swam again, and I shook it off. Teenagers or no, I'd had a bad feeling about going out all night, and I refused to ignore my gut anymore.

"I'll be fine. I've done it before. Remember?" I didn't ask again before I climbed onto the railing.

Taking in a big breath, I prepared myself for the pain to come. I reached above my head, gripping the edge, just as I did last time. I pulled. Something tore, seared with pain, and tugged at my gag reflex. My legs were dangling from the edge when I heard Heego complaining to Bonnie about her delinquent friends getting him into trouble. I grinned at the irony of it and pushed through the pain to pull myself upward. The skirt I wore was too long for proper leg functionality, and I regretted the outfit choice the moment I finally reached the top safely.

"Hey," I whispered down over the edge, blinking away the white spots in my vision. "I'm going down to open a window. Just wait there." I scurried to the window and stopped, calling down to them again. "We should probably call San Dimas."

Cassius's room was dark and empty, just as it had been. And just as before, he was nowhere to be found.

"Cass?" I whispered, not wanting to make too much noise in case someone dangerous was in the house.

Incredibly dark, the space was nearly impossible to navigate. Cassius, having grown up in the house, had probably moved through it with ease and could've been anywhere at that point. Not wanting to waste too much time screwing around in the dark, I made my way downstairs to open a window for Heego. He was the cop; he could deal with the criminals. I'd had my fill of crime fighting.

"Cassius?" I called again at the bottom of the stairs. Silence. Only the ticking of the standing clock by the front door could be heard. "Come on." I began to grow worried what could have happened to him in that house in those precious seconds he'd been alone.

Wasting no time getting to the window, I tried the largest, which sat to the left of the foot of the stairs. As I pulled back the curtains, muted light spilled into the room. I pulled on the window, but it didn't budge. Heego met me on the porch, his brows pulled together tight, grimacing from the other side of the glass. Flipping the lock back and forth did nothing. Then I caught sight of why. Nails. Scads of them, jutting out here and there holding the slider in place.

"That bitch," I whispered. Pointing at the nails, I said through the glass, "Nailed shut."

Heego threw his arms in the air, exasperated. He pointed to the other two windows in the rose room, and I nodded. They would be nailed shut too, I knew in my gut, but I'd check anyway. Heego's eyes went wide, and he slammed his hands against the frame of the window.

Hands came through the darkness behind me, and I was off my feet and moving backward. The curtains closed, blocking Heego and his horrified expression from view. I kicked my feet through open air and tried to scream. A hand covered my mouth, pushing my chin painfully against my throat. I thought I'd pass out and began to panic at the sensation of not being able to breathe.

Curtains closed, the space was again drenched in darkness. It didn't matter. I knew I was headed for the basement. That basement had held too much torment in a matter of a day, and there was no way in hell I was going down there willingly. I fought. I fought harder than I ever knew I could.

Sending an elbow behind me, I made contact with something that brought an oomph from my attacker. I shook my head hard and fast like a pit bull, trying to free my face from his hand. The basement door clicked and popped open. It was now or never.

Planting my feet on the ground, I bent my knees and readied myself for a fall. Still backward, I pushed off on my long legs and down we went. My attacker held on to me all the way down, his body guarding mine from the pain of the stone steps. We hit the bottom in a puff of dirt and agonizing groans.

"Jesus, Pennington, what were you thinking?" said a deep voice I couldn't quite place in my stupor.

A groan rumbled through the chest of my attacker. Morgan Pennington.

"What... in the hell... are you two doing here?" I asked breathlessly, my voice hoarse, wind viciously knocked from my lungs.

"Get up, Morgan," Brady Miles said, nudging Morgan in the side with his foot and ignoring me completely. "Come on, I got it. We gotta get outta here."

I mumbled but realized my words were hardly coming out a whisper. Puffing dirt with my breath, but not much more. *Where the hell is Cassius?*

"The bitch tried to kill me," Morgan grumbled.

"I told you to check on the noise upstairs, not bring it down here with you. Now get your ass up before she wakes up and sees us."

They hadn't seen Cassius. Whatever they'd been doing, they didn't want me to see. Knowing their feelings toward Cassius *the freak* Shooster, his fate would have been far worse than mine. I decided to lie there and wait them out. No use in letting them know they'd been caught. I only hoped Heego came barreling in before they flew the coop. Or Bonnie. I'd take Bonnie.

"Clarabelle's waiting at the well. We have to go, now." Brady urged his cohort, pulling him up from the ground, dumping my body off him and onto the dirt floor.

I lay there still. Listening to every word they said.

"She'll be there when we get there," Morgan said.

"You know if Penderhaus is here, she's got that freak with her. You think Elroy is gonna be able to let you slide twice? They've got his nuts in a vise as it is. This is your saving grace, bud. Now let's go."

Morgan huffed, and they both made their way to the stairs, leaving me to rot in the basement like cowards. Neither one acknowledged me further or made any attempt to help me. For all they knew, I was lying there dying. I was, but not in that sense.

"Flintlock Sheriff's Department," a muffled voice called from somewhere upstairs.

"This is the Flintlock Sheriff's Department. You are trespassing on a crime scene. Come out now," another voice said.

"Here," I did my best to yell out to them, but my body was weak. Weaker than I'd anticipated.

Footsteps overhead warned me of coming officers. Heego had called in the cavalry. Probably in desperation after he witnessed my kidnapping. I tried to sit up, but my arm had had its fill of work and refused to function like it should. Above my head, heavy *thunks* from boots stomping gave way to an all-out scuffle.

The scuffle ended as quickly as it had begun, and footfalls moved swiftly above me. Someone was coming for me. They had to know I was down there. Consciousness was fading. If it hadn't already been black as pitch in the basement, I'd have said the world around me was fading to black. I forced my eyes to stay open, naming each character from every Disney movie I'd ever seen in my head.

"Penderhaus," a gruff voice called to me. "What, d'ya fall down these steps in the dark? Serves you right, breaking and entering." It was Sheriff Floyd standing over me.

"Morgan…" was all I could get out before my eyes fluttered closed and the world was gone.

I woke up screaming. The pain in my arm seared through the muscle, bringing bile up my throat, burning my already irritated airway. A rough, strong hand hefted me by my arm through the house and out the front door. I had no memory of walking up the stairs or even getting up from the ground.

"He wasn't breaking in," Heego said from afar. "Pensky, get him out of those cuffs," he yelled.

Tears streamed down my face. I could hardly form thoughts, let alone words. My stomach churned, and I heaved over, retching limply onto a pair of shiny uniform shoes.

"Well, dammit, Penderhaus, you drink too much?" Sheriff Floyd yelled at me, flinging yellowy barf from his shoe.

"Hey," Heego called. "Sheriff, what's going on here?"

"Heego, you're off duty tonight. You go worry about your high school girlfriend."

"She's an adult. And she's not," Heego said about me. "She's hurt. You need to call an ambulance. Now."

"Dumb girl took a fall down the stairs in the dark is all. Probably drinking. You buying these kids booze too?"

"Let me go," I huffed. "My arm," I cried and gritted my teeth through the pain.

"She's in pain, let her go."

Yelling from the street caught my ear. Cassius was screaming nonsensically; only my name could be understood.

"Elroy Floyd, you let my daughter go right now," Mom screamed, barreling up the walk.

His hand released, and I tumbled to my knees. My lanky body fell against the aging porch, echoing a thud beneath the planks.

"Frankie, your daughter is drunk and incoherent. She broke in here with her boyfriend there and destroyed my crime scene."

"Morgan," I mumbled. "And Brady."

"Prudence, I'm calling an ambulance," Heego said.

"You could have a head injury."

I shook my head slowly. "My arm." I tried to prop myself up on my good elbow but didn't even bother. I was too weak.

"You son of a bitch," Mom yelled, and a loud smack cut through the commotion. "Do you know what you've done? Do you?" Mom patted my head. "Just rest, baby. We'll get you to the hospital and get you all fixed up."

Her reassurance didn't do much for my morale. My eyes hadn't opened fully since I'd lost the world in the basement, but I knew nothing was right. Just like Phillips had said. There was so much more to the story than anyone knew. Anyone but Sheriff Floyd, the Shoosters, and apparently Morgan and Brady. It felt in that moment that I'd die before ever knowing the truth.

"Prudence," Cassius screamed to me, seeming closer than before.

"She's had too much to drink, that's all." The sheriff stood strong on his lie.

"She's dying, asshole," Mom screeched.

"Oh, now, there's no need to be dramatic."

"Rhabdomyosarcoma. Stage three. Size of a lime right there in that bicep. If you don't back up out of my way, you'll see dramatic."

I wished I could've seen the sheriff's face when she said it.

"Like cancer?" Cassius asked, and every last ounce of joy I'd felt in the moment was sucked away in those two words.

I forced my eyes open, watching through murky slits. "Cass," I breathed. I wasn't sure if anyone heard me, because no one answered me.

"Sheriff Floyd," a familiar voice said, and I forced my eyes open fully. "I thought we discussed the jurisdiction here? You stay out of my crime scene, remember?"

"Sergeant," Sheriff Floyd said curtly. "We had a call of breaking and entering. We are local authority responding to a crime. These kids broke in here and trashed the crime scene."

"That's a lie," Cassius yelled. "Someone was in there, and Heego was too short to climb in the window, so I climbed in the window. I was arrested in the kitchen."

"It was Morgan and Brady," Bonnie said, repeating what I'd been saying, only loudly enough to be heard.

Sheriff Floyd scoffed. "My officers didn't find anyone else here."

"Someone was here, sir," Heego insisted. "Someone grabbed Prudence in the dark. I couldn't get a look at him, but it wasn't a few seconds later the sheriff cars pulled up and an officer had Cassius in cuffs coming up from around back." Heego's voice trailed off at the end as though he were lost in thought.

I tried hard to stay with the conversation. I knew what happened. Morgan and Brady had broken into the house for a reason. A reason I was beginning to think had everything to do with Sheriff Floyd.

A siren cut the conversation short. Heego shouted at the ambulance to guide them toward me. I wanted to stay. The pain would subside eventually, and I would be fine. The fall down the stairs hadn't hurt me, not in the need-of-a-trip-to-the-hospital hurt. I didn't think. The hurt I felt had been there far longer. The swimming sensation in my head, if I was being honest with myself, had begun the moment I woke up for the day. Whatever was happening to me had been a long time coming.

Gentle hands worked me over. The sweet scent of perfume wafted past my nose. I opened my eyes to a lovely pair of crystal-blue eyes hidden behind a pair of glasses. They curved into half-moons with a smile. I couldn't tell if the eyes belonged to a woman or man, but in the moment, it didn't matter. They were kind and caring and would do their best to ensure my health.

They hefted me onto a gurney and into the back of an ambulance. I swallowed back the urge to vomit into the oxygen mask with the movement. Straps and metal clicking and locking. Bright light, blinding overhead. Pain.

Please survive. Please.

"Prudence," Cassius called to me from outside the ambulance. The syllables of my name a song of hope over the sounds of my medical emergency. "Are you dying?"

No, I wanted to scream at the top of my lungs. *I won't leave you*, I wished I could say. But nothing came out when I opened my mouth.

"Come on, Cass," Bonnie said. "We'll go see her." I hoped she'd take care of him no matter what happened to me. "We can't go with her." She tugged on his sleeve.

"No," he said, jerking from her grip. "Prudence Penderhaus, I love you."

Tears streamed down my cheeks. There was no telling if he really knew what love was, but in the end, I knew I didn't. That didn't stop me from screaming inside, *I love you, too, Cassius Shooster.* Instead, I raised my hand a foot off the gurney and gave him a thumbs-up.

Snap, snap.

"I'm right behind you," Mom yelled. "I'm right behind you."

The doors slammed shut, closing out the drama I'd created. *Nothing here is right.* I played that sentence over and over in my head. The sheriff, the Shoosters, Morgan, Brady, and who knows what other Flintlock resident had been harboring secrets for more years than I'd been alive. I wished my dad were still around. He would have gotten to the bottom of it all. He would have blown the lid off the whole thing. Lying in that bed, headed to the hospital, I knew I was the only one who knew Brady and Morgan had been in that house for a reason. It would be up to me to find out what. If I survived the night.

$/3$

THEY LEFT THE BONE BEHIND. MY PRETTY SURGEON HAD been right, almost. She couldn't get it all. But most. I'd worked myself too hard and my body couldn't take it anymore. Two days after I arrived in Marysville ER, they sliced me open and took my invader, fearful its rapid growth would soon destroy my scrawny muscle, taking with it nerves and lymph. It'd been terrifying and lonely. I'd been hidden, kept captive, hostage if you will, in room 227 by my mother and the medical staff of the 2nd-floor recovery unit. The night I went to the hospital in an ambulance was the last night I'd seen home in a week.

"I miss your face," I said into the phone as soon as he answered.

"Good morning, Prudence. I miss you too." He choked out a chuckle. "Your face too, I mean." Shuffling in the background seemed to take his attention. "How long until you are free?"

"Mom said I have to be home at least a day."

"How long has it been?"

I looked at the clock. "Three hours." I snorted.

"Twenty-one to go," Cassius said with a laugh that I wasn't totally sold was honest.

"Don't feel discouraged. Mom told Sergeant San Dimas-high-school-football-rules the same thing. He'll be by tomorrow to handle this Sheriff Floyd business." Which I was looking forward to with eager anticipation.

"Are you comfortable?" he asked suddenly.

"I am." As comfortable as I could be with stitches and whatnot going on in my arm. "I love my window seat. Thank you so much. You guys did a great job." I ran my hand over the cotton cushion.

"Heego taught me how to build with wood while you were in the hospital. I had figured you would need somewhere to lay about and look at the world while you heal."

I'd gotten word through Bonnie just that morning that he'd been convinced I would be all better after my surgery. Cassius Shooster seemed a more clever boy than that, but I didn't have the heart to bring it up. What would be the point?

"You figured right because that's exactly what I'm doing right now." I sat, smiling on my new-to-me bench. Bonnie had persuaded them that recycled materials were better for the environment, so I was sitting on what once was a handful of scrapped wood pallets and a cushion made from a few old band shirts.

"I'm glad you like it. I smashed my thumb with the hammer. Your mother cried when she gave Bonnie those shirts, also."

I looked down at the shirts in question. Recognizing the familiar Bon Jovi design, my eyes welled with tears. They'd used my dad's old band T-shirts. I couldn't believe my eyes. I hadn't even known Cassius had brought it back since borrowing it.

"This is.... I love it. I can't believe the Bon Jovi shirt survived."

"Sergeant San Dimas-high-school-football-rules gave me my house back on Tuesday."

I choked. "You're living there by yourself?" I exclaimed loudly.

"With Heego. At my house with Heego," he clarified.

"Oh." I was honestly concerned. "I guess with your parents locked up, the house is yours by proxy." I wasn't sure how healthy it was for him to live in the house where he'd been held captive for the majority of his life, but, oddly, I kind of trusted Officer *no first name* Heego.

"Sergeant San—" He cleared his throat, stopping himself. "—told me I could live here until they find property records. And my birth records. Otherwise I'm useless."

"Cass, you're never usele—"

"We smashed the rose room with the hammers," he

interrupted with a smile I knew was spreading across his face.

I wished I could go back in time and be present for that event. In my head, Cassius had pretended each was his mother's face and any vengeance rotting inside his soul was released with the action.

Movement outside caught my attention, distracting me momentarily. A large white truck with no emblem was parked in front of the late Mr. Horowitz's vacant house. Men in blue coveralls hauled boxes from the truck to the house. I hadn't known it had been for sale, just empty.

"You're getting neighbors," I said absently, looking through the window at the scene.

"I know. They've kept me awake two nights in a row with their incessant drilling." His annoyance radiated through the phone.

"Drilling?" I leaned forward and peered out the window for a sign of the homeowners. "What kind of people are they?"

"Dunno, haven't seen 'em," he said, sounding like he was chewing. "I have to hang up and eat, Prudence." And he did. Without another word.

"Obviously Heego hasn't gone over phone etiquette yet," I said to my phone, watching the screen go dark.

Out the window, the men in coveralls continued their dance. Man, truck, box, house. Another man, truck, box, house. No happy homeowners. No kids running amuck around the feet of the movers. Just plain brown box after plain brown box going in for almost an hour. The lawn visible from my Thyme-facing window had been trimmed and cleaned of debris. All those layers of soggy leaves gone. Crooked fence sent straight again. Would they have done all that work overnight? In the rain?

Drilling in the middle of the night at a house no one had lived in for months and hadn't been for sale. In a town no one would move to willingly. No homeowners seen by observant neighbors. Directly beside the now nationally—or at least county-wide—infamous spook house. Something was afoot at the Circle K.

As if a hidden boy, a murdered child, police corruption, and my impending doom wasn't enough, I was now presented with yet another Flintlock mystery. Who the hell was moving in to 19 Marigold Lane?

For more information about
Autism spectrum disorder visit
WWW.AUTISM-SOCIETY.ORG

If you, or someone you know,
is suffering from abuse, there is help out there.
WWW.CHILDHELP.ORG/HOTLINE

For more information about childhood cancer
and how you can help visit
WWW.STJUDE.ORG

R.M. Gilmore is a paranormal and mystery/suspense writer and creator of the occult bestselling Dylan Hart series. She resides in the Pacific Northwest with her teenage minion, bearded man-child, and toys still in the box. With an awkward and incessant sense of humor, it is likely she will die laughing.

"Star-crossed lovers and dead things. It's what i do." – R.M. Gilmore

For more information visit

WWW.RMGILMORE.COM

Made in the USA
Las Vegas, NV
05 December 2022